What Once Was Lost…

by

Catherine Young

For all my friends and family who encouraged me to finish this book.

Acknowledgements

With special thanks to:

Emily Hall-Roberts and Lynn F Weston for encouraging me to take the plunge and self-publish.

My daughters, Frankie White and Hannah Bielecka, for supporting me always and for reading my many drafts.

Kay Stonham; her "Writing for Wimps" course inspired me to try writing fiction.

John Featherstone for his patience and skill in producing such an appropriate and eye-catching cover.

Finally, my many friends for helping me nurture and revise the book in its many forms over the year. You know who you are and, yes, I do want you to buy the final product.

Do not go gentle into that good night,

Old age should burn and rave at close of day;

Rage, rage against the dying of the light.

Dylan Thomas

Contents

Chapter 14: All's fair in love and war.

Chapter 15: A woman's work is never done.

Chapter 16: Don't trust what you see, even salt can look like sugar.

Chapter 17: Truth will out.

Chapter 18: Every cloud has a silver lining?

Chapter 19: Ignorance is bliss?

Chapter 20: Sufficient unto the day is the evil thereof.

Chapter 21: If you play with fire, you will get burnt.

Chapter 22: Forgive and forget.

Chapter 23: The wages of sin is death.

Chapter 24: Desperate times call for desperate measures.

Chapter 25: Needs must when the Devil drives (again).

Chapter 26: Tomorrow is another day.

Chapter 27: A friend in need is a friend indeed.

Chapter 1: Marian

There's no Fool like an Old Fool

The air is so heavy with incense I can't breathe. The holy pictures are covered with black cloth. Not out of respect for us mourners but because it's Lent. The time for confession, penance and redemption. Not for me. I stand there, unforgiven and in silent shame; as still as the Madonna statue with her child. I pray to her for forgiveness but she knows I am unworthy. A man rises from the crowd and enshrouds my face with the cloth, forbidding me to speak my truth. He runs off with the child. Again I can't breathe, can't move. I'm too ashamed to beg for help yet unable – or unwilling – to release myself from his commandment.

It's dark, too dark. Suddenly the darkness lifts and I have to shield my eyes as the garish sunlight blazes across my metal bed, flooding my care home room with its harshness. Sonya, my carer is there, standing over me. She's gripping a pillow in her hands.

"Quiet, Marian. Why you make such noise?" She walks slowly backwards, staring down at me while shaking the pillow. "I am only taking pillow. Why all that screaming?" She laughs, and turns away as she scolds me.

"I couldn't breathe! You – with that pillow – you were – I know it!"

The pillow is still in her bony hands. Her white uniform on her skinny frame hurts my eyes. She walks away as if my words, maybe even my life, are of little consequence. As she leaves, she tells me that she will have to suggest to Dr Campbell that I need more my medication,

"These dreams make you crazy. You need peace. I need peace from you."

She strides to the door, and even though I don't speak her language, I know she's swearing.

"I'm still a person, you know, I'm not mad. I just want to find my baby"

At this she turns, almost looking at me,

"Oh dear, you have bad mood today, isn't it Marian? You have baby dream again? I get you up ready in good time. You go nowhere and I have medication to fix and many room to tidy. I take you there in two minutes." The door slams shut behind her. I sink back into my pillows, soft and unthreatening now, and wait like a patient child for her to come back to wash and dress me. Why does she scare me so? I try looking back to find a reason for this fear but it is lost, like much of my childhood. Memories are slippery things, apt to slide sideways from your mind, just as you try to catch hold. So why am I so sure of the baby that everyone denies? Maybe they are right and it is just a false memory or wishful thinking. I'd be depressed if I could be bothered. How, in a few short weeks, have I come to this? This is not me. I should have paid more attention when Tracey hauled me off to the GP.

*

"Have a seat, Mrs. Norman, and – Tracey, isn't it? I haven't seen you since you were a little girl. How are you?" The GP ushered us into his surgery, without so much as a brief glance at me and, without a second thought, Tracey took the seat next to Dr. Evans, the GP I'd had for more years than I could remember. I sat at the end by the door. They talked over Tracey's many concerns about me while I studied the instructions for dealing with anaphylactic shock, strokes and epileptic fits on the posters decorating the walls. Quite educational, although I'd known most of it from my time as a teacher, even kept up my First-Aid training until I retired. The background noise stopped and I became aware that they were both staring at me. I'd obviously missed something important.

"I said, when did these nightmares start, Mrs Norman?" I hate that patronising tone.

"They're not all nightmares. More lost memories; a bit jumbled…"

"Of course, Marian – may I call you Marian?" He never had before. We'd always had a suitably formal relationship. I didn't see why it would change now, after all these years, but it seemed churlish to object so I just smiled. He took my silence for consent.

"Marian, the loss of a dear spouse can affect the mind in strange ways. You're now on your own, is that right?" We all knew I was, what was his point? My only interest was in finding out the truth of my past. Surely that's why we were there?

"I want you to check my records back to the 1960s in Brighton. I gave birth to a child there. I know I did. What happened to him?"

I saw the glances they exchanged. I'm not daft, nor blind.

"Mum, I already asked him to check, when you first started on about all this. He's just told you that but, as usual, you were off somewhere inside your head." She fixed me with one of her looks. "There is absolutely no record of an earlier pregnancy." And she tried to reach for my hand – to comfort me, I suppose. It wasn't comfort I needed; instead I stood up to go.

"Please sit down, Marian, I can see this is distressing for you. I'm going to put you down for some bereavement counselling and, in the meantime, some Amitriptyline." That condescending smile again, "Try to get out and meet other people as much as possible; they run some good classes at the Age Concern centre just off the High Road…"
I didn't stay to hear any more.

I never could get away though; after the swimming pool incident people kept coming to ask me questions, to assess me, to judge me. Quite rightly, they found me wanting.

Can they really have someone sectioned on such flimsy evidence? Of course now whatever I say is merely considered the product of my supposed dementia, or whatever pretext they used to have me hidden away here. Like a dirty secret.

*

As I'm wheeled into the large day room, I check all the chairs and I see Gwen – the only person I could really trust – sitting on one of the few comfy chairs over by the bay window, well away from the group of women playing a noisy game of armchair charades.

"Oh Gwen, I'm sure she was trying to kill me!" I grab at her hand. Why do I say it? I know it sounds ludicrous.

"Don't be silly, girl," she takes my hand between hers, "You said that last week when poor old Sonya, all she do is make a mistake with your medication. Tracey soon sort it out and now you're fine."

I know she's right but I also know that there is something very wrong about my being here.

"Then why do I feel so weak – so weak I can't even walk by myself now? I was as fit as a fiddle when I came here. Now they say I need this," and I thump the heavy old wheelchair.

"Don't fret so, they look after you. That's why you here. Your Tracey will cheer you up. Is she coming today?" And she peers out of the large picture windows as if she could conjure her up for me.

Her interest in my family always makes me feel blessed that I have children and grandchildren, then guilty for not cherishing them enough. She has no one. She left all her family behind when she came here, back in the sixties. She won't talk about them. She sits there, in her favourite floral-patterned armchair which almost swallows up her tiny frame. She's draped in the strange assortment of clothing they've arranged over her fragile limbs. I draw myself closer to her and she gives my arm a rub. The beige cardigan smells musty and has frayed, grubby cuffs that cover most of her beautiful, brown hands, while the elasticated skirt has been fixed with safety pins as it's at least two sizes too big for her. If you don't have visitors, there's no one who cares that much if you don't always get your own clothes back from the laundry.

Gwen rises to stare out of the window. She lifts up her hand and smiles a greeting. I look. There is absolutely no one there.

"What on earth are you doing..?"

I look out the window again. There really isn't anyone there. Just privet hedges and fading hydrangeas screening us off from the rest of the world.

She waves again.

"There's no one there." I have to check one last time.

"No. Not yet. But there will be, in a minute," and she looks at me so seriously that, for a moment, I think she must be joking.

She continues to execute a perfect "royal" wave for at least another couple of minutes as I settle myself down beside her.

"But Gwen…," I stop. No. I can't believe it. My Tracey's there. She's looking paler and older than when I last saw her as she shuffles up the path. When she sees us, she lifts her head, straightens her shoulders, forces a smile and begins to stride towards us, waving. Gwen beams at me.

"See..? Now, when's lunch coming?"

I smile back but I can't help wondering why Tracey looked so troubled when she thought no one was looking.

Chapter 2: Felicity

There's No Such Thing as a Free Lunch.

I'd always wanted a career in politics so, when the chance came, I didn't stop to think about the consequences. I really should have. Or maybe not. I found out a lot of things about myself, some things not so attractive.

My family's good at nepotism. After all, that's how my brother Ed got his job on The Edinburgh Post. It came as a surprise though, until that sunny afternoon, I was sure that, as far as Daddy was concerned, it was a waste of time to help me in my career; all he seemed to expect of me was to make a good marriage.

My parents live in a huge house in Surrey; Georgian, I think, set in beautifully landscaped grounds, with a large drive and stables. An impressive staircase in the entrance hall swoops up to the first floor; Daddy's forbears scrutinising every visitor. I've had several friends who said they felt their disapproval so strongly that they felt they couldn't come back, not even for my twenty-first bash.

My bedroom was in the east wing with delicately flowered wallpaper growing up the walls in pastel shades of pink and violet. I hated it, once I'd grown out of my Jane Austen phase.

"It's a lovely room for a girl, why would you want to change it?" my perplexed mother wanted to know, the one time I tried to express my opinion. There never was much point in my having an opinion in our family. That was men's business.

The floor in the entrance hall was so well polished that our two Dalmatians would skitter along, like Bambi on ice, barking in unison, as they came to check out anyone with the cheek to enter their front door. Today it was my turn to receive their spirited reception.

*

"Darling Felicity how lovely to see you," Mummy enfolds me in her arms and her Chanel perfume wafts around me. Despite myself, the smell turns me back into my childhood self again.

"Guess who's here? Your Uncle Charles, isn't that just lovely?" I feel myself blushing as my stomach tries crawling up and out of my mouth. Why do you do this to me,

Mum? I know he's Daddy's oldest friend but I find him so hard to cope with.

Still, I quickly check, my lipstick in the hall mirror and untie my pony tail, shaking my hair so it trails down my back.

"Oh darling, you do look stunning," Mummy strokes my hair, messing it up. So irritating. I smile at her, check the mirror one last time, smooth my hair back down again and follow her into the drawing room.

"Felicity, darling, you remember your Uncle Charles, don't you?" Stupid question.

"Yes, Daddy, of course I do. How are you Uncle Charles?" I give him my practised smile from across the room. I wish he didn't make me feel so nervous. He sweeps his hand through his luxuriant hair, much greyer now, and sends me back a stunning smile. He's standing in the bay window that overlooks the grounds at the front of the house, sun streaming in around him and flooding the room with a winter's pale light. I know all his tricks. I have to admit, though, he is still quite handsome.

"Come here my dear, haven't you a kiss for your poor old uncle? It's been so long. What a beautiful woman you have become." He holds out his arms while his eyes walk up and down my body. I wish I'd worn jeans; or at least shaved my legs.

Mummy links my arm in hers and steers me right into dear old Uncle Charles's moist lips.

We reminisce about the "lovely" times we used to have back in the day. Uncle Charles was a regular visitor. He's Daddy's best friend from Eton; a great support to Daddy, especially during the financial crisis of 2008. We nearly lost the family home. Ed told me once that he suspected that Uncle Charles had paid for our school fees too, although how he would know that, I'm not sure. He and Daddy hardly ever say two words to each other and Mummy wouldn't know, she's from that generation that leaves everything like that to their husbands. A different time.

She's in full flow now, lots of happy little stories of when Ed and I were children and Uncle Charles used to visit almost every weekend. How differently people remember the same things. Eventually old Mary, who's been with us for centuries, breaks through the golden-coloured memories,

"Lunch is served."

At last… I wonder how soon after lunch I can leave without upsetting everyone?

I don't get off that easily. As soon as we are finished with the cheeseboard, Daddy and Uncle Charles grab the port and basically *demand* that I join them in Daddy's study. I look to Mummy for support but I just can't catch her eye as she turns to go out of the room.

Daddy's study is in a part of the house that somehow never catches the light and always smells of tobacco and fusty trousers. He has those hideous stag heads on the wall, even though I don't think he has ever been on a shoot. They eye us glassily as we each take our places in this dance which I could tell was the prelude to something important, I just didn't know the steps.

"So, Felicity, is it true; you want to pursue a career in politics?" That sensuous voice.

Always scared of giving him an inadequate answer, sounding stupid, I hear my voice rise an octave, like a little girl's.

"Yes. I'm working as an intern for our local MP. I expect you know him – Mike Brown." Of course he knows him; he knows everyone and everything that goes on at Westminster. Idiot.

"Of course," Uncle Charles smiles indulgently, "he is a reasonably capable chap, not one to set the world alight, but steady," and he hands me the extraordinarily large glass of port my father has poured. I'm locked into his blue eyes. I need both hands to steady the glass. My nails, painted what I'd earlier thought an on-trend and attractive light blue, suddenly look rather garish and decidedly unprofessional.

"Charles has a proposition for you, sweetie." At this I sit down quickly to regain some control, place my glass on the teak side table before it spills and tug at my skirt to cover a bit more of my legs. Charles walks over to the window and looks out. Daddy fiddles with his cigar, trying to get it to stay alight.

"No doubt you've seen this video clip that became popular on social media; the one they're calling "Stripogranny"? A poor old lady, clearly a little unhinged, took off all her clothes in a public swimming pool. Lord knows why. Then, would you believe it, she started dancing around in the showers. Stark naked. Extraordinary! A rather brash young lad caught it on video with his smartphone and posted it. It seems to have caught the media's attention. It even made the local news. Naturally I have asked for it to be taken down and for the DPP to investigate the young man's actions."

He turns and smiles. I hadn't even heard of it but I nod. Don't want to seem lacking. Daddy nods back at me approvingly.

"Well, Felicity, the fact of the matter is," and he turns away to look out of the window again, "I recognised the poor woman involved – from way back in the past, of course. Her name then was Marian Alsop. I feel an obligation to do what I can to help her and her poor family. I was their MP back in the 1950s. Good Catholic family. They must be utterly embarrassed and she clearly needs help."

"They must, indeed."

Did I just say "indeed"? Out loud? I take a gulp of port and immediately regret it. Cloyingly sweet and sickly.

Uncle Charles is not used to being interrupted. He swivels round and looks at me as if reconsidering the whole idea of continuing. Shit! I hold my breath. I need this, it could be so, so good for me. I very slowly put my glass down, straighten my back and try to look professional. I really do want this. Working for Uncle Charles… on my CV..! Daddy would be so proud. I hold my breath. The impassive grandfather clock over by the corner ticks away several agonising seconds. Eventually Charles smiles again and the whole room takes a breath.

"Hmm… well, what I propose is that we get our Mr Brown to release you from answering e-mails, or whatever it is you do, and have you seconded to me so that you can do some real work. If you do well, I could offer you a permanent position. What do you say?" That smile again. How could I ever say no?

"I think she'll say thank you very much, won't you Fliss? It's a great opportunity, no, I tell a lie, an honour to work for a cabinet minister, especially one held in such regard as you, Charles," Daddy turns and looks meaningfully at me, "It could lead to a permanent position, old girl."

Why don't you just get right on down on all fours and lick his boots, Daddy. Or worse. He's always like this when he's with Uncle Charles. I smile demurely like the good girl I am and say "Yes, please".

The story of my life. Stitched up like a kipper, as they say. Not that I'm complaining; it would be excellent for my career. If I do this well – and honestly it can't be that difficult – working for Uncle Charles could be my route to some amazing opportunities for a career in politics. Just think of the contacts he has, the networks I could form. Lunch with my parents is not usually so worthwhile.

He tells me to find out where this woman lives, her present name and all her background details such as family and stuff. I'm to report to him only, I get a pay-as-you-go mobile and the use of my own office (more like a cupboard as it turned out, but it was all mine) and my own expense account, again to be claimed through him. Why all this cloak and dagger stuff? Highly suspect. Then again, that's what makes it so exciting. She's probably the mother of one of his many girlfriends from the past and he's being put under pressure to help her out. Maybe I should… but really I *don't* actually care what it is. It could be a real step up for me

Even so, much as I admire Uncle Charles and his work in Government, I want to get away as quickly as I can without appearing rude or ungrateful. Richard said he might be able to come to the flat tonight and I've bought two bottles of his favourite Merlot.

"Are you back off to London?" he suggests as we get ready to leave, "I could offer you a lift, maybe even a little drink to celebrate our new… relationship."

That smile. Sparking an uneasy feeling, a memory perhaps? A brief warning light flickers at the back of my mind and I have to force myself to maintain eye contact, "That's so kind but I have my car here and I'll need it to follow up on our little project,"

"That's my girl, keen as mustard," and Daddy slaps me on the back, breaking through whatever was going on between Uncle Charles and me. Charles laughs, kisses Mummy good bye and strides off to his black Jaguar parked across the drive without a backward glance. He could at least have said goodbye to me too.

*

It takes ages for me to find a parking space for the mini on Putney High Street. I have to leave my car in a dark alley just off the High Street and walk back to my flat. I've never been afraid of walking around London alone at night, although I know some women are. I refuse to submit to some night time curfew. I make sure I have my phone in my hand though, you can't be too careful. I'm proud of my independence.

When I think about what her life has been like, I feel sorry for Mummy, even though she drives me mad. She's never had a career or done anything much. I guess she was born too early; her whole life has revolved around the men in her life. I won't make that mistake. I'm careful to choose men who won't get too serious so that before you know it, it's all the old "Let's get married and have kids" stuff. Richard, the guy I'm seeing now, is cheating on his wife, even though she's six months pregnant. He's not someone *I* would want to have a child with. I like him well enough and we have fun but it's a relief to know it can't go anywhere.

I'm not saying I'll never get married. I'm only twenty-three; at least seven years before my clock starts ticking.

Once in my flat, I walk over to the kitchen area, pour myself a large glass of Merlot and settle on the window seat overlooking the High Street. I'm proud of my flat; I know Daddy paid for it but it is all mine now and I love the feeling I get, walking in to my very own space. No one can touch me here.

Right, let's look at this video clip. See what all the fuss is about and get started on the next bit of my career. I shan't use my phone. This is an important placement for me so I'll give it the full treatment of my brand new lap-top. Besides, I'll get a better look at the old dear that Charles wants me to find. See what she's like. I walk over to the table and open up my laptop; a present from Richard. He laughed at my old one, saying it was next to useless. I actually preferred it but it wasn't worth arguing. I checked the time on my Fitbit, another present from Richard. He wanted me to make sure I did enough steps every day. Yes, I had time before he was due.

It didn't take that long to find, even though it was no longer on any UK web-sites. This Jason White who had posted the clip had a steady hand for someone laughing so loud. You could see everything. And I mean everything. But as I'm watching her being led away, it occurs to me that she's probably quite a bit younger than Charles. Yes, he's kept his looks with careful grooming and that, but he must be in his eighties now.

I even find and upload the clip of the original local TV news report:

Our reporter, Mike Sargent, is in Finchley with 15-year-old Jason White who uploaded the video."

The camera cuts to a young, not so fresh-faced, boy in what appears to be a concrete walkway in a run-down council estate. Behind him stands a group of local youths, pulling faces and hurling obscene gestures at the camera.

"So I'm in the Lido, right, and I hear all this shouting and that, so I look up and there's this old granny, like, and she's in the showers at the edge of the pool, taking off her kit. So I pick up my phone and within seconds she's, like, totally stark (BLEEP) naked! Then this lifeguard comes up, yeah, and she's fighting him off at first but then she, like, changes her mind and sinks into his arms like he's some old lover or something and she goes off with him, singing and waving to everyone."

At this Jason's "audience" behind him whoop and shout, their gestures becoming ever more grotesque. When asked by the beleaguered but infinitely patient reporter to describe the woman, White said, *"She was well fit for her age, if that don't make me sound like a pervert.* (Raucous laughter from behind Jason.) *"Anyway, when I uploaded it on Instagram, my mates thought it was jokes so I put it on YouTube for a laugh."* Thankfully, at this point, the shot returned to the studio:

"After overwhelming protests, Instagram and YouTube removed the video. There are also calls for Mr White to be charged under the invasion of privacy laws but, although the video may raise serious issues about privacy and the care of the elderly, it is nice to know that help is always at hand – even if it is only a hand carrying a lifeguard's towel!"

The newscaster shuffled his papers with a smile, the programme's credits began to roll and the clip ended.

Well that's a good start; it was at Finchley Lido in the borough of Barnet. I can drive up there tomorrow and ask around, see if I can find out who she is. This is too easy. I celebrate with another glass or two of wine. By the time Richard arrives, I'm a little worse for wear. He doesn't like it when I drink too much so we end up arguing and he just walks out. I don't care. I have the possibility of a glittering career in politics. I just hope that the price I pay for working so closely with Uncle Charles is worth it.

Chapter 3: Tracey

Blood is Thicker than Water

It was Tuesday so I went to see Mum at lunchtime. It troubles me that she is getting worse but Dr Campbell assures me that patients - or 'clients' as she likes to call them – often react this way when they first arrive. She was adamant that they soon get used to the change and settle down to accept that this is the best place for them. Whatever fancy names she calls them by, most people here don't seem to have many feelings either way about their surroundings or anything else, for that matter. I can't help thinking that I shouldn't have let her be placed here after all. Still, she's here now and he said it was the very best place for her. He did seem to know what he was doing. Well, I'm sure she'll get used to it eventually. She's already made friends with a funny little old Jamaican lady.

I arrived in time for lunch which was not so good for me as I've never liked scrambled eggs. The aroma of the lukewarm egg slithered around the room and mingled with the smell of old ladies. I took one look at the rubbery substance floating in its watery liquid and pushed it around my plate for a while before I finally gave up. Instead I busied myself with the stainless steel teapot and plastic mugs.

"That lovely little Polish girl says you've been having some bad dreams again," I said, keeping my eyes on the teapot, "Going on about lost babies and accusing her of trying to kill you?" The silence lasted almost long enough to become uncomfortable but, God bless her, Gwen broke it,

"I'll have mine black, please; I don't trust the milk in here. They put stuff in it. Like they do to the sailors" Gwen reached for her mug.

Taking her cue for distraction from Gwen, Mum joined in, "How are Tom and Emily? Coming to see me soon, I hope?" She's always trying to make me force the kids to see her. As if they would do anything I ask them. Anyway, I've told them; they wouldn't like it here. The less they know, the better.

"They put bromide in sailors' tea you know, to make them less randy," Gwen added.

We both turned to Gwen.

"It's true! Look it up if you don't believe me. I'm sure you can goggle it or whatever." She looked around the room as if someone might volunteer the opinion that she is right.

"It's Google, Gwen," I'm used to Gwen and I wasn't going to let go of my line of thought, despite their attempts. I turn back to Mum, "You have got to stop all this nonsense, Mum." I have to pacify her. "They'll never let you go to The Grange if you keep this up."

Was she upset or angry? I've never been able to tell with her.

"Good. I don't want to go there now. I want to go home. I want to wake up in my own bed and then do whatever I want. Eat porridge for lunch and wear jim-jams all day, if I like. It's no one else's business!"

I could see she wanted to stamp her feet like the petulant child she's become lately but she couldn't, sitting there in her ridiculous wheelchair. I can't understand why they insists she needs it. She's always been so active. I took her hand and spoke slowly and gently; she suddenly seemed so frail.

"Mum, we had to sell your house to get you in here." I try really hard to keep my voice gentle; I have to persuade her that this is the right place for her. "They say you need someone to see that you don't come to any harm and I can't do that. Not twenty-four hours a day. This is a lovely place. They'll give you the best possible care for your condition. When you get better we can try The Grange in Brighton again." Of course we all know this will never happen.

 "Why can't I come and live with you and Nigel and the kids? I'd be no trouble and I can help them with their homework and look after them after school before you get home…" Close to tears, I realised she had lost all sense of time and I swallowed down the lump of sadness in my throat,

"Mum, Emily's twenty-two, Tom is eighteen and living in sin with some older woman he's only just met. They don't need help with their *homework!"* My patience was cracking but still she didn't stop.

"Anyway, what condition? I don't have conditions! That's just something doctors say when they don't know what's wrong; like viruses. Isn't that right, Gwen?"

But Gwen was too busy, leering at one of the young male nurses.

"See that one with the nice bum..? I've had him," she said with a wink.

*

Thank goodness for Gwen. I don't think I could stand these visits if it wasn't for her. I do worry about what I've done to Mum, but I was told – quite firmly - that it was the best place for her to make sure she doesn't come to any harm. She's so resentful now, so negative and she refuses to settle here. She's always enjoyed a project, something to drive her on and now she's latched on to this stupid fantasy of a baby that doesn't exist. Who knows where she got that idea? Now she's accusing the staff here of all sorts, even of trying to kill her. It may be part of her illness, like they say, but that doesn't make it any easier to cope with.

"You've got to stop this nonsense, Mum," I told her, keeping my voice low so that the nurses don't hear, "Dr. Campbell says your delusions are getting worse and that they'll have to transfer you to a more secure unit if you persist and I really don't want that." I could hardly get the words out, my throat was so dry, but I had to make her understand,

"But it's true. Why don't you listen to me? Why won't anyone listen to me..? Just because I'm a bit older..? I'm still the same person inside, God help me! A little forgetful, true, but you don't stop being who you are, just because you're old! I need to find out what happened to my baby."

She was on the edge of one of her tantrums and I'd been told by Gwen that emotional outbursts are often punished at Golden Meadows with an increased dose of Valium. I looked quickly around to check. Luckily, no care workers were in earshot.

I tried again to talk some sense into her and took hold of both her hands and made her look into my eyes,

"Don't you remember, I took you to your GP and he checked with your records right back to the 1960s. No sign of any pregnancy. You're just making yourself miserable with this obsession. You're like a child that cannot accept that just because you want something, it doesn't mean you'll get it..." I don't get a chance to properly explain.

"I hate it here. *They* all hate me here. Take me home, please Tracey." I had to look away. I couldn't deal with her begging me like this, whining like a child. I shook her hands away and got up to look away, out of the window. Anywhere but those pleading eyes,

"Nobody hates you. You always think that – no matter where you go."

We've had this conversation so many times before, all my life , it seems.

I heard her sigh – or was she crying? She touched my arm and I turned back to her,

"At some point in your life, Mum, you're going to have to accept that you're a good person and the world is not against you."

"If I was such a good person, why did I make your dad so angry? Why was I such a useless mother that you had to look after yourself and Darren?"
"Mum, that was only in the early days; once you got involved with the school and started to look outside yourself you were fine." I knelt down and put my arms around her, something I hadn't done in years and as I felt her trembling, I couldn't stop myself any longer. I too started to cry. She clung to me like a baby but within seconds we had to pull away. It was too intense.

"Mum, I know this wasn't what you wanted but I was told it really was the best option for you, especially after the incident at the lido."

Life had been difficult for all of us since then. A succession of police, social workers and a psychiatrist all came to our door. At the last Party meeting Nigel was approached by someone who implied that it might have damaged his chances of becoming the ward's next Parliamentary candidate. He was advised to sort it quickly and, as ever, it was left to me to pick up the pieces. So I did what I thought was best.

"Was that why you sent me away? To this place of purgatory, this waiting room for the damned?" she shouted at my back.

"Mum don't be so melodramatic, you know I don't believe all that Catholic stuff and I doubt that you still do either, except when it suits you." I turned to face her to see that she, too, was still crying. Why do we always do this to each other?

The visit ended with us both sitting in isolated misery. Next to each other but miles apart. I can't help wondering if I've done the right thing.

Chapter 4 Marian

There's no Place like (a) Home

Of course Tracey brought it up. Even now, I can't understand why everyone made such a big deal of it. We all make mistakes.

It wasn't my fault; I didn't have my glasses on. You can't swim in glasses; you'd look ridiculous. And when I don't have my glasses on, I can't see so I just end up living inside my own little bubble.

*

I've always loved swimming; the lightness you feel in the water, the way it holds you, and the freedom your body has as it moves through its caress. I'd started swimming every morning once I'd given up teaching. After I'd made his breakfast and seen Bob off to work, the day was my own and a good few lengths of the pool would set me up for the day and keep me relatively fit. Of course, he made me stop when he retired but I took it up again after he died. It was a great consolation. Today I've done ten lengths, non-stop and as I walk to the showers, I rejoice that I can start my life again, brimming with hope for my – I suppose you would call them – my "golden years".

The soothing feeling of the warm water flowing down my body in the shower, chasing away the coldness of the pool after my swim, makes my mind wander. I'm thinking back to the conversation I'd heard earlier through the partition wall of the cubicle as I'd got changed…

"Come on sweetie, let's get you nice and dry. Come on foot, foot, foot! That's right, now the other one; foot, foot, foot! Well done. Did you enjoy yourself? You were so clever." It's a man's voice, but very gentle.

I can hear the child's whiny response but can't quite catch the words.

"Just let's dry you up all nice and warm and get you dressed, my lovely, then we'll see about going to the café…no, no I didn't promise, I said we'll see… no, no don't cry sweetie; that doesn't mean we won't go, it means we'll see. Now just pop your arms in here, no not that way, we'll get all in a twist…" and it goes on like this for all the time it takes me to struggle out of my clothes and into the new tankini that Darren bought me in Brighton. What a sensible invention! A top and knickers for swimming. Why didn't they think of it years ago?

Anyway, we all emerge from the cubicles at the same time. The father and his little boy head towards the café and I start for the pool. Little boy? Throughout the overheard conversation, it had never once occurred to me that the child was anything other than a little girl.

Later as lather my hair, I realise that it was because the father had spoken so gently and lovingly to his child. Bob had never spoken to Darren like that. I remember overhearing him telling Darren off for trying to sit on his lap,

"No, no. You're far too old for all that now. Six year old boys don't need kisses and cuddles, that's just for sissies and Mummy's boys. From now we'll just shake hands, eh? We'll all be men together, yes?"

I heard my beautiful little son's voice agreeing; trying so hard to be big and manly. Ironic really, the way he's turned out.

I found myself wondering, as I've done many times since Bob died, what my first little boy would be like now as I rinse my hair. So long ago but the memories keep coming back these days. Without warning, I have a flashback to that terrifying night. His poor little body haunts me...

The shaking starts again. My mind shuts down. Once again I've lost control of my body. I can't breathe. Let me get this tankini off. Aah, that's wonderful. The warm water soaks right through to my poor old bones. The memories fade. I could stand here for ever.

What? There's someone grabbing me from behind. I scream for help. He's trying to tie me up with some sort of a rough towel or something. Get off me! You're spoiling it all. You're not allowed in the ladies changing rooms anyway . . . what are you doing here? Then I look round and remember; the showers are by the pool, not in the changing rooms. I'm naked by the pool and everyone's watching me. There's that shame again, that terrible shame. I'm really cold now. I can't stop the shaking. I hear a cheer go up. I can't see them well without my glasses, but I hear them cheer. I help him cover up my body. They go on cheering, louder; and I begin to smile. The young man is very gentle with me now I've stopped struggling. He leads me away, and I'm laughing.

Even now, I can't stop laughing, remembering, "He was a nice young man though," I told Tracey.

"That's hardly the point, Mum. If you were a man you'd have been charged with indecent exposure."

"Indecent exposure? Like when Sonya stripped me naked then left me in a bath until it got freezing cold?"

"Mum, I promise you, you just imagined it. I checked it out with Dr Campbell and she made a thorough investigation. Poor Sonya was distraught, she works so hard and you still won't trust her. You must have been dreaming again." I don't believe her. She always thinks she knows best,

"Well, when they finally do kill me you can tell yourself it was only a dream!"

Tracey sighed, "You're always so dramatic! I know you hate it here but it's for your own good. Trust me."

*

They've come to torment me again. In their white, shiny clothes; faces behind white shiny masks. He's there. Mum too - or is it Tracey? The doctor picks up the knife. Sonya shines a light into my eyes. It's so

bright. I can't see them anymore. I know
what they want. I need to get up, to run
away - but my body refuses to move. There's
a searing pain somewhere down below.
They've done what they wanted. The blood
seeps from my body. It's warm and wet and
I'm helpless as they take his broken little
body away.

"Oh, not again! I always changing sheets,"
Sonya rips the duvet off my still almost-
sleeping body. She looks down at me,
disgust blazing from her eyes and mouth. I
cringe there in shame and my own urine.

"Please don't hurt me again," I hear my
voice whimper. Is this really me, helplessly
lying here in my own filth?

"No, no, don't be crying, is not helping! "
Sonya hauls me out of bed with such ease
that I feel I'm flying through the air. How
have I become so insubstantial? How long
have I been here? One month? Two months?
It feels like forever. Am I just briefly
passing through?

Years ago, in another life, I was a teacher. A
good one too. So long ago.

*

"Mrs. Norman, can I have a quick word?" Once again Darren's teacher leads me back into the classroom. The eyes of the other Mums in the playground burn into my back as I follow the teacher into the school. I know that they'll be whispering to each other about me again as soon as I've gone in.

"Has he been in another fight? It's not his fault; they call him such terrible names..."

"No, it's…"

"Oh is it about my note about the PE? …He really does have a bad leg this time..." Have they discovered the bruises?

"No, Mrs. Norman. It's not about Darren. It's about you."

"Oh!" I shrink back. What does she know? How did she find out?

"We were wondering if you would like to volunteer to be a parent-helper. We think it would be good for Darren - and possibly for Tracey too, although she seems to have settled much better into school than her brother…"

Was it really Darren she was concerned about? I don't know. I was at a very low ebb. Maybe she knew I was in need of a reason to get out of bed in the mornings. It worked. Bob didn't like it but this time he couldn't say no. From the start, it made a difference. I finally managed to get the kids into school every day. There I could forget my troubles. I loved working with the kids, seeing their faces when they finally "got" something – a new skill, or a difficult concept. I ended up becoming a teaching assistant and eventually trained on the job as a teacher. I was a good teacher too, maybe because I enjoyed it so much. Within a few years I became a Deputy Head of our small primary school. Bob resented every moment that I was out of his sight, his control.

*

"Well now Marian, how are we today?" Dr Campbell's jaunty voice clashes with the coldness in her eyes and startles me from my memories. She frightens me more than most. She wears a dark green dress over her brown tree-trunk legs. She advances towards me and I'm reminded of the nightmare trees in Burnham Wood moving in for the kill when I took Year Six to see Macbeth at The Unicorn Theatre

"We have little accident again, yes, Marian?" Sonya betrays me with a smile. I hate her. My body's shame is exposed once again. Dr Campbell and Sonya confer in whispers almost out of earshot, something about increasing my drugs, possibly intravenously if I don't respond. I know that they think I can't hear. They turn to look at me and nod at each other.

"Yes, that would be best. I'll notify the relatives today." Dr Campbell fixes me with her professional smile and raises her voice an octave.

"We must try and stay positive, Marian. It's no good feeling sorry for ourselves, now, is it? It will only upset your daughter. Sonya says she comes to see you almost every day. You're a very lucky lady. I hope you realise that."

Sonya hands me yet more pills with a glass of water. I'm sure I've already had them this morning. I start to speak but they turn and walk out together, tree-trunk lady and the pale ghostly nurse, leaving my door wide open – with me on display in my dirty, wet nightie - to anyone who might come along. I shiver with cold and shame.

I sit back and shut my eyes for a minute. When I open them there's a lunch sitting on the table. It's mince with peas and mashed potato, one of my favourites. They've pushed the table closer this time and for once, I can actually reach the plate of food easily, thank goodness. I gratefully launch myself at it but one mouthful is enough. It's stone cold. I try to swallow it down. There's that choking feeling again. Memories of somewhere dark and scary flash through my head. Too quickly. Where was I? A place of pain, even death? Did they take my baby from my body, like in the dream? Sometimes you remember things in dreams that you don't know when you're awake. I slump back in my chair. I don't know whether I want to scream out my anger and frustration or to just sit there wallowing in self-pity. How is it that I can't even recognise my own memories or feelings anymore? Have I completely lost my mind, my sense of who I am? It will only get worse when they increase the drugs.

No. I *am* still me. I use my anger to push the table away then push down hard on the arms of the chair, my arms shaking with the effort, but I am determined to stand. Several times my wrists scream at me and I have to sit back down. But I won't give in now. One more push and I'm standing. A wobbly stand, true, and still needing the chair's arms, but I've done it. I release the stale air I'm forced to breathe in this place with a triumphant rush. Slowly, step after careful step, I reach the door and slam it shut on them all.

This is *my* space, my life. I start to hum "No, no, they can't take that away from me…" and I stand a little taller and straighter. I'm still smiling as I stagger, less tentatively than before, back to my chair. I remember what Gwen said and I hide the pills in a tissue, put the tissue in my drawer and drink the water. I drift off to sleep again and wake up still feeling stronger.

Gwen is sitting in the chair by my bed, clutching her treasured bible:

"I had a dream that God spoke to me," her eyes are shining with a religious fervour that I've not seen before. "He looked like that man on the TV," she says, "the one you keep watching. That politician."

"What did he say?" The skin on the back of my hands feels strangely prickly and I'm a like a schoolgirl again. I don't know why. I try to concentrate on Gwen's ramblings to steady myself.

"He said "I am imni, omni, imi…"? Oh, I know… "I am impotent" and then he went back up to Heaven holding you on his lap and with a host of angels singing Alleluias at his feet." Her smile is beatific at the memory.

"Do you think he might have said "I am omnipotent"?" I gently suggest.

"Oh yes. That's it. He couldn't have been impotent or he'd never have gotten Our Lady up the duff with Jesus, could he?"

But I couldn't laugh with Gwen. I was too busy trying to control the cold sweat that had gripped me and it wasn't just because I was still in my damp nightie. I really must get out of this place and find out exactly what happened to me back then.

Chapter 5: Felicity

If A Job's Worth Doing, It's Worth Doing Well.

I didn't dare fail Uncle Charles. Few people ever did. So I was really careful with my research and I presented him with what I hoped was a well-written and thorough report on the woman, now called Marian Norman, and her family: her address – obviously - and further details surrounding the lido incident and other involvement with social services and her GP.

There had been several minor incidents since her husband died to give the woman's family, and the local authorities, concern about her mental health. I found an address for the daughter. She was now Tracey Dawson and she lived with her husband Nigel and their two children, Tom, aged eighteen and Emily, sixteen.

Marian's son, Darren, lived with a Kevin Bryant in Brighton and they were on the local authority list as potential adoptive parents. I couldn't see anything that should worry the Party or Charles. The only vague link was that the son-in-law, Nigel, was hoping to be selected as the Party's parliamentary candidate at the next election.

Charles picked up on that as soon as I gave him the report, "Ah, yes, Nigel Dawson. I shall have a word with him. Find out when his next constituency meeting is as soon as possible."

I made a note to remind myself.

"The grandson, Tom. I want you to get to know him, if you know what I mean. On the QT, of course."

"Sir?"

"You're more or less the same age, aren't you? Maybe you have a few years on him but that could work to our advantage. He'd be in awe of you, you'll have no trouble wrapping him round your pretty little fingers."

"Sir, I'm not sure I'd feel comfortable…" I couldn't help stepping back a little.

"Nonsense. Don't ever let feelings dictate your actions if you want to get on in politics. One just has to keep the situation under control. You wouldn't think so to look at her, but this little old lady could cause problems for the Party. Looks can be deceptive, can't they? After all, I'm old, I know. But I could still ruin a young researcher's career, couldn't I?"

Was that a threat? No, surely not. That's silly. This is Uncle Charles, Daddy's best friend. I've known him all my life. I try to smile. He continues as if mothing has happened. I was clearly being oversensitive.

"I need you to get close to the family. The obvious way is through her grandson. Find out precisely what the family knows about her history and about her present state of mind. Get contact details for her GP. Keep an eye on her for me. Find me some leverage. There could be a bit of a media storm if this story is not contained. Do you understand what I am saying, Felicity?"

"Yes, Sir" Although I wasn't really sure.

"This could be a great opportunity for you - if you bring it to a positive solution, of course. You want a Parliamentary career, I hear?"

Of course I did.

There's little that happens in the Westminster village that Uncle Charles doesn't have a hand - or even a whole arm - in. This project is really a dream come true. Support from Charles Davidson was a guarantee of a successful career in politics. I can do this. How hard could it be? All I have to do is to keep an eye on the old granny and her family. I'm still not sure why it matters so much to him.

*

It wasn't difficult, tracking down Tom Dawson. You'd have thought his generation would have a greater understanding of privacy settings on social media. Maybe they just don't care, naively think they've nothing to hide. He looked good in the photo I'd downloaded from his end-of-year school magazine: "The Boy Most Likely to Hack into Langley." He didn't look that geeky. Shiny brown hair, nice teeth. Rather attractive, even though his attempt at growing a beard had clearly some way to go. Actually, the more I looked at him, the more attractive he seemed. Pity he's so young. My love life's been a bit of a desert lately.

After that row we'd had on the Monday night when I'd been to my parents, Richard ignored my texts for several days. When he finally got in touch and said he wanted to come round, I told him I had to work.

"What do you mean, work?" He was so dismissive, "It's not like they pay you."

"But it's important to me. And besides, I am getting paid now."

"So now you're a career girl?"
"Woman."

"What?"

"I'm a woman, not a girl. You wouldn't like me to call you a boy…" I trailed off. I didn't really want to upset him. Too late. I could kick myself.

"Oh no. The feminist card. Well, I tell you what. You let me know when you're not too *busy* to see me and I'll see what I can do." He cut the call. I was stunned. It was the first time ever I'd said no to him. Clearly he didn't like it. Well, screw him. I don't need him. I don't need anyone. I finished off the bottle of Pinot from the night before and cried myself to sleep.

I looked back at Tom's photo. Young - but why shouldn't a woman go for someone younger? Men do it all the time. I tried to distract myself by flicking through the other photos. These comprehensive kids and their attempts at irony. They think they're so clever, taking the piss out of American yearbooks, yet look how influenced by American culture they actually are. Jeez! I must relax, I always revert to type when anxious; becoming the snobby rich kid. Sometimes I wish I had a normal upbringing. But not too often.

*

I tracked him down to a club in Camden. He was messing around with a group of teenagers, probably his mates from school, most of them with fake IDs by the looks of them. He was by far the best looking guy there, but then most of them were all arms and legs, gawky and spotty. There was about eight of them, all standing at the bar. I realised, a bit too late, that it might not be so easy to get to know him. I took a swig of my Corona - from the bottle, obviously. Didn't want to look out of place. Could I really do this? Maybe I could get out of it by telling Uncle Charles that he was gay or something? I can't just walk up to him in front of all his mates. But, then again, it would be awful if I failed. Catastrophic for my career and I can just imagine what Mummy and Daddy would say if I didn't measure up to Uncle Charles' expectations and he let me go. They are always telling me how immature I am and that I should be more like my brother Ed, how I never stick at anything …blah, blah, blah. So many levels to their disappointment in me.

The boys were getting louder and louder as the drinks took effect.

"How's your Gran, Tom?"

"Yeah, the Gran I'd most like to…"

"It's not funny!" Tom's attempts to shut them up only led to more vicious taunts and laughter from the group. He pushed his way through the ring of boys and went to sit down with his bottle of Becks in a corner by the door. He looked pretty miserable. His mates stayed by the bar, getting more lairy by the minute. A group of girls walked in off the street giggling and shouting back at the boys, giving as good as they got. Tom was no longer their target. Brilliant! My chance.

"Hello you, do you mind if I sit here?" I didn't wait for a reply but sat next to him in the corner. I flicked my hair and licked my lips, shiny with bright red lip-gloss. I made a great show of making a few lines of coke. Fake, of course. I didn't want to get arrested and blow the whole job. Blow! Very funny.

I did my best flirting although I've never had to take the lead before. It's more natural for the man to do the chatting up. Luckily, Tom was not backward in coming forward,

"Well hello, please help yourself," and he grinned as if he meant much more than to help myself to the chair.

"Is that..?" he paid more attention to the "coke" than to me at this point.

"Try some, I've plenty more at home."

I was a bit worried about him sniffing up the talcum powder. I really haven't had much experience of drugs apart from the occasional spliff. Always too scared. Both of being caught and of being out of control. But he rubbed it into his gums and seemed happy enough. I copied him. He might be younger than me in years but he seems more experienced or at least more street-wise than me. That made me feel a bit better about the task Uncle Charles had given me.

"Why is a beautiful lady all alone in a place like this?"

Corny, but I guess you have to go through all the motions. I found myself blushing – really?

"Waiting for you of course," he didn't know how true that was.

Well, we went through all the usual chit-chat and by the end of the evening and quite a few bottles later, I'd forgotten all about

Uncle Charles so when he asked if he could see me home, I had no reservations at all. I really liked him. He so enjoyed walking out the pub with me, showing all his friends that he could pull an attractive, older woman.

"Shouldn't you phone your parents to tell them where you are, Tom?" I asked when we got to my flat. I turned to look at him but he was wandering about the place in the same way that most people do in museums or art galleries. Staring respectfully at everything and walking quietly as if any noise would reveal that they shouldn't really be allowed in such hallowed surroundings.

"Wow, is this really all yours? You don't share it with anyone?" he absent-mindedly picked up an old photo of me as a child with Mummy and Daddy while still looking at the paintings on the opposite wall. I quickly took it from him and placed it back, face down, on the bureau.

"Is this real?" he was looking closely at the painting of a sea-scape that Charlie, a once promising graduate from St Martin's, had given me as a twenty-first birthday present.

"Of course it's real. What do you think it is?"
"No, I mean, it's not a print, is it?" he

looked back at the print of 'The Kiss' by Klimt, "what about this one?" I couldn't stop myself. I laughed. "I wish I could afford the original."

I was beginning to regret bringing him home. He really was looking very young and now he knew where I lived. This could get messy. But Uncle Charles had told me to do it and I desperately wanted him to see that I was good at doing whatever he asked me to do. Shit, no, that sounded wrong. I wanted to succeed in the given task. That's better.

So I poured us both a large glass of Cabernet Sauvignon, just a cheap supermarket one.

I handed him a glass, "Shouldn't you ring your parents? They'll be worried. It's after midnight."

"No, it's fine. Dad won't even notice I'm not there and, right now, I don't care what Mum thinks; I'm that pissed off with her. It'd do her good to have something real to worry about," and he took a huge gulp of wine.
"What do you mean?" I thought he was showing off.

"She's always worrying about Gran. Always has, even before Gran started acting a bit weird."

"Weird?" This was interesting. A good start. "Yeh, since Grandad died it's a bit like she's lost it, acting out, getting angry at Mum, going off on random midnight walks, even made a fool of herself in the Lido. She forgot the showers were at the side of the pool or something and started to take her kit off," and - would you believe it, Tom laughed.

"What?" I hoped I sounded surprised.

"No it's not really serious but of course Mum blew it up into a big thing. Took her to the GP and she's now got her into her in a care home. She hates it there. So I don't care what Mum thinks any more," and he came over and sat down next to me, finishing off his wine as if, that too, was an act of defiance. I couldn't think of anything to say to that. I could never talk about my mother like that to a complete stranger.

But I had to make it so we were no longer strangers and after we had finished the bottle of wine, I applied myself to the task with due diligence. I actually forgot all about Uncle Charles and the lady at the lido.

The chemistry was there from the start and I felt surprisingly uninhibited, taking control and showing him what to do with a woman's body. His previous experience was all from internet porn and he had no idea. Our first attempts were almost thrown off course by his expectations of what women liked. But he was a quick learner. And so enthusiastic. He was young, yes, but a welcome change from my usual types. I actually felt he liked me and I could not believe how exciting sex could be. Tom was more than grateful, but in the sober dawn that followed, I think we both felt more than a little embarrassed. After polite discussions about who would like to shower first and then what to do about breakfast, I offered to drive him to the nearest tube.

"Thanks, yeh that would be good. Thanks," Tom wanted to leave as much as I wanted him out of the flat. Neither of us knew what to say and we couldn't look each other in the eye. It was totally embarrassing

"Can we..?" And simultaneously, "How about..?"

And that broke the ice again as we both laughed and then realised that we both wanted to see each other again. So he never did go home. Amazing! So easy. I still couldn't grasp the idea that he didn't care what his family thought but I did try to make him phone his mum to tell her where he was.

He sent her a text; I felt a bit used, as he clearly just wanted to upset her, but at least it made us equal. In a way.

We got on surprisingly well that weekend, spending most of it in bed, with the occasional foray to the fridge for food and alcohol. Once we'd got the porn stuff off the agenda, I realised how good it felt to have sex that included an emotional connection. With all the others it had always been a simply physical, almost competitive, activity for me and always led by the man. Sometimes in the past, I have to admit, I wasn't all that keen but it was easier to give in than to argue about it. In fact, that's how it was with Richard. He was so demanding and never wanted to take me out, he always just wanted to meet me at the flat and have sex and when I finally said no to him, he disappeared.

By Monday morning I was exhausted, but in a good way. I didn't mind: it's true what they say about teenage boys and older women. We had a great time. I couldn't help snuggling up to him. Not like me; the original ice maiden but he made me feel secure. Strange.

*

For the first week every day started the same, "Time for some early morning delight!" And there he would be, cup of tea in each hand, naked as the day he was born and clearly ready for some more action. So tempting. I could just while away every day like this but – Uncle Charles's project. I had to get on with it. He'll be expecting another update any minute now. So, after one more day of this pleasant self-indulgence I jumped right in, "Listen, Tom, I know you're getting a weird kind of pleasure out of wearing my clean knickers, but don't you think you need to get a change of clothes from home? I could take you there in the car..?"

"No, I don't want you meeting my bloody parents. They'd spoil everything."

He'd told me a lot about how awful his parents were but I soon realised it was all just typical teenage boy stuff; nothing that I could use as a lever to find out more about his grandmother. I was terrified of failing Uncle Charles so I try something else,

"I could drive you there, wait outside and then we could go on to the old people's home to see your gran. I'd like to meet her." Strange but true, but for the wrong reasons.

"You're joking me. You know how awful those places are? She and this old dear started fighting over bloody biscuits when I visited her the other day. They both wanted the last of the Gypsy Creams; almost came to blows..." He gazed out of the window. "Mum was right, maybe I shouldn't have gone. I had to find out the address of the home by looking through the files in Dad's office. They really didn't want me and Emily to visit her."

Interesting... I wanted to ask why they weren't supposed to visit their own gran but this was clearly not the time.

"I can't bear seeing her like that. It's like she's become part of the place. Lost herself...and it smells." He look so sad, I wanted to hug him.

"But you keep telling me how she "gets" you and how great she is. I'd really like to meet her, honest. And I think you should carry on visiting her, even if it is difficult."

I have to meet her, it's the only way, although it scares me. What if I say something wrong and get found out? He shrugs but I can see how he likes the idea of showing me off to his gran, and - of course - getting a free ride to his parents' house.

So we drive to some dreary North London suburb. He directs me to this mock Tudor semi lurking in a row of identical houses; each with their dropped kerbs and hard-standing for the mothers' SUVs and the fathers' BMWs. I don't know what I was thinking. I had no plan of action. The consequences of failing Uncle Charles came to mind and I think I panicked. I marched up to the front door and knocked before he could stop me. I could have blown everything. His mother certainly would have killed me if she'd been in. Well, I would have gone for any woman several years older than my eighteen year old son if she'd lured him away to her flat. Luckily, no one *was* in.

"You're mad," Tom says. I think he was right.

"That's just the way I roll," I drawl in a mock American accent and we both giggle with relief that my bluff hasn't been called.

I need to get in that house to "progress", as Uncle Charles would say, my involvement with the family. I knew now that Tom's mum had a difficult relationship with Marian and that it was her who had put her in a home, isolating her from her grandchildren. Although what I'm supposed to do next I don't know. As I said, I have no plan of action. No doubt Uncle Charles has; but I'm only on a need-to-know contract.

*

While Tom gets his things together upstairs, I have a nose around the.., what do they call it.., "lounge" I suppose. All the usual stuff: stripped floorboards, gaudy rugs and modular seating in grey brocade to go with the feature walls of Graham and Brown wallpaper. Everywhere else is a slightly different shade of off-white. The obligatory reed diffuser wafts a bland chemical fragrance over it all. A few prints and loads of family photos in those tacky mass-produced frames, stuck together, supposed to give the impression that someone had just artfully arranged them in tasteful little gatherings on the wall. Just as I realise I'm being bitchy and on the defensive because it feels more like a proper home and not like our family mausoleum, one stops me dead. It's Uncle Charles - next to a middle-aged couple who, from the other photos, must be Tom's parents. What? Why did he send me here if he knew them all along? So what is the link with the old granny? No… A dreadful thought struck me. Could Charles seriously be Tom's secret grandfather or something? Shit! I have to sit down.

I'm still there when Tom comes down.
"You ok? You look really pale," he says.

"Um, yeah, sure," stay neutral, Felicity,
don't blow it, "Just tired. I didn't know your
parents knew Charles Davidson..?"

"Who?"

"This guy here, he's often on the telly. He's
a politician actually. Even you must have
heard of him." I still can't steady my voice
but Tom doesn't appear to notice.

"No, I'm not into politics, they're all the
same - you ever heard them on the TV?
Load of posh blokes shouting at each other,
just a game for them. I don't give a toss
about any of it, it's mad." Annoying and
immature but I let it go. He is still young, I
suppose. God! What am I doing? All I want
to do is to make a successful career in
politics so that Mummy and Daddy could be
proud of me. Maybe –with Uncle Charles
help – I could become a researcher or even
an advisor. I would really knuckle down and
take it seriously then. Show my family that
I'm not just a pretty little face. But this is
getting too weird, isn't it?

"But why would your parents pose for a
picture with him?" I'm genuinely curious.

Tom walks up to the photo and looks at it as if he's never seen it before.

"Oh him. He's been helping Dad get nominated to stand for parliament or something. Yeah, and he helped Mum get that place for Gran. They only met him a few weeks ago; couldn't wait to have that photo up there," and he laughs, actually laughs.

"What?" My knees and the tops of my thighs start prickling and I have to get up and walk around. What is happening here?

"Yeah, Mum took her to the GP, like I said, so Uncle Darren arranged for her to go to this place near him and Kevin in Brighton. Gran was dead excited, but apparently this posh guy in the photo comes along, tells Mum this other place is better and takes her there to look at it. Next thing I know Mum tells me Gran's not going to Brighton any more. Shame really. Brighton's cool."

I sit down again. Is Charles playing me? Rumour has it that he plays god with everyone. I'm actually beginning to believe it. The top of my legs start to tingle even more, as if I were standing at the edge of a precipice about to fall at any minute.

"When did this all happen?"

"Oh a couple of weeks ago, I think. They met at one of Dad's political meetings. He offered to help and it all takes off. Yeah, Mum goes down to this new place on the Monday, Gran was in there by the weekend. That photo was taken just before me and you got together. That night was magic." He makes a dewy-eyed lunge for me but I'm in no mood for teenage lust. I need to get away.

"Let's go," I snap, "before your parents get back. Unless *you* want to stay here. But I'm going right now." The look on his face makes me regret taking it out on him. "Come on, have you got all your stuff? Let's go and see this Gran of yours." I say.

"Hang on I can't find my blue backpack. I asked Emily, my little sister, you know, to put it somewhere safe for me..."

We can't wait any longer; his mother might come back at any moment. I'm not good at direct confrontations. I can't help myself; I grab his sleeve,

"No, let's go now, you can come back for it later."

So we leave and all the way to his gran's care home, I'm trying to work out if I can find out what Charles is up to without blowing my chances of promotion and upsetting my parents. More to the point; have I really been screwing around with Uncle Charles's grandson?

Chapter 6: Marian

Nothing Ventured, Nothing Gained

I felt safe when I lived in my own little terraced house in Finchley. I knew where everything was. I loved my garden with its small lawn where the crocuses came up every year, the rose bushes and the lavender and, of course the beautiful magnolia tree with its old gnarled branches and ostentatious spring flowers. I would sit in my little summer house at the end of the garden on summer evenings with a sneaky gin and tonic and even an illicit cigarette when Bob was too busy watching the boxing or cricket to worry about what I was doing.

For all his faults, I was lonely after Bob died. I realised then how totally dependent on him I had become. Over the years, Bob and his temper had managed to alienate all my friends and family, so they stopped coming round. I kept meaning to contact my old friends after his funeral but somehow I had neither the courage nor the energy to do it. I told myself every day that I'd do it tomorrow.

One day the loneliness got so bad that I decided to do something. As I drift off, lying

in this antiseptic room with its carefully
controlled heating, I think back to that cold,
wet summer's day. I saw myself, lying alone
in the double bed that now seemed far too
wide; the urge to stay there all day…

*

Birds squawking a dawn cacophony. The
empty house closing in on me. I am
suffocating here. I drag myself up and across
the floor, wrap my coat over my dirty
nightie and slide my feet into my old
slippers. The need to get out of this house;
this cold and empty life, pushes me on,
down the darkened hall and out of the door.
It slams shut behind me as if it, too, is sick
of the sight of me.

I look at the street of identical houses, their
windows not watching me like they usually
do because it's too early in the morning to
care. It's raining; any sensible person would
go back in but, no, I shall walk bravely on
and "screw my courage to the sticking post."
Yes, I love that quote, where's it from?

Just a minute, what's that sound? Am I near
the sea? I've always loved the sea. I need to
go back to the sea; it's important though I'm
not sure why. I follow the sound of breaking
waves … What? Oh, it's not the sea after all.

No, just the endless waves of traffic on the North Circular road. So close to the cemetery. Bob lies there. Safely tucked under the pitiless soil.

The waves disappear, lost in the noise of the cars and lorries. Stupid old woman- what was I thinking? I creep as close as I dare. Look at all these people getting on with their lives at such a pace. The filth from the road sprays up at me, drenching my slippers and coat. The rush of wind from each vehicle drags me towards those diesel monsters. There's no freshness to this rain. Is it that acid rain I've heard about? The touch and smell of it scorch my eyes and throat. I scream against the traffic and lose. Hurtling along, the rest of the world ignores me. Until I step out.

A lorry blasts its horn. The driver shouts abuse. His vile words linger in my head as he swerves into another lane. I fall back onto the muddy verge and curl into a ball, sobbing. It sparks a memory; the smell of bleach and fear, a dingy room, me sobbing, just like now. Something dreadful happened there. No, it's gone again. What's the use? Come on now, pull yourself together. I straighten my hair and clothing and stand up to my full five feet one inch. With all the decorum and dignity I can muster, I stand at the roadside, waving down the traffic. Ages pass by but at last a young couple stop. Their shocked faces demand an explanation from me.

"Is it Christmas yet?" I ask them.

Of course, I know it's only June but what else can I say? Our family had a saying for when life was bad and it was; *Never mind, it'll soon be Christmas.* The young couple don't seem to understand.

The warmth of their car envelops me as the young woman folds me gently into it, and gradually I hear my sobs subside. "I'm so sorry…"

I let them drive me all around North London, pretending to look for my house until, eventually, they – like everyone else - give up on me and take me to a police station.

They hug me goodbye. I don't think anyone has touched me for ages. I can't help clinging to them like a little lost child but they're not mine to cling to. Then the kind policeman gives me a lovely cup of hot sweet tea. It tastes like nectar, even though I don't usually take sugar. I pretend I can't recall my name because I like being here with people interested in me.

"I know I knew it when I left home… it must be written down somewhere..." I scrabble around in my bag, pretending to look for my name, when a young black girl, about twenty-something, walks in.

"Hello, there. My name is Shireen and I'm a social worker. I've come to help you sort this silly mess out." Oh no. Is she going to take me away? Mum always said they'd take you away and put you in a home if you were naughty. Didn't that happen to me once? The image of endless dark grey corridors flashes into my mind. My mum being held back by Father Michael. The overwhelming fear forces the truth from me.

"It's ok. I remember now. My name is Marian Norman, of course it is, silly me. How could I forget?"

I like this girl. We talk for ages and I tell her all about Tracey and Darren and how well they look after me, most of the time. In the end Shireen drives me home in her own car, helps me find the right plant pot for the spare keys and together we look up the phone numbers for Tracey and Darren in the address book next to the telephone.

Whatever the social worker said to them worked; I got regular phone calls from them every week after that.

*

"Is no good getting comfy," Sonya pulls me back up to sitting, then swivels me around, edging my legs over the side of the bed, deftly manipulating me into the wheelchair, "Tracey here for you."

She throws a blanket over my nightie and wheels me into the day room. The news from Tracey is a complete surprise, even though Tracey insists that I already knew.

"Tom? In Cape Town? He can't be - that's in South Africa. It's miles away! He was here! I've just seen him." I feel suddenly bereft.

Tracey smiles that patronising smile that I hate so much, "No. You are funny, Mum. He can't have been here, not recently. Don't you remember – I did tell you - he came back home for some of his things? Remember? It was beginning to get serious with that Felicity. Wanted to move in completely with her, can you believe it?" I try to say something but she waves me away with an irritated hand. "Anyway, I was carrying his blue backpack downstairs, I wouldn't stop him moving out; it would only make him more determined. But then the bag split open and - guess what? It was full of drugs. I was so angry with him, Mum. He'd promised me that he didn't use that stuff anymore but there was enough there for him to be sent away for dealing. That's what Nigel said, anyway."

"Trust Nigel to think the worst of his own son." I thought I'd muttered it under my breath. There was usually no stopping Tracey in full flow.

"No, Mum, that's not fair. Anyway, we talked it over with…with someone who suggested getting him into some sort of rehab and he suggested this place in South Africa. It was cheaper than anywhere in England, even when you take into account the air fare."

"That's ridiculous, he just needs a bit more love and understanding, not being sent away. I should know." My poor boy; sent away. Who could I turn to now? I had hoped Tom would get me out of here somehow.

"It's not always about you, Mum," again the dismissive hand, "We contacted Jenny – you remember your cousin, Jenny?"

"Of course I do" I snapped. "Why does everybody think I'm senile or something?"

"We don't, Mum, it's just that you haven't been in touch for years," she sighed an unnecessary sigh.

"She was sent away to South Africa when we were teenagers…" I try to remember why. I close my eyes and think of my favourite cousin. We were so close once. What happened? Something bad, I think. I wish I could remember. But Tracey pulls my attention back to her.

"No. She wasn't "sent away", as you put it. Really, Mum. You do say some funny things. Don't you remember? She went with her family, paid for by some government-sponsored emigration scheme, but that's beside the point. The thing is, she checked out this place for us and, although it's costing us a fortune..."
"Nigel won't like that." I just can't help myself.

"Stop saying things like that. I don't know why you don't like him. He's agreed, Mum. He does love our kids, despite what you think of him. He wants the best for Tom."
"More likely he wants him out of the way so he can concentrate on his Parliamentary

career without scandalous druggie sons spoiling his chances…"

"Mum, I can't keep doing this…" And suddenly she is crying.

The silence creeps around us while we struggle to find a way back to the innocuous small talk people fall back on in places like care homes. I never could hold a grudge for long, no matter how hard I try. I've always been too needy. I sneak a look at Tracey while she's lost in thought. I didn't give her much of a childhood. I have to make up for it somehow and arguments like this will never do.

"So will you go to visit him?" I finally dredge up to ask my poor, long-suffering daughter.

"Go where? Oh you mean to visit Tom. Yes." Tracey seems pleased to break the silence too, so long as she doesn't lose face. There I go again, thinking the worst of her.

"We all have to go and do some family therapy. Nigel's not keen but I've told him it's like a three line whip and he'll just have to take time off from work and his political campaigning. The Party encouraged him too. They said he should go. It would look better if he supported his son's recovery or something. Emily's very excited – I've told her it's not a holiday but she can't wait to get out there." She looks out of the window, to avoid my eyes.

An even heavier silence sits between us.

Tracey takes a deep breath and whispers, "Actually, Mum, it scares me a bit. I'm not sure what's going to happen. Families are a mess and you're never quite sure you've done the right thing by your kids. They can always find something to throw at you."

I miss one of the few times that Tracey lets her vulnerability show because I'm still thinking about myself and my resentment, "Like you refusing to believe me, you mean?" I can't stop myself.

"Oh Mum, please, not this again. I've told you, I asked Dr Campbell to check yet again about your medical records. Nothing! No other babies, no other pregnancies." She's back in control again.

We sit together: the words have run out. Our bodies are close but our minds are in separate worlds.

*

"Marian, stop ringing alarm, you wake everyone up!"

Sonya bustles into the room, syringe in hand. "Here, this fix you. It's five in morning; your young visitors make you over-excited."

I'm just about to tell her I haven't had any visitors for weeks, even months, maybe years when she stabs my arm with her needle and life seems too pleasant to argue. But that doesn't last nearly long enough.

Tracey is waiting for me when I wake up again. A face like thunder. She goes straight into the attack.

"Sonya tells me you've been waking everyone up, ringing alarms in the middle of the night, going on about cameras and lost baby sons. Really Mum, we'll never get you out of here if you keep on like this. Are you still taking all your all medication?"

"It wasn't me…"

"You're just punishing yourself for not stopping Dad from sending our Darren off when he told us he was gay."

She leans into my face. "You haven't lost your son."

 I turn away from her hot breath. I made my peace with Darren long ago.

"Mum – listen- the medication will help you. You're not missing out any of it, are you?" And she starts to check my bedside table to see if there are any pills in the drawer. How dare she? She'll tell them if she finds the pills.

"Leave my things alone," I slap her hand roughly away from the drawer.

"Mum!" She is shocked and I am ashamed – but also angry. Tracey shifts uncomfortably in her chair, rubbing her hand. Once again, mother and child are torn apart.

*

Gwen and I have been allowed out in the garden, so long as we stay in sight of our key care workers. We call them our minders. Child-minders, or the heavies you used to see before Perestroika, "minding" the Soviet athletes and dancers? Are we naughty children or dangerous subversives? Probably both. Anyway, they always seem to be minding the two of us, in every sense of the word.

"Gwen, I think Dr Campbell's a bit odd…Don't you think there's something not quite right about her?"

"Who?" Gwen is sniffing the dead hydrangeas.

"Dr Campbell!"

"What? Other than the fact she's a very ugly lezzie and wears nasty clothes, you mean?" She has a way with words.

"No, it's not that. She's always checking up on me, giving me more and more drugs. She keeps a closer eye on me than she does everyone else here." I shake off the dark thoughts with a laugh. "Maybe you're right, she is attracted to me; likes the older woman."

"Well, you are a damned fine woman." She looks appraisingly at me, "I would..! You know...! If I were that way inclined. In fact I might anyway, I'm getting that desperate!"

"Thanks - I think" I do love Gwen; no matter what life throws at us she still makes me laugh. But today I need her help to sort out something in what's left of my mind.

"I had one of those new mobile phones the other day. Did I show it to you? I can't find it anymore. It has something to do with Tom but I can't remember. Do you remember if he visited me this week?"

"I don't get them mobile phones – how do they know where you'll be when they ring?" Sometimes Gwen's view of life confuses even me.

"You know, last week when your Tracey come visiting, Emily rang her here on the clever little phone she keep in her bag. Why did she ring here? How did Emily know she'd be visiting you and wasn't at home - did she tell her?"

"No Gwen; Darren says that they work through some sort of satellite system that tracks the phone. But why would anyone leave a mobile with me? I don't think we're allowed them. I don't even know how to use one." But Gwen wasn't listening.

"I had a dog that was sent up in a satellite, Laika, her name was. They couldn't get her back. She must have starved to death. Imagine how scared she was; she didn't know what was happening. She must have been so lonely, so abandoned. I wanted to go get her down from there. But I couldn't reach her. They wouldn't let me. I cried for months after." Gwen's eyes misted over into tears and I held her hand in mine.

"I don't think that was *your* dog, Gwen..." but she had withdrawn into that lonely place that I know so well. Everything's just too tiring to think about and all you want to do is sleep. I've lost whole years in that grey and self-absorbed place. I settled back in my chair, still clutching Gwen's outstretched hand.

Before I knew it, I was thirteen again.

*

"Don't leave me here," I begged, but with my eyes, not out loud. Not even this fearful place could make me speak. I looked into the long, long corridor with its doors. So many doors, all tightly shut. They refused to look at this shameful girl. Father Michael knew. My silence at confession hadn't saved me from his knowing. I watched him holding Mum back as the nuns led me away.

"There's your bed, third on the right, make sure you keep it clean and tidy." They gave me a rough grey blanket and a matching dress. They took away my own clothes…

I don't remember much else about the place. I wonder if that was where I lost my baby. I remember Mum coming to collect me. She dressed me gently in my old clothes and cried when she saw how small they were on me.

I wish she were here now, looking after me. I don't feel safe.

Chapter 7: Felicity meets Marian

You Can't Judge a Book by Its Cover

I'm still trying to get my head around the photo of Tom's parents with Uncle Charles when we arrived at the care home.

Oh God, that disgusting smell! As a boarder, I was used to the institutional pine disinfectant and boiled cabbage pot-pourri of my school but the walls and floors in the care home were also steeped in years of old ladies' urine and slightly bad eggs.

A skinny girl in a white uniform opened the door, smiling at Tom and totally ignoring me.

"Hello Sonya, how is she today?" Interesting, he knows her. No of course I'm not jealous.

"Same as usual Tom. She still think I try to kill her every day," and they shared a laugh.

"Let's go," I couldn't stop the edge to my voice so I tried to compensate by smiling at Sonya. Believe it or not, she totally blanked me and turned back to sorting out the drugs trolley. We wandered through endless green corridors.

The smell didn't get better when we finally found Tom's gran. Two little old dears holding hands, sitting side by side with their body odours and lavender water mingling with the rest. One black, one a deathly pale. One twinkling with unreleased energy, the other dazed and immobile. Was this really the same woman from the video? She was staring straight at us as we walked in, with no sense of recognition for her grandson.

"Look, Marian, it's your Tom and his new girlfriend. Ooh she's a stunner!" Marian's companion gently shook her friend's arm. Finally Marian blinked back into the room.

"Hello Tom, my lovely boy. I haven't seen you for ages. Haven't you grown?"

"You saw me the other day, Gran, but don't tell Mum." Clearly Tom was used to this. He dragged a couple of those plastic chairs, screeching across the linoleum floor, expecting me to sit on one. I couldn't help imagining my white linen trousers coming into contact with the mixed residue of bodily substances. What could I do? I had no choice. I sat down. The click of the clock counting out the silences seemed to get slower and slower. One old dear in the corner was crying and Sonya was trying to comfort her, without success. A group of women were playing a noisy game of cards over at the table and there was a solitary woman staring at the silent TV. No men, I noticed. Finally, thank God, Tom could stand it no more and he broke our silence,

"This is Felicity, Gran, I told you about her last time I was here, remember?"

"Of course I remember. Why on God's earth would you think I'd forget?" A bit harsh, I thought.

Undeterred he kept up a barrage of chatty banter, appreciated more by the little old black lady, who I guessed was her friend Gwen, than by his gran who kept disappearing behind her half-closed eyes. The only time she reacted at all was when Tom mentioned his Uncle Darren.

"Why won't he come and take me away from here?" I couldn't help but be fascinated by the way her tears found their way down the wrinkles on her face.

"I need to go to Brighton. He said he'd take me. How can I get there if he doesn't take me?" She was clutching Gwen's hand so tightly, I was surprised that she didn't react. Used to it, I supposed.

"It's the drugs," Gwen whispered to Tom, "she's not herself lately."

"She should do what I used to do when they kept giving me Ritalin. Stick it between the inside of your cheek and your gum." I stared at Tom. Ritalin? Wasn't that something they gave to disruptive boys once the educational psychiatrist had given them the ADHD label?

Gwen chuckled, "That's what I do. I keep telling her; no use fighting them. Pretend to be good and quiet, then they don't watch you so closely, but no, she take on so, they watch her like hawks. Sometimes even inject her when she get too distraught."

It came out before I could stop myself, "I'm sure they wouldn't give her the drugs if she didn't need them. They must know what they're doing."

The way Tom and Gwen stared at me! I felt like an idiot child. Am I really so naïve? Everyone seem so to know so much more of the world than I do. I suppose my life experience has been quite narrow up until now.

"They just keeping her quiet, make it easier on themselves," Gwen rubbed Marian's arm again, "She don't need all them drugs. They make her so weak, distress her with bad dreams."

"Gwen's right, Fliss. That's why my secondary school got Mum to take me to the doctors to get some Ritalin, the teachers couldn't handle me, said they'd expel me." There was more to Tom than I had realised. I didn't know if it made him more, or less, attractive.

"Wish we could get expelled from this place," I watched Gwen look wistfully at Marian, then out of the window.

"Will you take me?" Marian had suddenly come back to us. She looked straight at me and for a brief moment I felt we had known each other in some previous life. But that was stupid.

The other two turned expectantly to me. I didn't know how to react so I made some kind of polite noise and picked off some of my nail varnish until my thighs stopped prickling. Why does she think I could get her away from this place? Has she worked out that I'm not really just Tom's new girlfriend? That I have another agenda? No, how could she? That's just my guilt talking. Guilt? Why should I feel guilty? I'm not hurting him, we're both just having fun.

*

I was relieved when Tom said we had to go, even though I had probably missed a chance to get closer to Marian. If only I had been braver, I could have found out just what she knew that was so important to Uncle Charles.

"I don't think I can go back there again." I told Tom as we left. It was just too risky because there was something about the way she looked at me that was really unsettling. Then there was that photograph in Tom's house. I was glad of Tom's protective arm around me as we walked to the car. Funny, it didn't seem then that he was the younger one.

"But, she's not normally like that, well she wasn't, but she seems to be getting stranger- and skinnier, come to think of it – every time I see her – just getting old I guess."

I was trapped. Again. How was it that whenever my family, including Uncle Charles, got me into something, I felt I was being used in a way that I didn't understand and couldn't control? Maybe it wasn't only the vile smells causing this stomach-twisting nausea.

*

"Tom, I've changed my mind. I'm worried about your gran," I shook him awake. The sun was filtering its way through the gauze Tree-of-Life hanging that I'd brought back from my gap-year travels in India. It had woken me at five in the morning. Frankly I had been grateful. Relieved. I'd had the most awful nightmare where Marian and I were both trapped in a sort of very soft mattress and the more we struggled to get away, the more we were pulled into it. It wasn't scary in itself. But it came with such a strong sense of fear that when I woke I didn't dare go back to sleep in case of what might happen.

As I emerged from the dream and before I was fully awake, I thought again about the photo of Uncle Charles with Tom's parents. This job I'd been given, when he was clearly in contact with the family, felt wrong. What was he going to expect me to do next? I looked over at Tom. He looked much younger when he was asleep. Had I trapped him? Had I pimped myself out? And to what end? No, I'm just being silly. It was just that the night terrors that I used to get as a child that had momentarily come back. Probably the stress of meeting Marian. She was now a real person, not just a name in a job I had to do. It'll be fine. Won't it?

"Tom? Are you awake yet?"

"What? What time is it?" His blond hair, all tousled, and his sleepy little face made me forget those dark thoughts and want to mother him instead. That didn't sound healthy. Totally inappropriate, in fact, given what we'd been doing just a few hours before. I shook my head and pushed away his all too welcoming arms.

"It doesn't matter. It's just that I'm worried about your gran. I think you should keep a better eye on her, especially if you and Gwen both think they're giving her more drugs than she really needs,"

"It's ok, Mum goes there most days…" He sat up and started to reach for his phone.

"But it was her who put her in there against her will…" That photo of Uncle Charles with Tom's parents, what did it mean? "Hang on. What are you saying about my mum..?" His glare shot me dead. He turned back to his phone. The only sound between us was the clicking of his phone. I looked over his shoulder and he was texting his sister, Emily, about his bloody bag. I felt like snatching the phone out of his hands.

"You've got a point though." he said, finally turning back to look at me.

"What?"

"Ever since Grandad died, Gran has been obsessed about some baby she had, back in the day. No one believes her and now Mum gets really mad when she talks about it and shuts her up. What if she *is* telling the truth, though? You would go bonkers, wouldn't you, if everyone kept telling you that something you *know* has happened to you, has never really happened? Especially something as heavy as that."

I felt sick again. That poor woman. That's what this is all about. Of course it had happened and I know how. Or rather, who with. I should get out of this mess – but how?

"How about we get Gwen to help her skip her drugs? And maybe we could slip them a mobile so we can keep an eye on them..?" It was said in a moment of panic, fuelled by the lingering atmosphere of my bad dream, but he latched onto it and, typically, insisted we went back that same day complete with a cheap pay-as-you-go mobile.

*

Tom showed the phone to his gran and Gwen when we went back. They were sitting in exactly the same spot in the day room. It seemed that all the old dears had their particular places. Was that one of the few choices they had left to make, or did the home allocate them?

"The phone's been wiped. It has a sim card but there's nothing on the memory,"

"It's a bit like me, then" Marian laughed when he tried to explain. Gwen was totally confused.

"It just means that there are no phone numbers or photos stored on it," he explained and showed them how it all worked.

"What do you mean photos? I thought it was a phone, not a camera?" Now Marian was confused too. Once we'd shown them how the camera worked we had to take pictures of everyone and everything. Even Sonya came and posed with them although I noticed Marian scowling. She really doesn't like her.

"Oh I like that one; the one of you Tom, with me and Felicity. Can I have a copy of it? Put it on my dresser?" she begged.

Tom showed her how to save it on her phone and I sent it off to my home server, promising to send Marian a printed copy. By now I'd overcome my initial shock – I'd never been in such a place before. Mummy and Daddy's parents had been looked after at home; we had people in to help.

Soon Marian and I were like best friends – you'd think we'd known each other all our lives – and we started swapping stories about our families. The ones about Tom embarrassed him but he didn't complain too much. I was careful about mine, but then I've never been one to give away too much. Maybe that's why I never had any real close friends at school. Not that I wanted them. Daddy always said that things get messy if you get too involved with people.

While Tom was busy trying to explain the phone to Gwen, Marian quietly turned and whispered to me,

"It's not right, you know…"

"What isn't?" Marian's secretive grasp was hurting my arm.

"The way they all confuse you. Tell you that things that you know have happened are just not real. They assume that all old people get dementia and we don't. It's just them. They deliberately confuse you and then they give you the drugs to keep you quiet, just like Tom said."

So I smiled and patted the old woman's hand and tried a few soothing noises.

"Oh, I can see even you think I am being paranoid now. But just you wait, my dear, until you get old. Then you'll understand."

I took a chance; "What is it that they confuse you about, Gran? You don't mind if I call you Gran, do you?"

"I'd rather you didn't, it makes me feel so old. Call me Marian. I don't know why but I feel I can talk to you. Would you mind walking me to the toilet?"

Oh no, I'm not good with old people and especially if it was going to involve bodily functions. But, despite my misgivings about him, I still needed Uncle Charles' approval and to get that I had to find out something about this woman.

"Don't worry," Marian held up her arms to be helped out of her chair then whispered, "I just want to talk in private, you know…" and she nodded towards Tom.

We made slow progress. Marian slipped her old bony hand in the crook of my elbow and we tottered across the room. Once past through the heavy safety doors into the corridor, Marian let go and turned to face me. Was she going to confront me? Crossing my fingers, I bent down to hear what she was trying to say.

"I…I think – that sounds daft; I should *know* – but I think I had a baby before I had Tracey and Darren…" She took a deep breath, dropping her voice still further, "and it was illegitimate; not my Bob's babies. It was before I met him. I can't remember much about it all so I need to get out of here; to go and find out what happened to my baby. Will you help me?"

Tears of shame filled her eyes and she cast her head down towards the floor. I looked around for help but there was just the two of us. Alone together. What should I do? I held the older woman in what I hoped was a gentle embrace. This made Marian cry all the more until her tiny body was a mess of tears. I've been brought up in a family that doesn't appreciate even glimpses of feelings, let alone emotional outbursts like this. But at that moment I felt a stirring, an almost imperceptible feeling of sympathy for this frail, confused woman.

"It's ok. Hush. Don't worry, it doesn't matter now. It was all a long, long time ago…"

My hand patting Marian's back was brusquely shrugged off. She lifted her head and glared at me. So much for making an effort to be nice.

"What do you mean, "It doesn't matter?" He was *my* baby! What could you know about it? You're just like the rest of them." Marian's eyes, still full of tears, were now piercing me with such a ferocity that I had to take several steps back.

"Sorry, I...I was just trying…"

"Yes, yes. You're all very trying," Marian's laugh was harsh, "they tell me I couldn't have had a baby or it would be in my medical records. They say that everyone in my family says so. My cousins, my own children, they all think I've made it up. So obviously, I must be mad. I must take all those drugs - but I won't. Not anymore and now I have to get out of here before they start to inject even more of them into me." And she swept through the door into the toilets, clearly able to walk without help. I just stood there. I waited for the flush of the toilet, the bang of the cubicle door being opened again and went in to find Marian at the mirrors, trying to put her face in order.

"I'm sorry, I didn't mean to upset you..."
But she'd changed again; she smiled apologetically,

"No, I'm sorry. I'm just a silly old fool, I know you didn't mean anything by it. For some strange reason I thought you'd understand. Let's just go back, and please..." and she touched my arm,
"Yes?"

"Don't say anything about this to Tom, will you?"

"Of course not, but how long ago was it that you had your baby?" I felt bad but I had to get some answers for Uncle Charles.

"When I was a teenager in the sixties. He was my first and only love"

"But you must have been very young..."

"Oh I was, and it was so exciting having a man like him noticing me." She looked positively radiant at the memory. I felt sick.

"But Marian..." I stopped. What could I say? Who was I to shatter her happy memories? What good would it do now; things were very different back then. So I just gave Marian's hand a gentle squeeze as I placed it back in the crook of my elbow and led her back to where Tom and Gwen were still playing with the phone.

The rest of the morning was spent taking photos and explaining the phone to Gwen and Marian. It was obvious that the two old friends were totally bemused by the idea of a mobile phone that could also take photos, access something called the internet and everything else. I felt safer knowing that they would probably never remember how to use it. Still, I entered my number into it and surreptitiously slipped it into the pocket of Marian's blue cashmere cardigan.

*

On the way home in the car, I struggled with my promise not to say anything about her to Tom but then I decided that she would probably have forgotten all about it by now and certainly wouldn't have remembered the promise. Well, she couldn't even remember my name; calling me Tracey or Jenny - even Darren once.

"I'm afraid I upset your Gran. You know, when we went out to the toilet."

"Really? Well, it's not hard to, she's got a real short fuse lately. I told you about the Gypsy Creams, didn't I? And she's always upsetting Mum, accusing her of moving her things, interfering with her life…all sorts of random stuff."

"Well people with dementia can get aggressive, I've heard. So she didn't seem so volatile before?"
"What do you mean?"

I wasn't sure whether he didn't know the meaning of the word or how it affected his Gran so I just said, "One minute she's frail and tearful; the next she's like a wounded tiger. She changes in a nano-second."

"It's the frail and tearful I don't get, she's always been quite feisty. For an old person, I mean."

"But it's the sudden changes, Tom. It's as if something switches in her brain, almost changing her personality."

"I thought you liked her..?"

"I do, don't get me wrong. I'm just wondering whether the authorities have got it right and she really does need to be in a place of safety like that." That much was true. I really had been shocked by the mood swings.

Tom stared at the greyness of the M25; for once it was almost empty and we were making good time. I didn't want to continue

the conversation as it was clearly upsetting
him and I was beginning to really like him –
and Marian, if it comes to that. Still, I had to
succeed in this job… project… whatever it
was. I can't disappoint my family again.
They'd been so happy that Uncle Charles
had taken me on. I couldn't bear to let them
down again. I took a deep breath,

"She told me that she'd had a baby, back in
the sixties, but that none of your family
believed her…"
"Well it would have been hushed up,
wouldn't it? They used to send them away
and not let them come back until the baby
had been born and adopted. Even in my
Mum's days it was the worst thing you
could do if you were a girl…"
"If you were a *girl*? Jesus! It takes two you
know."

"Yeah, obviously, but wasn't it always the
girl who got the blame, who had to hide it
all away? Mum says there was a girl at her
school who got herself pregnant: her mother
brought up the kid like it was her own and
this girl had to pretend she was just its sister
with no say in her own baby's life. And that
was in the eighties, long after Gran's time."

"When *she got herself pregnant*? There you
go again. Blame the woman. Thank

goodness it wasn't like that when I was growing up." I'd never stopped to think about it before and here I was, coming over all angry feminist. Weird.

"Yeah, well you rich kids could always go to Harley Street and pay for your abortions anyway, not like my gran. She didn't get a choice." That brought me up short, I'd been so angry, I'd almost lost sight of what I was supposed to be doing. I needed to find out what he actually thought of Marian's story. "So you do believe her?"

"Only because no one else does."

"But she would have been a very young girl; she married your dad at seventeen."

"That's why Mum never believed her… Wait… how did you know that?"

Shit! Think, Felicity, think. I looked back at the road.
"You must have told me. Yes, that night when you were so angry at your mum and dad. You were so pissed, I'm not surprised you don't remember. I got your whole family's history."

I think he believed me but it was clear I needed to be careful and try to remember what I'd found out for Uncle Charles and what I'd heard from Tom. But what Tom had said about girls getting themselves pregnant actually got me thinking. I'd have been in big trouble with my parents if I'd got pregnant so young. They would have dealt with it quickly, all sorted with a quick trip to a discreet gynaecologist, without any discussion with or about the father. Money and contacts, that's all it takes. Not like those girls in Rotherham and all the other towns. They were blamed for being groomed and raped; got called prostitutes and druggies. Working class girls with little or no support. Young teenagers, just like Marian must have been. No one believed them either, until much later. Poor Marian. I really did like the old lady. She seemed to lose years when we talked. By the end of the morning, I'd forgotten just how old she was. It was like talking to a normal person.

I looked over at Tom. I needed to talk but he sat there, miles away from me, fidgeting with his phone, scrolling vaguely through his Instagram pages. I searched for a neutral subject.

"So, did you like the photo we took?" I asked, keeping my eyes on the road.

"S'alright" was the clipped response.

"She's a character, your gran, isn't she? And that Gwen…"

"They're ok." He looked away, out to the fields beyond the hard shoulder of the M25. I tried a few more times to start a conversation about Marian, but had to give up. I had clearly strayed onto sensitive ground here. Several miles passed heavily by.

"I'm going home tonight…" he casually threw at me, carefully avoiding eye contact.

"What? Why? Are you not coming back to the flat?" I couldn't believe everything was going so wrong, so suddenly.

"Oh yeah, I just need to pick up that bag. It's got some stuff in it. Some really good stuff. Columbian." He smiled.

"Oh. So you'll be back tonight?"

"Of course I will, I don't want to spend any longer than I have to with them."

So I was being over-anxious, expecting him to be sensitive. He was a teenage boy, after all. Totally tied up in his own life.
"Yeah, just drop me off in Barnet and I'll make my own way home on the bus. I'll be back about sevenish."

How I wish that had been true.

Chapter 8: Felicity

Needs Must When the Devil Drives

After a sleepless night when Tom didn't return, I drag myself into work to find an envelope marked "Private and Confidential" on my desk. It's a report on Marian written by a Dr Campbell who is, apparently, her designated medical practitioner at the Home.

To Whom It May Concern

Private report on Marian Norman, nee Alsop

Marian Norman was admitted to Golden Meadows Care Home on 30/08/2019, under Section 3 of the 1983 Mental Health Act, granting us the power to detain and treat her mental disorder, to be reviewed in six months. She is very resistant to treatment and her son is becoming uncooperative, repeatedly questioning our treatment regimes and declaring his intention of removing her as soon as the order has run its course. Her daughter, who acts as the main carer, is more amenable.

She was admitted under the Mental Health Act after an incident at the local authority swimming pool in Barnet to which the police were called. Records from her GP showed repeated bouts of depression and anxiety throughout her teenage and adult life. More recently, following the death of her husband, concerns were expressed about her increasingly erratic and sometimes dangerous behaviour whilst living on her own, often wandering along busy dual carriageways, possibly contemplating a suicide attempt.

She is vocally resistant to the drug regime which we have tried to impose. Because of our rigorous observation, there has been no evidence that she has yet been able to avoid taking the medication, although we have, on a few occasions, had to resort to administering the drugs intravenously or by single injections. This may be our primary method if her total quiescence is not achieved soon.

Her general health has rapidly deteriorated since admission; she frequently fails to eat her meals and has lost a substantial amount of weight. We have yet to discern whether she is doing this deliberately. She no longer takes care of her appearance or general hygiene. She has had several attacks of urinary incontinence. She suffers from muscular atrophy, possibly from lack of use due to her lethargy. She also suffers extremely vivid nightmares and frequently wakes up screaming.

Her medical records, going back as far as the 1950s, have been checked. There is no record of any birth other than those of her two known children, Tracey and Darren, nor of any miscarriages or abortions.

There is, however, circumstantial evidence of abuse, both in her childhood and as an adult and it may be this that has caused the schizoaffective disorder which I would diagnose as her major problem. This would explain both her depressive mood symptoms and the psychotic symptoms that she displays in the form of hallucinations. She frequently hears voices and interprets the world around her in an unusual way; for example insisting her TV remote is, in fact, a mobile phone. She also suffers from the delusion that she is being controlled or even harmed by staff here. She is often very confused and frightened, particularly when she first wakes up.

These symptoms are frequently seen in people who have been through difficult periods or trauma in their lives and Marian falls into that category. As a child she was admitted to The Victoria Hospital in Lewes, Sussex, with severe injuries to her genitalia, allegedly caused by an accident on a bicycle. This was not followed up by social services at the time as child abuse was not a common consideration back then. In addition, as an adult, she was admitted several times to the Whittington Hospital, London with suspected non-accidental injuries. As she always gave vaguely plausible reasons for the injuries and never once accused her husband of assault, the police could not take it further. She was unusually emotionally dependant on her late husband as is often the case in abusive relationships and his recent death could have triggered the onset of her borderline personality disorder.

■■■■■■■■■■■■■■■■■■■■■■■■■■■■■■■■■■■

Even given the unprofessional tone of the document, I'm still shocked. Borderline Personality Disorder? Amy Winehouse, Princess Diana and Marilyn

Monroe - don't people say that they all
suffered with that? They didn't end well.
Maybe she's more disturbed than Tom
thinks.

And – shit - this report can only have
reached my desk via Uncle Charles. Why is
he giving this to me? To highlight my
inadequacy in not getting it myself. So is he
in contact with this Dr Campbell? Why does
he need me? He knows Tracey too. This is
so messed up. What if Dr Campbell finds
Marian's mobile and tells him? Would they
realise that it was me that gave it to her?
Would Marian tell them? Oh shit, I can't
imagine why I put this placement in
jeopardy like that. So stupid. But if he is in
touch with Dr. Campbell and Tom's parents,
if they're all in this…this *thing* together,
what does that mean for me?

Then I check the memorandum: Charles
Davidson expected to see me at eight-fifty
this morning. I check my watch: eight-forty-
five. No time to get my head in order.
Racing along the corridors to his office I
finger-comb my hair and pinch my cheeks
and lips to make it look as if I've been
awake long enough to put on make-up
before arriving at the office. What if he has
found out?

*

Why did I bother? I've been sitting here for
fifteen minutes, feeling more anxious by the
minute. Typical power play by dear old
Uncle Charles. Still, at least I can try to
think stuff through. That report with its tone
of underlying collusion, like a private
conversation between them. You wouldn't
present that to a case conference - far too
unprofessional. I'm no psychiatrist but I
would have thought there would have to be a
lot more information gathered before anyone
would make diagnoses like that. And, from
what Tom said, Charles actually organised
her placement there… not something you'd
do without a bloody good reason. And all
that emphasis in the report on achieving
"quiescence" and imposing drug regimes…it
makes me think she wasn't quite so paranoid
after all. My heart's thumping now, what
have I got mixed up in? Exactly why is he so
involved? It would really damage his
reputation if it got out he was having old
ladies locked up for no good reason. More to
the point, what does he want of me?

His PA glances up at me with a puzzled
frown and I realise I'm hyperventilating,
probably mumbling to myself too. I must

calm down. This whole project is gnawing away at me. I'm clearly not just doing a straight-forward piece of research, am I? Why do I feel like I'm selling my soul along with Tom's grandma? Well, I shan't tell him anymore than I need to; definitely nothing about my relationship with Tom. Worst of all, I feel there is something almost incestuous about his asking *me* to this this dirty work. Like he knew he could manipulate, no use, me. Oh God, I feel sick, I have to get up and pour myself a drink of water from the dispenser over in the corner. The perfectly groomed PA watches me all the way there and back. I smile at her but she just looks back at her computer.

After another ten minutes I am finally ushered in. I sit. The chair he provides for others is shorter by several inches than his. Never one to miss a trick. I shuffle a little and can't help a nervous cough escaping.

"So you made direct contact with her?" He scarcely looks up from his papers but the tension in his voice reminds me, as if I needed it, to be wary. I try the light hearted approach:

"I did. She seemed to me a normal, slightly forgetful old lady, a little spaced-out but that would be a side effect of the drugs she's on.

Nothing out of the ordinary. She is convinced of the baby story but nobody in the family believe her. She seems pretty harmless…"

There's a sudden coldness in the air and I realise I've given the wrong answer. His face gives nothing away but, knowing him so well, I can sense the tension in his whole body. There's a pulse in his neck that trembles when he's angry or frustrated. He starts to pace the room. I can't look at him, I just sit there fiddling with my watch, trying to think of something to say to make everything right again. I just don't get why he's quite so tense. So, he had a fling with her, maybe there was a baby. Most people wouldn't care nowadays. Anyway, it's unlikely to break; no one, apart from Tom, seems to believe her.

His shadow breaks through my thoughts and I see he is standing by the window, looking down on me. He stands there for a good two minutes, in silence, presumably calculating his next move, then surprises me by saying, "You have done well, little Fliss. Both Marian's family and I are grateful."

I open my mouth to speak but I have no words. I have no thoughts, or none that make any sense. Just an unpleasant feeling deep in my stomach.

"In fact you have been so thorough that I feel your talents are wasted here. I have organised an opportunity for you to broaden your expertise. The Scottish Independence issue continues to be a thorny one for the Party and the Government. There's an opening in our Edinburgh office for a dedicated and bright young girl like you."

Edinburgh? Really? And that's supposed to be a reward?

"You have an older brother, Ed, who lives in Edinburgh, am I right?" He knows I do; he knows everything about our family.

I nod, my throat is too dry to release any sounds. I'm being sent away? A treat or a punishment? Was it because I gave her the phone?

"I've arranged, with your father's help, for you to spend a little time with young Edward, all expenses paid, before you start work there officially next month. Your brother's rather keen on the idea." Now I know he's lying, but his face moves into one of his special charming "smiles" that defy anyone to argue with him.

"But what about Marian, er… Mrs Norman?" At last I get something out of my stupid mouth.

"Thanks to you, she will be taken care of. As I said, the family is extremely grateful."

He hasn't mentioned the phone, he doesn't know.

"But what about the baby? Shouldn't we try to find out if it's real and if it is, to reunite them?" I have to make some sort of effort for Marian.

His smile falters, but then he laughs,

"You read the report. It was a shame that *I* had to procure it, but no matter now. No one will ever find a shred of evidence that a baby existed. Every member of her family believes that she is delusional. There is nothing in her medical records that point to any pregnancies other than those of her known children. It is done. You need no longer concern yourself with her. I think perhaps you've become too emotionally involved. I'd expected you to be more circumspect, but I suppose it is what it is, as they say. Now it's time for you to move forward. Trust me, she will be more secure in her next placement. They have more efficient protocols to ensure she takes her medication."

He walks towards me as he is talking, then looms over me so closely that I can't stand up to try and make myself feel less vulnerable. His eyes rove over me while he assesses my reactions. I sit there like a child, looking down at the fingers on my lap. I do not object. Do not speak out. I hate myself for being so pathetic. A phone rings in the next office. An eternity shuffles slowly by. Abruptly he turns his back on me,

"Off you go then, Fliss. Give my regards to your brother. Your new contract will be drawn up and sent to you within the week." I had clearly passed some sort of reliability test, no mention of the phone, and was now being released back into the wild, or at least somewhere that was a long way away from Marian and Tom.

*

I stumble out of the office and make straight for the nearest toilet where every part of my body shakes in a macabre version of St Vitus' dance. I throw up repeatedly until there is nothing left but bile. I didn't sign up for this. I want get back to my normal life – away from intrigue and suspicion. Away from Uncle Charles. And Marian. Am I now the one who is paranoid? Couldn't it all be kosher? She could just be a slightly delusional old lady…couldn't she? But I know that's just what I want to believe. Never confront difficult situations or feelings, me. Uncle Charles had said that all her family think she's delusional but I know Tom believes her. Oh shit, have I ever told Uncle Charles that?

I try phoning Tom's mobile. I could do with hearing his chirpy voice. It goes straight to voicemail but I do hear his voice. A disembodied Tom tells me and anyone who calls him that he's been sent away. To a rehab centre in South Africa. Tom, "sent away". The only member of the family that Marian could rely on. The only one who believed her? Did I tell Uncle Charles that he believed her? Oh shit, I can't remember, I hope I didn't.

Now Marian is alone in that place with only crazy old Gwen to support her. Oh no, didn't Uncle Charles say something about sending her to a new, more efficient placement? And now I'm being sent away too. Worse still, my family will all know I've failed again; failed to live up to Uncle Charles' expectations, failed in yet another job. With that freaky synchronicity that we have, Mum's number lights up my phone and, unusually, I answer straight away. I need some comfort. I don't get it,

"Can't you do anything right? We arranged this fantastic chance for you with Charles and you go and mess it up. What were you thinking? What have you done? I thought you wanted to make something of your life. I never had your chances. I can't believe you've just thrown it all away."

"Mum," I tried to explain, "There's something that doesn't add up here..."
"Yes. Your incapacity to stick at anything. Your father was right; we should never have bothered to send you to University, should have encouraged you to marry Oliver when he proposed."
"Mum, I was only eighteen and I wanted more..."
"Well you've blown that, haven't you? And no political career now, without Charles' support. Ring me when you get to Ed's. Hopefully I'll have calmed your father down by then."

She cut the call, leaving me feeling even more alone than the way I'd felt on the first day at boarding school, seven years old. I thought of Marian; how alone and vulnerable she was.

I scroll through my phone to the copy of the photo I'd made of her with me and Tom. Poor woman. Then I saw the photo I'd copied of Tracey, her husband and Uncle Charles. Smiling at the camera, they give nothing away. The anger I feel overwhelms me.

Without realising it I'm pacing up and down in the confined but safe space of the office toilets: the chemical smell of jasmine failing to mask the murkier smells. Several Felicities pace with me as I look at those complacent faces on my phone. I stop, look at my reflections in the mirrors and stand a little taller. There is something seriously messed up about all this. I need to do what I can to fix it. I no longer want to be the useless little girl that my family sees. I punch in the number of the mobile we'd given Marian. After a long silence at the other end, I ask, "Marian? Is that you?"

Then I hear Marian, "Who is this? Where's Tom?"

Chapter 9: Tracey

Blood is Thicker than Water

My bloody mother! She twists me around until I've no idea where I'm going. She's done it all my life. With a well-timed histrionic cry for help, she blows me off course, every single time. They all tell me: my friends, my husband Nigel, my daughter Emily, even my brother Darren. They say she just knows which buttons to press and when. They're right. Take yesterday. There I am in the middle of a crisis with my son and she decides yet again that she can't stay in the home; they're all in a plot to kill her. It takes me all my strength not to say I'll help Sonya hold the pillow down myself next time if she carries on. But I say nothing. If she only knew how highly regarded that home is and that, if it hadn't been for Nigel's contacts, we'd never have got her in there.

I always try to stay calm and talk her down, putting my worries about Tom on the back burner. Like the time Tom was caught at school selling drugs, and she decided I hadn't called her enough. Wandering off in her nightie and pretending she thought it was Christmas. Ha! Darren fell for it, said we hadn't given her enough attention since Dad died. I said his death was a blessed relief. No more bullying from the old bastard, excuse the language. At least he'd stopped beating her by then. Why hadn't she stood up to him, for all our sakes, instead of wallowing in some deep depression? I'd never stand for it. If Nigel ever hit me, it would be the first and last time, that's for sure.

I hated our old house, identical to all the others on the estate; part of the new town development in the 1950s. The original inhabitants of the town resented us council tenants. I guess they thought they were better than us; most of them owned their own homes. We weren't poor but we were definitely working class; no books in the house, we ate mostly microwave meals in front of the TV and we didn't talk "proper". Even at that age I knew I wanted more once I'd grown up and had a family of my own. Things got better once Mum pulled herself together and realised the benefits of a decent education; for us, but more surprisingly, for herself.

But back in the earlier days most of the responsibility for our family fell on me; she was far too depressed. So many times I came home from school to find her still in bed and I'd rush around trying to get the house tidy and get her up and dressed before Dad came home. Typically, Darren was oblivious to it all; just expected me to sort it out for him in true little-brother fashion.

*

"Mum! Are you in? We're home." The only noise is from the TV which never gets turned off. I draw back the curtains at the front room windows and open them to get rid of the fog of stale air, tinged with the sad tang of tobacco. I find a cup of milk for Darren to drink, it's only slightly off. He doesn't notice, he just watches children's TV while I shake the lump of grey blanket on the settee.

"Mum, it's 4 o'clock. You have to get up. Dad will go mad if he finds you like this again. Come on. "

"No just leave me alone. Just get yourself some tea; there's still half a tin of baked beans in the fridge from the other day. You can make toast for you and Darren. I've got a headache, leave me be, there's a sweetie."

In the kitchen, I hold my breath as I plunge my hand into the cold, grey water in the sink and pull the plug. I've a bracelet of greasy scum around my wrist as I try washing the dried-up Weetabix and Dad's egg and bacon remains off the plates that fester there.

"Marian!" the door slams. Dad's home early. I don't want to hear this. Not again. I drag Darren upstairs with me; out of the firing line. I don't want him getting in the way of Dad's bad mood again. Darren's snivelling about missing "his programme".

"Let's play Top of the Pops, you can be Rod; I'll be a backing singer" I turn on the music centre that Aunty Jenny gave Mum when she went to South Africa with the rest of her family. I turn it up as loud as I dare. As we dance, we try to drown out the noise of my mother's cries and our father's fists with the loudest singing we can manage: "Wake up, Maggie, I think I've got something to say to you oo oo..." But what my father has to say to mum still pierces through both the walls and our singing. Afterwards, we all sit round the tea table as if nothing has happened. Mum's face looks blotchy and a bit bruised but Dad acts so sweetly to her that you'd think he was in the first fling of love.

No one ever talked about it. Not even
Darren and me. We still haven't and
sometimes I wonder if mum's loss of
memory isn't a blessing. She seems to have
wiped Dad completely from her life since he
died, so now there's just each day as it
comes. Only now she keeps on about this
lost baby. That bloody baby. She's totally
fixated. She never mentioned it when Dad
was alive. I think she believes that finding
this so-called baby would solve all her
troubles, make her happy. Thanks Mum,
what about me and Darren? Don't we count
for anything? But no, that's all she seems to
care about lately. I'm glad we were able to
arrange for her to go to Golden Meadows. If
she'd ended up near Darren in the Brighton
home it would have been so much more
difficult for me to keep an eye on her.

Now I must put all this in a box, put the box
on a shelf, so to speak, and concentrate on
my son, Tom. I hope that clinic in South
Africa can sort him out. I have to be there
for him in a way that Mum was never there
for me. This hurt can't keep going on for
generations.

*

I look at the gated entrance; in the bright
Cape Town sun, it's like every other rich

(still usually white), family's fortified residence in Hout Bay. Sheer concrete walls tower into the blue sky, their starkness slightly softened by the bright purple bougainvillea. Here, though, the security measures are there to keep my son and the other addicts inside, as well as providing the protection that the privileged few need against the poor at their gates. I look at Nigel and try to gauge his first reactions as he stands there looking ridiculously out of place in his suit and tie – I feel so responsible. But then I always have.

"There's a bell here, shall I ring it?" I ask - almost hoping Nigel will say no and we'll just get back into the rental car and drive away.

"No, I'll do it." He takes on his head-of-the-house stance and rings the bell in what would have been an authoritative way, had he not jumped back several yards as a massive Alsatian dog bounds out, all noise and teeth. It hurls itself against the tall metal fence to either eat or greet us at full volume. Emily screams and hides behind me.

"Get down Bruce! He's fine really; once you get to know him. Hi there guys, you must be Tom's family. Come in, come in.

Take no notice of him; he's a great big pussy-cat. I'm Sally, the House Manager."

A slight, blonde-streaked woman in her late forties, wearing a faded T-shirt and denim shorts punches in the code to open the gates. She maintains a constant stream of trivial chit-chat, at full volume, as she ushers us past the swimming pool and into the main building on the other side of the courtyard. Nigel keeps his eyes all the time on the "pussy-cat". Like me, he's seen a documentary of the way the South African Police used to selectively breed these dogs to encourage their violent natures - even creating a hybrid wolf/Alsatian strain.

We're taken into a room – all pine, with floaty gauze curtains and white furnishings, patchouli wafting in the air – and it gradually becomes clear we are not going to be seeing Tom today.

"You'll be glad of the chance to put your heads down. How was your flight? Was the change at Jo'burg ok? I've arranged for you to stay in a flat nearby. It's still early in the season for us so I got you a good deal on the rental flat. It's a ten minute drive away – you do have a car?" Without waiting for an answer or to take a breath, she's off again. She gives us directions to the flat and then outlines the programme for our week here. With typical English reserve, we just sit, obediently sipping our cups of rooibos tea while she extolls the virtues of their centre and tells us about the programme here.

"We also take great delight in encouraging our clients to interact with the local community and try out new experiences."

Her voice became even higher as she soared on a self-belief I could never accomplish, even if I had a million lifetimes.

"We want them to regain their joy of living without having to rely on props such as alcohol, drugs, food or even shopping to fill the emptiness in their lives."

She smiles, finally giving us space to make a comment, if not burst in to a round of happy-clapping or a chorus of "amen". We continue to stare at her, stunned. As a family, we have been happily reliant on such "props" for several years, if not decades. Then it seems we have homework to do as she gives us a whole sheaf of papers to read before we come back tomorrow.

"I'm sure it must be possible to go over and greet our son, having come all this way?" Nigel stands and stares down at her. Once again he is eager to reassert his authority. Neither his clumsy attempt nor my hostile silence have any effect on her.

"No, sorry. He's in yoga at the moment and then we have a group therapy session." She then also stands up, disconcerting Nigel by being several inches taller than him. "It's best if you prepare yourselves this evening and come for your preliminary meeting with Alan, our psychotherapist, tomorrow at 10.30. Be prompt, mind, we run a tight schedule here."

So, with a heavy sense of anti-climax, we leave the Centre and return to our hotel in the leafy, but reasonably priced suburb of "Gardens" in Cape Town itself. None of us know what to say, what to do; the silence is so heavy we can hardly find the energy to even look at each other. So we unpack and sit down to try and read through the mountain of literature that we've been given. Nigel and Emily don't last long. It has been an exhausting day. After they've gone to bed, I walk out into the cool night and look at the stars from the balcony. The sky is so clear here that it scares me - and the stars are different, unknown. I decide to phone my Aunt Jenny.

*

The next morning we drive back to Hout Bay and take a walk on the beach to pass the time until we're expected at the Centre. Even though it's autumn in England, the South African spring still hasn't really arrived here and, of course, we'd brought the wrong clothes. We'd assumed South Africa would be hot, or at least warm, all year round. It was warmer in England and we shiver in our late summer clothes, despite the several layers we'd struggled into this morning to try and keep warm. But the sunshine, though weak in terms of heating our chilled bodies, gives a glorious light to the white sands and blue sea of the bay.

Despite the beauty of this place and Emily's delight in being here I can't hold in the news from Aunt Jenny any longer. It's time there was more honesty in our family. I feel terrible for what I've done to Mum. What she must have gone through and I let that man talk me into putting her into a home she hates. She's got so frail and thin. She is literally half the woman she was. When we get back I'm getting her out of that home as quickly as I can. I must explain to them, whatever the cost. I grab Emily's hand and twist her round to look at me,

"Listen, no matter what is said today, we must remember that whatever your father and I have done, it's always been because we thought it was for the best. I have only ever wanted the best for all of the family …" I am suddenly lost for the words to explain it all and I find myself crying; something that I never did, until recently

"Mum..!" She snatches her hand away. Like *my* mum she has never been one for physical contact and emotional displays.

"God, Tracey, Emily knows that – it's your son that has the problem, not you!" Nigel snaps and the two of them stare at me as if it's me that needs therapy, not Tom. I blow my nose and close myself down again. I just can't face it yet. Also, it might mean the end of Nigel's political career and possibly my marriage.

We walk on, picking our way along the sands and back over the grass to the car park, each with our own silence stalking us. I can't help feeling now that it is the silences - the unspokenness of things, of our thoughts and feelings - that that have held my family together through the generations. Take them away, start revealing our true thoughts, our true selves and the family will crack under the strain, bringing down each of us in turn, Mum included. But maybe it's time..?

When we arrive at the centre this time, Tom is waiting for us. He looks a lot thinner and vaguely worried but gives Emily and me a big squeezy hug, then he and Nigel tap each other's backs to show that, even though they have their arms around each other, it isn't the same as a "girly" cuddle; it's man-taps.

"Come on then, peeps – it's Show Time!" Tom laughs and takes us across the garden into a large round room with six chairs set out in a circle in the middle. As we stand there in uncomfortable silence I wonder how Mum is. I'm not sure she understood me when I told her I would be away for a week or so.

I feel so far away from her here in Cape Town. But then I feel so far away from her even when I'm sitting right next to her in that home. Since talking to Aunt Jenny, I'm beginning to have such doubts. Why *did* I agree to send her there? I feel the guilt battling with my sense of duty. He'd told me it was for the best and – at the time - I believed him.

*

The atmosphere in the big meeting room is heavy with the weight of the countless family traumas that have been unpacked in this room. Tom looks almost as worried as I am. Fearful of the words that will unlock the family chains that both bind us together and keep us all in our own distant loneliness; always searching for the next thing that will fill the holes in our souls. But now we have a chance to put it all right and all I can feel is that fear. Fear of the words that may change things forever and fear of the words that we fail to say that should be said.

Sally bounces in. "Come on now, don't be shy, please take a seat. You sit there, Tracey, next to Emily and you, Nigel, opposite Tom and next to me," Sally is using her bright 'there's-nothing-to worry-about' voice. She arranges the seating as if it were the most important point of the morning. Alan, the psychotherapist, walks in and immediately the mood in the room is charged with an expectant energy.

"Hi guys, let's warm up by introducing the person sitting on our left to the rest of the group. This is Tom…"

Believe it or not, we obediently make the introductions even though we all know that everyone here knows everyone else, so it seems a bit awkward, but at least you find out whether your voice is going to work. And so it goes on like this for a fair twenty minutes, all polite, superficial storytelling.

One minute we're laughing as I retell the story of Tom coming home from infant school, all puffed up, telling me, "I can count to ten – even with my eyes closed," and the next minute Emily and Tom are at each other's throats again. Only, here in this sterile room, very politely at first.

"You always were teacher's pet, Em. What about that time when that old cow, Miss Perry gave me the exact same assignment that you'd had when you were in her group? You got an A. I copied it word for word two years later and she gave me a C."

"You shouldn't have copied, should you? Always riding on the back of what I do. You get away with so much more than I ever can just because you're the baby. At least I never did drugs…"

We all shifted in our chairs. Nigel coughed quietly.

"Shall we take a look at how that made you feel, Emily?" Alan lit Emily's fuse.

"Well look at us! All here because of poor Tom's problems," and she makes her fingers into speech sounds. I feel Tom bristle from across the room.

"He gets to have nearly three month's holiday…"
"It's not a holiday, Emily, we do a lot of hard work here," Alan tries to get back to the positivity we'd all promised to share at the beginning.

"Oh yeh, in between riding elephants, watching whales and spending time on the most beautiful beaches *I've* ever seen. Do you hear what I'm saying?" She turns on me, "How come I never get the same attention? Just because I'm always the good, responsible one? It's not fair. When you're not busy worrying about him, you're stressing about Gran. What about me?"

She's got a point. That's exactly how I felt at her age. All mum's attention went to Darren; first when he did so badly at school – she even became a school helper so she could keep an eye on him – and then when he announced he was gay at sixteen. Who knows their own mind at sixteen? I was sure it was just more attention-seeking. Dad went mad and refused to have him in the house. So lucky little Darren got to go and live in Brighton with Aunty Olive. Not quite South Africa, but certainly better than staying behind watching my mother crawl back into her shell when Dad refused to allow her to go back to work.

"I know how you feel Emily…" I try.

"No you don't, how could you?"

"Yes, why don't you expand on that, Tracey? Tell us how you feel and then we can look at both your and Emily's feelings together." My fists clench involuntarily, that's a surprise; I'm not a violent person.

So I tell them a sanitised version of my childhood. They don't need to know that their grandad was a violent drunk. How could that help anyone?

"…I always felt I had to keep the peace, keep everyone happy. But nobody ever did that for me. Not even Mum." As I falter to an ending, Nigel coughs again and sits back further into his chair, I look at him and I felt tears prick my eyeballs. My throat constricts and I can only just about squeeze out the words I'd not said for many years;

"And I love my mum. Why isn't she ever there when I need her? Helping *me*?"

Tom snaps his head towards me,

"But it was you who put her in a home! She didn't want to go; she could have lived with us. You abandoned her! You got her locked up there and now you've done it to me too. Why, Mum? Or are you just following the family trend? Sending away embarrassing problems so they no longer exist in your fake version of petit-bourgeois reality?"

Nigel is about to get up off his chair but is stopped by a glance from Alan. Emily reaches out to hold my hand.

When it's obvious that I cannot respond, Alan turns to Tom,

"Tom, it's clear that you feel strongly about something here and I think we should explore it; does everyone agree?" As if we could ever say no. Don't question authority; never make a fuss, that's our family motto.

"Gran is in that looney-bin of a care home now because she's an embarrassment to Mum, which is ironic as Gran sent her own son, my Uncle Darren, away because he embarrassed her and, when she was a young girl, first her baby was sent away and then she was too - because they were both a shameful embarrassment to her parents!" Tom's words tumble out in a messy rush and I stare at him; where has all this come from?

"What are you talking about? Who told you all this?" Nigel's confused, not just by what Tom says but also, I think, because the person he now sees in me is so very different from the one he knows. I never cry. Never make a fuss.

"Yes, Tom. We hear you; can you explain in more detail what you're feeling?"

I have to stop this.

"Tom, Nigel, stop. You don't know the whole story; your Aunt Jenny says ..."

One look from Tom froze the words in my head. My mind went blank. Had she really meant it? I couldn't remember her exact words but I knew it changed everything. Before I could gather my thoughts, Tom was off again.

"I know, Mum, that when Gran was young she ended up in the nut-house after being sent away a couple of months before - possibly to have this baby boy that she keeps

144

on about? It used to happen a lot in the old days, we all know that. Fast forward a few decades and she sends her second boy, a legitimate one this time, away at the age of 16. Jump to the next generation and here I am; stuck in a rehab in South Africa, far away from any prying eyes. It's like a social history: "Things to Send Your Sons Away for Through the Ages." In the 1950's if he was illegitimate. In the 1970's if he was gay. In 2020's if he's on drugs. What will it be for your son, I wonder Emily?"

"Nice one Tom. You practise that little tirade in the mirror this morning?" Emily was squeezing my hand so tightly that my rings hurt. I have to put a stop to this but it's too late, too complicated now. I can't tell them.

"All that stuff about a lost baby is rubbish. Your Mum looked into it…" Nigel looks to me for support.

"There are some things you don't know, Nigel, things I didn't know until yesterday…" I take a deep breath, maybe we *could* all start again, truthfully this time - no matter the consequences. It's like they say, 'if not now, when?'

At that precise moment the door opens and a worried secretary throws into the mix: "I've got an emergency phone call from the care home in England, I'm afraid your mother has disappeared."

I feel the breath leave my body as if I had been punched, my head lurched and suddenly I know that it's all too late. After a long shocked silence, Nigel responds true to type; finding someone to blame, "She's in a wheelchair, for God's sake! They were supposed to have a fool-proof alarm system. Someone must have abducted her. It would probably be your wretched brother Darren. He never agreed with you arranging for her to go there."

My thoughts are much darker, given what Aunt Jenny had told me about Charles Davidson. I wish now I had never accepted his help. Has he had a hand in her disappearance? But now I couldn't possibly tell my family. I'm too scared and ashamed.

Chapter 10: Marian

Tread on a Worm and it will Turn

 "Aren't we going to turn off clock? We wake everybody with noise!" Sonya bustles in and hits the clock on my bedside table.

"I didn't set an alarm; I was having a little afternoon nap…"

"Afternoon nap? Is 9.30 in morning. Time for getting up and start another day."

"But my mobile phone went off. There was a call…" For once, Sonya actually looks at me instead of somewhere just above my head.

"What..? Mobile phone? Oh no, that's not mobile. Who you ring – the TV people?" Sonya laughs at me again.

I look at my hand and I am holding something, but it's not a mobile; just my TV remote.

Sonya unfolds my arthritic fingers and, without a word, turns off my TV; right in the middle of a news report about yet another powerful man and young girls.

Once I'm up and dressed, I stretch out of my morning stiffness then search my room for the phone. The one that – like my baby – nobody else believes in. The one that Tom and his girlfriend took photos with when they visited me the other day.

I haven't imagined all that, surely? Still, life takes on a strange quality in here, with no outside pegs to hang it on. One day merges into another and, before you know it, a whole week's gone by. Nightmares and daydreams jostle in your head and eventually you're never sure of anything except the daily routines of institutional life. But listen to me, the philosopher without a beard! All I want to do is to find that damned phone; to see if it's real.

Where's my cardigan? I'll go and see if Gwen's going to breakfast... what's this? Here it is. So I haven't imagined it after all. In my pocket the whole time. It's like a trophy for the remnants of my memory. When I look at the thing I see that it has "missed call" written in it. How clever, but who could be ringing me? I throw it away as if it were burning my fingers. It lands on the bed and I'm trembling with fear. It scares me because I don't know who gave it to me. It could be anyone. No, you're being silly. It must be Darren. I press another button and it says "number withheld"? Why doesn't Darren want me to ring him back?

I wander into the dining room and ask Gwen what she thinks.

"He probably rang you by mistake; thought you were one of his playpals."

"I think you mean toy boys and he doesn't do that anymore. Not now he's got Kevin. And anyway, if he did, why would he withhold his number"

"Well, he wouldn't want his mum to know he was still chasing "toy boys" when she's so sure he's settled down with a nice young man, now would he?" Her logic is faultless. I give up. I'll think about this phone thing later – if I remember, of course. Right now, I need to get to the breakfast buffet before all the bacon is gone.

"They'll take it off you, you know" Gwen whispers so close to my ear it makes my spine tingle.

"Why?" I place a protective arm around my two rashers of healthily grilled bacon.

"Because they don't want you to talk to people if they can't hear what you're saying. They keep a check, you know. In case you say something bad." I wonder at Gwen's paranoia, once it dawns on me that she's still thinking about the mobile phone and not my bacon.

"What could I possibly say that would have any effect on anyone or anything?" I know my place in the world. Women of my age are more or less invisible.

"Just don't trust anyone," she says darkly and she picks one of the precious rashers off my plate with her fingers and eats it before I have time to object.

*

I'm dozing on my bed while the News is on. There's something about that voice; where do I know it from? They're insisting that single mothers should not be given benefits. I was never given the benefit; no one ever seemed to care about what I wanted. I learnt early that it was no good arguing, nobody listens to little girls.

I'll just have a few more minutes… When I wake up I'm several hours ahead, into Question Time. That same voice. My heart is beating far too fast, it's really frightening. Am I having a heart attack? I reach for the alarm button, then I stop because I realise what is happening. It's even worse than a heart attack, it's that voice, here, on my TV, in my room. My mouth fills with saliva and I retch. Nothing comes up. My heart is still racing and I realise I'm crying. I am unable to move as the voice goes on;

"It is unacceptable that a family on benefits is better off than a hard-working household. We must enable families to get out of this dependence on the state. It is the right thing to do." The self-assured politician on my TV smiled at the jeering audience and leaned back in his chair, watching the other panellists fighting to be the first to respond to his comments.

Is it really him? It couldn't be. That would be… But, yes… it is him. The one they said I must never see, or even think about, ever again. But no, it can't be; why is he on TV? If it is him, why do I only just recognise him now? My mind's playing tricks again. I take several deep breaths, then look at the TV again. I'm beginning to calm down; my heart isn't jumping as it was before, thank the Lord. I lay back on my pillows and watch him. He is a handsome man, so in control, so persuasive. As I watch, back in control now, I can't help myself; wouldn't it be nice if he really was the one? That we really did have a child together…I would be so proud … No, stop this! You can't let your imagination run away like this.

"It is imperative that our young people assume responsibility; so many young men abandon their children and expect the state to support them and the single mothers they abandon so wantonly…"

He's talking about people abandoning their children. I'm confused and my heart begins its racing again. Is he talking about me and my baby? People on TV, talking about me? Don't be so stupid; this really is paranoia. The ravings of a mad woman. No one's going to be talking about me on the TV, are they? I can't possibly know him. I sink back into my pillows, head spiralling in pain and confusion.

So I must belong here. I need to be looked after. I close my eyes and drift towards the sanctuary of sleep, blocking out once again all thoughts of my first love. And then I remember what Tom says; "Rage, rage against the dying of the light."

I suddenly remember a bit more and sit up again.

He *did* bring his young lady to meet me. I knew it. That must have been before Tracey sent him away. Or is he back now? Who was that girl? Such a pretty girl but there's something about her that I don't know if I can trust. Who is it she reminds me of?

*

"I think it's Amy Winehouse," says Gwen when she comes to see me the next morning.

"Why? She looks nothing like her, she has lovely long blond hair, not black and pushed up into a stupid beehive thing." I pass Gwen the sugar bowl from my tray. She takes sugar lump after sugar lump, "What are you doing? That's far too much."

"I'm just making sure I'm getting my penny's worth from all the money the council has to pay for me to stay here," she says, stirring it all in. "Something's eating away at that girl, you mark my words. But she's on your side. Maybe she have a plan to get us out of here."

Gwen is always talking about us doing some kind of breakaway from this place.

"Have you been doing what I told you to do; taking the tablets and sticking them under your tongue?"

I nod.

"Then get rid of them once they leave you alone. Flush them down the loo and no one's any wiser. Sometimes I think about saving them up for when it all gets too much as well, but there's still life in this old girl yet!"

I clutch my bag. I haven't even told my best friend about the collection of pills in the lining of my favourite handbag. I don't know what I'm saving them for, just that they might come in handy some time.

"One day I'll be well enough to take you away from all this." Gwen has that look in her eye again; the one that means trouble. "Come on; let's take you for a spin in your old chariot. It'll do you no good lying here, feeling sorry for yourself and I'm bored without you." She points to the dreadful wheelchair I had to use when I was still taking their drugs and could hardly stand.

"But I don't really need it any more…"

"You need to keep 'em fooled or they'll suss you're disposing of the drugs."
"You've watched too many films, you know."

Almost before I've sat down, Gwen races me up the corridor. I cling tightly to the sides of the chair and shut my eyes. I say a little prayer to thank God that none of the nurses are around. At last we reach the day room. I can breathe again. Oh no, I'm spinning round in the middle of the room. Myra is the only other person there. She is sitting in her usual place close to the toilet, looking vaguely in the direction of the TV. It's on, but with no sound.

"Sorry, Gwen's gone a bit mad." I call to her. No response.

What's that ringing sound? Have we set off some alarm? No. It's coming from my handbag. Oh yes, it's that wretched phone. I try to smother it, just in case, but it keeps on ringing.

"Sit still" Gwen says and she steers me straight into the garden. I hesitate by the edge of the patio. "Well, what are you waiting for? You can tell me all about it when you get back. Go on, I'll head 'em off at the pass!"

I watch her going back into the day room and taking up a position right in front of Myra. We both know what happens if Myra can't see the TV. As I search my bag for the phone I hear Myra scream at Gwen, then;

"Come on then, Myra, I dare you." A few more unintelligible noises come from Myra as she launches forward, only to fall on the ground. Gwen sits triumphantly on her back.

I don't wait to see any more. No one notices me wheeling further out into the rose garden. I decide to be brave and I look at the damned thing. At least I might have a clue as to where it has come from. Now how does this thing work? It's still ringing. I need to talk to Tom. It must have been him who gave me the phone. He's the only one I can trust now. I see a number and I press the green button. As I lift the thing to my ear, a voice I almost recognise says,

"Marian? Is that you?" Who is it? It's not my Tom.

"Who is this? Where's Tom?" I fumble with the shaking phone. My hands are itchy with fear. I check behind me. I'm alone in the garden. No one else here yet. What if they catch me? Who is this person? Is she going to hurt me? I clutch the thing tightly but say nothing. Just like before. Secrets are safer if you say nothing at all.

"Hello Marian. Are you ok? I've been worried about you in that home..."

My heart lifts and I'm no longer shaking. Someone outside this wretched prison of a care home knows who I am. I begin to hope that I might live my life again. Begin to reclaim my past and make amends. I take a deep breath, look back at the dining room one last time and ask, "Can you come and take me away from here?"

Chapter 11: Marian

God Helps Those Who Help Themselves

"What you do, sit in cold? You silly old lady, come I take you to lunch," Sonya goes to grab the wheelchair but this time I'm not going to cooperate. How dare she? She's bullied me enough. It's time to take a stand. I laugh – maybe too loudly - at the thought of me "taking a stand" in a wheelchair that I don't need. Sonya draws back as if I've slapped her. My hand's firmly on the brake. My other hand clutches the phone inside my cardigan pocket. I really do exist to someone; someone not part of this concrete suburban prison. I could even get back to being myself again. The person I was before they dragged me in here and tried to kill me off with their drugs and bed-rest and wheelchairs.

I'd been dying, worse, giving away my soul, bit by bit. Now I have hope. I can go and find my past, my baby. I feel my strength charging through my body but I'm not getting out of this chair; I like the pretence. So I look straight ahead, chin out, refusing to look up at this slip of a girl who has controlled almost every aspect of my life for the past few months.

"Please take your hands off my chair," I use my best "teacher voice"; the one my kids hated when they were little. "I am perfectly fine out here. I just need some time to myself in the fresh air. That's not a crime, is it? Surely you can allow me that. I am paying your wages, don't forget." I smile inwardly at my new assertiveness.

"But your lunch, it get cold. You need come inside, don't be silly lady." Sonya glances fearfully back at the door, back into the building. I know she's paid to see that the old ladies in her care are cleaned and fed on time but today I'm not concerned with other people's worries.

"If you call me a "silly lady" one more time I shall lodge an official complaint. Please inform the kitchen that I would like a cold lunch served in my room and I will come in when I am good and ready." I'm actually enjoying this little exchange.

She's looking shocked and a bit scared – of me, what a turnaround. Eventually she whispers something to the burly man next to her and they slink back inside to regroup.

Now my hands are shaking. My whole body buckles. Thank god for the support of this damned wheelchair. I can't help chuckling to myself. Who would have thought I still had it in me? I hope Felicity arrives soon, though, because I'm not sure I can manage it if they come back again. It's getting cold, too. I wish I had a blanket to snuggle and hide under.

I hear the chatter of the other inmates as they eat their lunch and then the clatter of plates as it's all cleared away. I wonder what Gwen is doing? Now it's gone deathly quiet, even the birds in the willow tree behind me have stopped chirping. I'm beginning to feel a little lonely and with every minute that passes, I'm a little bit more certain that Sonya will come back. Maybe with scary Dr Campbell or, worse, with her needle of death (that's what Gwen calls it). I'm going to miss my lovely Gwen. Should I go back for her? No, they'd never let me out again. Maybe I shouldn't leave, maybe that girl's not really coming…

Is that the back gate?

Do I recognise this young girl, in a bright yellow t-shirt and jeans, smiling as she walks towards me? Long blonde hair and a beautiful smile. So it can't be Emily, can it?

Surely not. Or maybe it is. They grow up so quickly; changing looks like I used to change dresses. It's no wonder I can't always remember them.

"Hi, Marian," the girl waves as she walks up the path by the rose garden, "are you ok?"

I clutch the arms of the wheelchair again; I'm still not letting go of the pretence until I know that this girl's safe. I also need its support; not in body but in spirit. I don't answer. I'm not sure what she wants me to say. The girl kneels down next to me – how patronising.

"I'm absolutely fine, just a little stiff from sitting here waiting for you." My voice sounds harsh, even to me.

"Sorry, the North Circular was rammed."

I smile as if I understand this strange explanation.

"Have they not been out to take you back in? It must be gone lunchtime by now."

"They tried, but I decided to take no more nonsense from them. Sonya and one of the men came out to get me but I told them I wasn't ready. Poor old Gwen held them off as long as she could, I suppose. She's

probably still causing havoc to distract them.
"

We both laugh at this and the tension
between us goes.

"I'm Felicity, Tom's friend," the girl says,
"we met before...?" She's looking a little
nervous.

"Yes, yes, of course. I knew that. Where is
Tom? Is he coming to take me away? " I do
miss that boy.

"Tom's in South Africa, didn't Tracey tell
you?" Felicity doesn't look at me but keeps
her eyes on the building.

"Nobody tells me anything," I start to say
but then a vague memory begins to surface
at the back of my mind. But why would he
go all the way to somewhere like Africa?

"Is he safe there?" South Africa is so far
away.

"Safer than we are here, I should think.
Would you like to get away from here?"

Silly question; of course I do. I nod.

"Well then, we need to get away before the
others come back. They won't let me take
you out officially so we'll have to sneak out.
Are you up for that?"

Her enthusiasm is contagious; I haven't felt like this for years; an adventure! Then again, is this girl trustworthy? I don't really know her. Aah, but Tom does and he likes her. And how else am I ever going to get out? I can't stay here. I'll never find out the truth. I shall have to put my faith in her, at least until we get away from here.

It's only when we're safely in the car, driving away that I think about Gwen again. I don't mind leaving behind all the rubbish that Tracey packed up for me when she was putting me into the home. But I shall miss my best friend.

*

The car purrs on round the North Circular, past London and on through some beautiful countryside. The sun is shining, there's no one trying to force drugs on me and I can be myself again. I'm enjoying dozing along with the gentle rocking of the car. I feel safe.

The girl's voice breaks through, "Maybe I should take you to your son."

"My son? We're going to find my son?" I can't believe it. That's all I've ever wanted.

"Of course, He's in Brighton, isn't he?"
"In a better place," I'm still half-asleep.

"Well it's certainly better than that dreadful home. He can make arrangements to put you into the one you wanted to go to all along."

What? Now I'm really confused. Has this girl found my son already? She can't have done but I test her out,

"It will be hard to find him. It's been years."

"Not that long, surely. Didn't he come to visit you? Haven't you stayed with him and Kevin in the flat before?"

Kevin? I don't think I like Kevin. Who is he? I can't quite remember. Why is she taking me to his flat? Are they in on it together? I panic,

"Stop the car, now! You're just like the others. I thought you believed me. Stop the car!"

I grab hold of the steering wheel. She pushes me hard. For such a skinny girl, she's very strong. It really hurts and I let go. The car veers across a couple of lanes into the oncoming traffic. She's screaming, out of control. A car is coming straight at us. I close my eyes. Please don't let me die now, I haven't found him. I feel the car lurch sideways and hear the hooting of the other car as it swooshes past us. The girl regains control and gets us safely back to our side of the road.

"You stupid woman! You nearly killed us. What were you thinking?" she shouts, "It's a good job there was only that one car coming. We could have been killed!" Her face no longer looks pretty; her eyes are staring and her mouth is distorted into a snarl. I'm really frightened.

I make myself as small as possible, hunched down in my seat. I whimper, "I thought we were going to find my baby, my poor little baby boy. Why did you say we were if you don't believe me?"

The car pulls to a halt as soon as the girl finds a safe place to stop. She just sits there, head and hands on the steering wheel. Wait, is she crying too? After a while she lifts her head and turns to me with a smile: the smile you have when you're placating a mad person or trying to ward off your child's next tantrum.

"Marian, you know Tom and I believe you. Why else would I come for you? Come on love..." She puts out her hand to me. I slap it away. I am so confused; first she shouts at me, now she smiles...

"Don't patronise me with your "loves". Do you even know my Tom? I don't really know you." I turn my head to the window. I don't want to listen to her. Who is she anyway?

Silence for a while, then the girl reaches over to the back seat and retrieves her handbag. Her eyes are still angry even as she smiles, "Look. Just have a look at this photo for me."

The girl thrusts one of those new phone things in my face. I don't understand; there's a picture of me on it. How did she get that? There I am, sitting with my lovely Tom and this strange girl. I stare at it for a while. Things drift back to me. This girl is Felicity and she helped me get out of that awful home. She's Tom's girlfriend. I love that boy. Then vague memories seep through the mist of my fear and anger and I'm aware of yet another loss in my life.

"My Tom, my little boy. Where have they sent you?" I snatch the thing from the girl and hold it close to my heart.

I must have fallen asleep for a while but then I hear one of my favourite songs. It's really romantic – a young man describing his feelings for the girl he wants to make his wife. How lovely. Charles said he would marry me but I can't remember him being very romantic about it. Bob was even less romantic. I sometimes felt he thought he was doing my mum and dad a favour by taking me off their hands. These young men seem so much better these days. What do they call it? Being in touch with their feelings.

Just as I'm enjoying the song Felicity turns it off. I make her turn it back on but it was the News; something about some silly actresses trying to tarnish the reputation of a man, just because they regretted having sex with him. They've all got tongues in their heads. They could have said no. Of course Felicity doesn't agree with me but that's the younger generation for you.

Anyway, I fall asleep again and before I know what's happening, Darren's there, taking me out of the car and into his flat. I'm so pleased to see him but he keeps fussing around me and asking how I'd got to Brighton. He's seen the car. What's he talking about?

It turns out that Felicity denied that she knew me; said she'd picked me up from the Prom. Stupid idea bur Darren seems to believe her more than he believes me so I give up arguing. I have bigger thing to sort out. Now I'm in Brighton, I'll be able to find out the truth about my past and what happened to my baby. I haven't felt so exhilarated in years.

Chapter 12: Felicity

When the Going Gets Tough, the Tough Get Going

Yes, you just carry on sleeping, no worries that you just nearly had us killed, you silly old fool. What were you thinking? Jesus! Still, I guess you've been through a lot. Can't have been easy back then, getting pregnant... what did they say? - "out of wedlock". So Victorian: wed*lock.* Such a strange word. I suppose back in the day you had to be *locked* to a man by marriage to have any status, certainly to be allowed to have children. Even after all those years, Marian was still wracked with shame that day in the home when she told me about the baby she had before she was married. Unbelievable.

God, I'm bored. I'll put the radio on, just low – don't want to wake Marian. Can't face having to talk to her again. Oh not that song again, it gets me every time and now my favourite grey silk shirt has got tear stains on it. Stupid song. Why am I crying over some sentimental crap about his hand fitting hers? I hated it when it first came out; now I'm crying because he says he dreams of her as his wife. I punch the radio off. Not everyone needs someone else to share their life with… even hoping to die with. Jesus! I'm fine by myself, thank you.

I guess I must be tired and strung out. I'll get Marian to a safe place as soon as possible, then get away, out of this mess.

"I liked that song," Marian moaned from her foetal position on her seat, "It was lovely. Would you turn it back on please??" But, of course, it had finished and someone was reading the news:

"… and in the last week, several more Hollywood actresses are coming forward to back up allegations against the powerful film producer…" I turned it off. I did not want to talk about this with Marian, of all people.

"I don't understand how they can do that after all this time. Surely the actresses would have spoken out at the time, if it were true..?

"Sometimes, Marian, women are too afraid or feel ashamed at the time and they bury the memories. It sometimes takes someone else to vocalise their distress before they can see it in themselves and then start to deal with it." God, I sound like some trendy psychiatrist.

"Nonsense. They went along with it at the time. They should have just said no." She looked stubbornly out of the window. Marian clearly didn't see the irony of this. Should I unravel this tangled mess, let her realise the similarities in her own experience? No. I've done my bit, getting her away from Uncle Charles and that home.

You're probably right, Marian." I said.

We drive on over the Downs in silence; Marian dozing while I try to work out how to make sure that Charles never finds out my part in Marian's escape to Brighton. I'm still hoping I can regain his approval.

Maybe I should take this broken woman back to the home right now. I could pretend that I had just taken her out for a ride or something. No, that wouldn't work, Charles would be told. He'd suss that out right away and that would definitely be the end of my career in politics.

I can just see my prospects drifting away with me shamed up in front of Mummy and Daddy. No, not an option. Perhaps I could still drop her off at Darren's? I needn't give my name – Marian would probably never remember it. I could leave her and run before he has a chance to ask any questions. Yes, that's it. That way, the poor woman is out of Charles' clutches and he'll never know I was involved. I carefully retrieve my phone from where it had fallen onto her lap. She stirs but only to clutch her handbag more closely to her.

*

 The sat-nav seems to want to do a complete tour of Brighton and its one-way systems but eventually we draw up alongside a row of tall terraced houses. With just a touch of some lovely Farrow and Ball paint, a few carefully trimmed olive trees and a damned good clean they would be perfect, what with being fairly central and near the big Queen's Park. Worth a fortune. As it is, I count along the hideously brightly-painted houses. Why do they always think they have to do that with coastal properties? Eventually we reach number 23; the address Marian had given me. This one even has a rainbow flag covering one of the windows. Can't they afford curtains? I look across at Marian, snoring gently but still clutching her scruffy brown handbag to her breast as if it contained her life's treasures. A passing feeling of guilt strikes me as I quietly open my door and shut it behind me with a click. I really don't want her to wake just yet but walking on the gravelled path seems far too loud so I have to look back to make sure my strange little passenger was still asleep Oh shit! Literally. I just manage to dodge the mess left by what must have been a very large dog. Disgusting. I climb the steps up to the front door and can't stop looking back again and again at the sleeping woman. Why am I feeling so bad?

I ring the bell, oops! Maybe that is a bit much; the noise seems to go on and on, into the big old house, summoning someone, anyone, to take away my problem. A man's voice answers through the door's intercom. "All right, there's no need for all that. One simple push will do the trick."

"Hi, I'm looking for a guy called Darren? I think I have his mother here."

There's no answer and I'm about to try the button again when the double-sized yellow door is wrenched open, revealing a tall, thirty-something young man, in a brightly coloured shirt and black jeans. Any other time, I might have been interested, but not today.

No hi or anything, just, "You found my mum..?"

He doesn't even give me a glance, staring over my shoulder as if I'm keeping his mother hidden behind me. Actually I'm pleased. I don't want to give him time to ask any questions or to notice what I look like.

"Yes, I found her wandering along the prom. At least, she says she's your mother. She's a bit confused, doesn't seem to know where she is or how she got here. Says her name is Marian…"

He pushes past me, runs down the steps two at a time and, catching sight of the small bundle inside the mini, recognises his mother. With absolutely no respect for me or my property, he yanks the door open and wraps his mother in the tightest of bear hugs.

"Mum! What are you doing here? How did you get out of the home? How did you get here? Oh thank God you're safe."

He almost drags the sleepy woman from the car and, as if just remembering I'm there, turns his head over his shoulder to me,

"Thank you so much. Come on up. I've been going out of my mind with worry. I was about to phone the police. Where did you say you found her?" He's already half-carried his confused mother back up the steps, clearly expecting me to follow and explain the unexplainable.

"I'm sorry. I'm so glad she's safe but I really must go. I'm already late for a very important appointment. Sorry, bye!" I shoot back to the car and speed off before Darren can question me. I drive away like a woman pursued. I look at the grim terraced street around me. Why do people rate Brighton so much? Then I see the sea-front; the broad promenade, the iconic pier and the dazzling white hotels facing the sea. This is why. I slow the mini down. Why should I go all the way up to Edinburgh, just because Uncle Charles wants me out of the way? I'd be out of the way here. He said I could spend time with Ed before I started that new job. I'll get Ed to cover for me for a couple of weeks and have a little mini break here.

As I sit here, planning my escape from it all, I can't help worrying about Marian. I probably shouldn't have just left her there. There's clearly something going on and now I'm complicit in hiding it away, just like I always do when things get too awkward or embarrassing. If nobody talks about it, it fades away until it seems it never existed. Is that why Uncle Charles wants me all the way up in Edinburgh?

I'm still not sure if Tracey and Uncle Charles were working together in trying to silence Marian – I can't see what Tracey would get out of it. She seems devoted to her mother, visiting every day. Maybe that was guilt? Uncle Charles does have a way of making people do what he wants without them realising that's what's happened. Shit! I bet he got her to send Tom away, now I think about it. Whatever. I'm glad Marian's at Darren's now and not in their control.

At least, I hope Darren isn't involved too.

Chapter 13: Marian

Beware of Jumping From the Frying Pan into the Fire

Darren's flat is very clean and uncluttered but a bit too high up for my liking. I felt a bit like Rapunzel, at first, trapped in a tower. I used to get dizzy simply looking out the window. But then I would remind myself how lucky I am to be here and not trapped in that awful Home.

I miss Gwen; she'd love it here. I imagine us soaring over the rooftops with the sea gulls, our laughter drowning their raucous calls. Nowadays when I look out of the window, I feel elated. The whole of my beloved Brighton beckons me down. I'll bide my time, though, just a little longer, until I feel a bit stronger. I got so thin in that place. It was a shock when I saw myself in the long bathroom mirror. I hadn't seen my poor old body in a long time. Darren's been good to me as always. He's fed me some delicious meals, taken me for walks on the beach and the Downs and introduced me to all his fancy friends. They are all so different. Most of them loud and outspoken, saying things I could never have dreamt even thinking about but all of them with a zest for life that's really contagious. I don't ever want to live in a place full only of people my age.

There's no sign of that Kevin. I think Darren asked him to keep his distance for a while. Stay at a friend's or something. Thank goodness for that; I've never felt he was good enough for my sweet boy.

I can't sleep though; my leg's playing up again. Fizzing and itching to move about, keeping me from the welcome escapism of sleep. It's as if my body's telling me to run. Run from, or to? I'm no longer sure. I'll have to get up. I gingerly roll sideways off the large double bed; it seems far too high to me. Turning the door handle carefully to stop it squeaking, I creep out the room: "Like a thief in the night". I think that's from the Bible, or is it Shakespeare? But I'm not a thief, I just want to find my boy and that's not a crime, is it?

 I try not to disturb Darren with my night wanderings through his flat. I don't know why he doesn't have carpets. All these wooden floors are cold and it makes it difficult to be quiet. I have no trouble walking now. Since I've been back in Brighton, I've been walking along to the pier with Darren every afternoon. It's wonderful and it's brought back so many memories. Some make sense but others are weird and frightening. Those ones I shut back out.

Now what's this? A jar of jam, made by Darren, or maybe Kevin. It looks all right. I'll make myself a sandwich to go with the gin. I take my midnight feast back to my bed. The gin helps me sleep. Or so I tell myself. Now that nobody makes me take the drugs, life stares me in the face. It scares me. It scares me more than the diazepam dreams and the constant paranoia that gripped me so fiercely back in Dr Campbell's "care". What if I can't find out what happened to my son? Would that mean I really did imagine it all, like everyone says? No, I refuse to accept that. Tom and Felicity believed me.

My whole life has been mired in dreams. I need to find the reality. Who am I if I've lost my past? It's here, I know it is. Every time I breathe the air here, I know it's whispering its truth. It fills my body. My mind just can't grasp it long enough to remember. I have a memory of being on the pier here with Charles, feeding chips to the seagulls but other than that I can't remember much. Did I have the baby here? Why can't I remember?

Did they take him away? Surely there would be some record of it somewhere. There was a baby that had been adopted, gone to a "better place". I remember mum and dad talking about it.

The next morning over our shared breakfast of croissants and coffee, out on the roof terrace, so sophisticated, quite French, I asked Darren about the girl.

"Darren, do you know where my friend is, the girl who brought me here?" I poured myself a coffee and moved my chair a little closer to the edge of the terrace so I could look down to the busy streets below.

"She was a lovely girl, Mum, and very kind but you didn't really know her." He passed me some butter; he'd even taken it out of the packet and put it into a tiny hand-made dish.

"But Darren, I do know her. She's Tom's girlfriend." I ripped my croissant apart. "Tom's girlfriend? No you've got that wrong; she's far too old and posh for a little scroat like Tom."

I try to explain but he just carries on. Why do my children make me feel so invisible?

"She told me that she found you wandering along the prom. You must remember, surely. Come to think of it I'm surprised you were able to remember my address."

He put far too much butter on his croissant and then some jam as well! He'll make himself ill, or fat.

"So how did you get all the way to Brighton yet? I still can't believe it. You're like some homing pigeon; you've always loved coming here."

He's getting crumbs all over the place. Why doesn't he use a plate? I try to sound reasonable and I touch his hand lightly to make him look at me,

"I *do* know her, she's my friend - and she *is* Tom's girlfriend. They came to see me. She gave me one of those mobile phones and she called me on it to meet her outside the home, in the gardens. There's a photo of her, me and Tom in it. She got me out of that place and drove me down here." I put my croissant back onto the plate. It tasted very dry all of a sudden. Maybe I should have put butter and jam on it too.

"Mum that's what you said yesterday. I'd hoped that once you've had a rest, you'd be able to remember things more clearly. Why would she run off like that if she really is who you say she is? Don't forget, Mum, you do get muddled sometimes. And don't you remember, I checked in your bag? There's no phone there, look!"

He turned my bag upside down, letting all my make-up fall out on to his scrubbed pine table. Luckily the pills were safe inside the lining. I scooped up the make-up and snatched up my bag with its secret contents. I glared at him.

"How do *you* think I got here then?" I shouted. Then I remember, I must be careful. I'm beginning to lose my temper and that's when I say stupid things I don't mean and everyone thinks I'm going senile again.

"I really don't know," he sighed, "maybe someone else gave you a lift. Maybe you wandered out of the home and someone picked you up and you persuaded them to help you..?"

"That's ridiculous – why would complete stranger drive me all the way to Brighton. And you accuse *me* of being muddled."

I stood up with all the dignity my poor old legs could muster and slammed the door into my room. If only I could find the phone – or was it a camera? I can't remember. It doesn't matter. If I could find the…the thing, then maybe Darren would listen to me. I could show him the photo.

"Calm down Mum. I'm only saying, why did she run away then, if she was a friend of yours or Tom's?" Darren had followed me into the room. He laughed gently and I felt a comforting arm around my shoulders, "It's ok, Mum. We all get confused sometimes."

But I brushed his arm away as my eyes filled with frustrated tears. That's what happens when you tell too many lies. The truth runs away. I've definitely told too many lies in my life. I was too good at keeping quiet. Now I need them to hear, they refuse to listen. I lowered myself onto the bed and hugged the pillow. Darren tip-toed out of my room. I took a couple of my pills to calm myself. Later on I shall go and find Aunty Olive's house and get my bearings from there.

*

I'm back home again. Darren and Tracey have betrayed me. Right on cue they glide

*in. All slimy smiles and greasy words. They
won't let me leave. Keeping me hostage for
their father. He comes to beat me again.
They laugh as he forces himself into me and
their singing punctuates his thrusting. When
he has finished with me I run and grab the
door handle. It won't turn. A prisoner again.
I turn back and there they are, under the
raining blows of their father's fists. I can
never leave, even as the door silently opens.*

"No, no, I must get away. I have to. I'm
sorry. I must find him and say sorry!" I try
to shout down the song's accusation that I
had stolen his soul and caused him pain.
Silly me; it's just the radio. It's come on at
full blast, instead of the gentler ringing tones
of the alarm on the clock-radio Darren gave
me.

"What's going on?" Darren rushes back into
the room, still in the boxers that he sleeps in.
I must have slept all through yesterday.
What a waste of a day. I'll have to be careful
with those pills. He turns the radio down.

"You can't keep me prisoner forever, you
know. I have rights and I'm your mother!"

"What on earth are you on about? Have you
had one of your dreams?" He walks towards

me but I back off, still furious for some reason.

"That's right, mock me. Nothing I do or say is real because I'm a loopy old woman, I know. But I tell you this, my boy, I've done things for you and your sister that you'll never know. I've kept secrets for you, suffered all sorts from your father and this is the thanks I get. Oh what it is to have a thankless child!"

I am beside myself with anger but Darren just laughs at me, "Now don't go all Shakespeare on me, Mum. I'm sorry but it *is* funny, you getting so cross and melodramatic while you're still in your nightie..."

Oh no, I try to hide myself. I never let anyone see me like this. I have standards.

"Listen, I'll make you a nice cup of coffee and then we can talk about someone to look through the local records of births, ok? You're not a prisoner. I just have to keep a bit of an eye on you in case you get lost again like you did yesterday and end up being brought home by the police"

"I don't like coffee!" But he's already in the kitchen.

*

He's lying again. I've never been brought home by the police. There was that nice young girl who helped me the other day when I got lost looking for places, trying to remember. But no policemen. Everything has changed so much here. The streets that I used to know look completely unfamiliar. Even Auntie Olive's old house has been painted a bright pink. The young couple who opened the door had never heard of her. They were very kind, though and invited me in for a cup of tea. That's when the young girl in the blue suit and perky little hat came for me and brought me back here.

I'm getting dressed and about to turn off the radio when I'm distracted by someone talking yet again about what they call "historical child abuse". Such an awful phrase and I can't understand what all the fuss is about.

"Rumours being circulated on the internet allege that several women are coming forward to accuse an eminent politician of historical child abuse. No names or further information is being released at the moment and mainstream sites such as Google, Facebook and Twitter have taken down all references following legal advice."

Well, clearly, when it's young boys or very young children, I can understand everyone getting so het up. But I'll bet these girls all knew what they were doing. Lots of girls I knew when I was at school followed the bands around. They called them "groupies". Some of them made good careers out of it. It's just the way it was in those days. But now they mollycoddle their kids, don't let them grow up and stand on their own two feet or take any responsibility. Treat them like babies right up until their twenties or more. I was married by the time I was seventeen, two kids before I was twenty. That's not including my first of course, the one they took away. They'd have called him illegitimate, or worse, but he was my love-child. It really was love, despite the age gap. I suppose they'd say he groomed me or something ridiculous nowadays. The world's gone mad.

Now I'm feeling stronger I can think about finding out what happened to my baby; tomorrow I'll focus. I'll tell Darren the truth, well the bits I remember. I'll get him to help me. Maybe we'll find that guesthouse, even find the landlady, Mrs. Blakely. Strange to remember that name. It just came to me… I thought our room with its shiny emerald eiderdown was lovely but when I said that, it made Charles laugh. I loved to make him laugh. My darling Charles, he helped me to run away…

*

"Marian, let's not wait until you're old enough to get married. Let's run away now. I'll take you to the sea-side and we can sort everything out and then I'll bring you back to your Mum and Dad and everything will be all right again, ok?" He was standing with his back to me, rearranging his hair in the mirror. I was eating the last of the penny sweets he'd brought me. I just heard the words "run and away", which sounded exciting, and "sea-side" which was even more so. I'd only been to the sea-side once; with Mum to Aunty Olive's, who lived in Brighton.

"Oh yes please!" I was so excited, "Shall I go and ask Mum and Dad?" He turned round and sat next to me. He held my hands tightly, a bit too tightly, really, but I didn't say so. His face was so close to mine that I could smell the cigarettes on his breath.

"No, my love. You can't tell anyone. Not ever. Really. Never, ever. It's our special secret and you'll spoil everything if you tell. They'll never let you see me again." I hated that smell, and the taste when he made me kiss his mouth.

"Oh, ok." I turned away, partly from the smell and partly because I was really disappointed. I wanted to tell everyone we were going to Brighton; it was so exciting.

"Promise me you won't say a word, Marian, this is very, very important," and he let go of one hand, held my chin and forced me to look into his eyes.

"Of course I won't. I love you and I love our secrets and one day we'll be married won't we?" I tried to sound and look happy.

He let go of me then and returned to his mirror. I rubbed my chin.

"Yes of course we will. Now let's get you home and remember, not a word to anyone."

He actually brought me to Brighton of all places, I remember that. But we didn't see Aunty Olive. He arranged lodgings at Mrs. Blakeley's. No family. Just the two of us. All for my own good, he said. Back then I trusted him, loved him. Still do.

*

The only other man I've ever known, apart from my lovely dad, was my husband Bob. My parents were so pleased when we started courting. They thought no man would take me on after what I'd done. He was so attentive in the early days; older and dependable. He reminded me of Charles. That's why I married him. That, and my parents.

"He'll be really good for you, Marian," Mum said when I told her that he'd proposed. We were in the kitchen, sitting at the old Formica table while Dad did his Pools in front of the TV in the sitting room.

"He's got a good, steady job and he adores you. You can tell by the way he watches you all the time. He's bought you all those lovely clothes. We couldn't have afforded them. So clever of him to know exactly what size to get. He worships you; he's always coming round to the house, asking after you, even when you're not here. Your dad and I won't be around forever, love; you've got to think about the future." She poured me another cup of tea and smiled the smile of someone whose worries had been solved.

She carefully placed her cup on her saucer and searched my eyes, I could see her having second thoughts. "He doesn't badger you, does he?" Mum's face suddenly looked worried.

"No, he's happy to wait until we're married. Says that's how it ought to be. Why he respects me because I don't go flaunting myself like the other girls."
"Well, there you are then." She looked relieved. "It's because he's that bit older. He respects you and he'll wait. You can't say fairer than that, my love. Most men don't, as you know to your cost. You have to keep your wits about you not to get caught again."

"Mum..." I hated it when she talked about what happened back then.

"What? Oh yes, well sorry. That's all behind us now. You haven't told him..?"

"No."

"Best to keep all that tucked away. You weren't to blame, far too young. What he doesn't know can't hurt him."

But it did hurt him. It hurt all of us. I should have told him. He was patient with me at first but, like Mum told me, a man has needs. After a while he started taking what he needed. I wasn't strong enough to fight him off, neither physically nor mentally. I used to lie there while he did what he wanted, imagining myself somewhere else, somewhere safe. He became wilder in his demands, trying to get some sort of reaction from me. When I couldn't hide my revulsion any longer he took to drink. To assuage his guilt, to patch the hole I'd made in his sense of manhood? I didn't know. But I knew it was my own fault and the blows were welcomed as a just punishment.

But I can't sit around thinking about the past, I have a job to do. I feel alive again, having a purpose.

Chapter 14 Charles

All's Fair in Love and War

Marian wasn't the only one reminiscing. In London, Charles was thinking about the night he first met Marian, all those years ago…

I was babysitting with her cousin Jenny. The clue was in that verb. Why didn't it register at the time? Even now I still don't know how old she was – or have I managed to bury that fact? She burst into that room with such energy, such passion. It was beyond my experience or understanding that a woman or girl was capable of such strong feelings. But of course, my experience was fairly non-existent. I had no sisters or female cousins and so the only girls I knew were the daughters of my father's group of friends and they, like their mothers, seemed to have a limited range of ideas and even fewer emotions. I found them all very bland and boring, something the other boys at my boarding school and I had in common. We knew we would have to get married some day and produce a family with all the entanglements and paraphernalia that goes with married life. We accepted that as our given duty.

Even after I left Eton, I still failed to understand the attraction that most other men had for women. I preferred the company of men and boys. I bowed to pressure from my father, though, and started to "step out" with Jemima, the daughter of one of his business associates. As night followed day, we got engaged and it was about that time that I met Jenny at a disco…

The Party was holding its regular Saturday night disco for local youth in the new town cherry-picked for me. As the prospective Parliamentary candidate, I was expected to attend on a regular basis. The little terraced house that they had converted into their headquarters was poorly lit and full of teenaged bodies writhing about in dirty little couplings on the stairs, in the corners and even on the dance floor.

Although I would never admit it to my friends, and certainly not to Jemima, I found these parties strangely fascinating; full of the sons and daughters of the aspiring working class who had ironically destroyed the very town to which they had been relocated, in the hope that they could start a better life away from the smog and dirt of London.

"Have you got a light?" A girl's voice broke into my thoughts as a hand plucked at my tweed jacket. I looked down to see a skinny little thing dressed in what I assumed was her mother's blouse, tightly fitted around her waist but unbuttoned low enough to highlight some budding little curves. Her knowing blue eyes did not falter as she held my gaze as boldly as I held hers. I was surprised but also impressed. Even as I lit her cigarette with my new American Zippo lighter, she continued to brazen it out, cupping my hands around the lighter with hers and only looking away to blow the smoke over her shoulder.

"Thanks. You're Charles Davidson aren't you? I've seen your picture on the leaflets by the door. Aren't you going to persuade me to join the Party?"

"Well I rather thought that you would already be a member if you were here,"

"No, I only came because my cousin Dave said you lot had good parties and there's nowhere else to go in this boring town. You got any cider here?"

"No, we don't provide alcohol and you're far too young to be drinking anyway." I couldn't decide whether I found this little slip of a thing annoying or amusing. She was certainly different from the females I usually came into contact with.

"I'm old enough to know my own mind, thank you, so – if *you* don't mind -I'm going to find someone who's younger, less stuffy and a bit more fun than you," and she made a move to walk off but I felt my hand reach out to stop her. She clearly had no objection to the hand on her shoulder. Or anywhere else, I hoped. She turned back, smiling. A devious little smile, I thought,

"What's your name, little girl? I'm sure we can find a drink downstairs in my office if you're desperate and you're not afraid to be alone with an "old man" like me…"

"Afraid of you? Don't make me laugh, I'm Jenny Alsop and I'm not afraid of anything. You posh boys don't know how to handle yourselves without a nanny holding your hand," and she linked her arm in mine and led the way down the narrow stairs.

I looked around quickly to make sure we weren't seen before pushing her through the door and locking it behind us. I switched on only the small desk light and drew the thick orange curtains across the small window. I lifted her up and sat her on my desk.

"Here, drink this," I had a bottle of vodka in my briefcase and I poured us each a large measure into the plastic mugs by the sink, "it's best taken down in one. Go on, try it. Or are you just a little scared girl after all?" As I guessed, she couldn't resist the challenge.

"What have you done? What is that? Bleach?" she spluttered.

I couldn't help laughing as she coughed and held her throat, tears streaming from her eyes. Serve her right for pretending she was something she was not.

"It's vodka, the latest drink in town. Is it too much for you? Shall I take the little girl back upstairs to her little new-town friends?" I teased, walking towards the door, pretending I was ready to take her back upstairs.

"Yes. No. I mean, I'm fine. I just weren't expecting it, that's all."

She was a brave girl, I had to admit, obviously game for anything.

"It's easier the second time," I said, pouring her another and holding her gaze.

"I'm not sure. My dad'll kill me if he smells drink on my breath and he's coming for me at half past ten," she hesitated, but just a little, before drinking.

"How sweet. But vodka doesn't smell. So this will be just our little secret. Just you and me. No one else need ever know, eh?" And I moved in to kiss her, pushing her slowly back across my desk.

She let me kiss her full on her mouth, then I started teasing her with my tongue and gently biting her lips. After a tantalising minute she pulled away giggling and sat up. I played it cool, not giving in to my frustration.

"I like a lady with a sense of humour. You will be my secret little lady tonight, won't you?" and I poured her another drink.

She clearly enjoyed being called a lady and drinking what she obviously saw as posh, fashionable drinks. I stroked the back of her neck and explained, "We have to be discreet because of my position. The newspapers would love to find some gossip about me, and the Party workers can be very petty and jealous. I'm not thinking of me, I'm a man and it's ok for men to play around a little. But not a pretty little thing like you. They would make your life a misery. People will talk. You would get a bad name. You know how it is for girls. I want to protect you from all that."

She gave me a lop-sided smile which I took to be agreement so I kissed her again; tenderly at first but then more fiercely, pushing my tongue between her teeth and into her mouth. She gagged a little but didn't push me away so I pushed her backwards again, down over the desk. Her skirt was beginning to ride up even though she tried to pull it back over her legs and I found it so exciting that I pushed my body between her legs and still she didn't really resist. Not really.

Then I put my hand under her blouse and put my hands under her bra, caressing her cool, naked breast. Even now she didn't say stop. I couldn't believe my luck. She just lay there and let me do it until she suddenly seemed to realise what was happening.

She pulled away, "I can't do that. Not yet, and certainly not on a first date,"

"Oh come on. I won't do anything else. I just want to touch you there. Just once?" I was desperate now and could hardly control my breathing, let alone the bulging pressure in my pants. She can't stop now, she'd let me go so far. It wasn't fair.

"No. I'm sorry." Even she was breathing heavily and I could see that she wanted it.

I tried another tack, "Well just let me see your breasts. I won't touch them. Just let me look. I bet they are beautiful. Go on, my sweet little Jenny, just let me see. What harm could it do? Look. I'll stand way over here," and I moved away from the desk to the other side of the room with my hands open, arms down by my sides. I knew if I could get her to take her blouse off, she'd have to let me go all the way.

"Show me. Take off your blouse and bra. Please. Then I'll know you really care for me and aren't just leading me on. I promise I'll stay right over here," and I walked backwards, eyes pleading with her, towards the door.

She was just about to relent when someone tried to get in the door.

"Charles? Are you in there? Come on, we must go." It was a woman's voice. A posh voice; bloody Jemima. She had to go and ruin it for me but surely, if I saw this girl again, she would give me what I wanted. I had to persuade her first to keep quiet. I walked back and gently put my finger on her beautiful, slightly swollen lips.

"I'm going to wait outside, Charles. If you're not out in 10 minutes I'm going without you and you can find your own way back to Berkshire from this God-awful place!"

We heard her leave and Jenny got the giggles. I held her face in both of my hands and, turning on the old Davidson charm whispered,

"Listen. If you want to see me again and I'm pretty certain you do, you have to promise me that you'll keep our love affair a secret. Promise me?" I hoped the word *love* would do the trick and it did.

"I promise, but when can I see you again?"

"Next Saturday, here. But only when I give you the nod. We'll come down here separately and carry on where we left off. Upstairs you have to act as if you don't know me and you can't tell anyone or we'll both get into terrible trouble. Understand?"

I was terrified that someone would find out, then not only would I have to give her up, I would probably get a bit of a rollicking from my campaign manager, even worse from my father. I kissed her, gently this time, and she whispered back, big blue eyes staring into mine, "I understand."

And so my first heterosexual affair began. I don't count Jemima. She insisted on waiting until we were married, and even then the sex was always a quick, furtive transaction. Jenny was nothing like any female I'd met before. She seemed assured of her own sexuality and revelled in it. I was fascinated and realised what a sheltered life I'd led. I found out then that the female of the species could be as exciting as the male. She took quite a lot of persuasion at first. The vodka that I always took with me helped, but she never really complained or asked for anything from me. That is, until she got herself pregnant.

I should have listened more carefully to my father. He was a man of the world and knew what was what. He'd warned me about consorting with girls who were not, how did he put it? Not like us. I now know he meant working class girls like Jenny, whose only way, he told me, to better themselves was to entrap someone like me by getting pregnant. I got the roasting of my life when I told him Jenny was pregnant. But he came through for me, or maybe it was more for his own ends. My eventual marriage to Jemima was part of a property deal he could not allow to be muddied by my "inability to keep it in my trousers." I think that was one of the many vulgar phrases he used.

He arranged for Jenny to see the requisite two psychiatrists who confirmed that her mental health would be severely damaged by allowing the pregnancy to go to term and he also paid for the private hospital fees. He consoled the parents by offering to pay for them all to move to South Africa, so long as they and Jenny signed some documents preventing them from disclosing any details about me and the appalling mess I had made.

*

On the night Jenny told me she was pregnant, I'm afraid my tendency to lose my temper, known previously only to my nanny and the younger boys at school, re-emerged. I raged at her and the more she wept the more furious I felt. I could have killed her. Perhaps if that tempestuous little demon hadn't rushed down to protect her cousin, I might have done.

She was a sight to treasure. So full of protective aggression. Such passion. She was young, yes, but that only made her anger more appealing. Her lithe little body against mine as she tried to prise me off her cousin was more like that of the younger boys at school and I felt a stirring. Despite my own experience and my father's advice, I was knocked sideways by this girl's angry innocence and beauty. Her short blonde hair, tousled from sleep and her furious brown eyes provoked such a reaction that I almost forgot about Jenny and the problem she had just given me.

"Get off my cousin," her voice was low for a girl and, despite the threat in the words, I bathed in its sensuousness. Jenny had stopped screaming by now and the girl had stopped beating me for long enough to comfort her cousin and to let me try to regain my breath and equilibrium.

"I'm sorry, Jenny," I forced my eyes away from her cousin to look at a red-eyed, snivelling Jenny, "I will sort something, don't worry. Everything will be fine." Although, at that moment I was not quite as sure as I hoped I was sounding.

"Go away," Jenny sobbed and I was only too pleased to comply.

*

My father's people sorted out all the arrangements and I was instructed to have no contact with Jenny again. But I needed to see that amazing little cousin again so I tried to arrange one last meeting with Jenny. She was reluctant,

"You should be marrying me, not getting rid of our baby," she complained on the phone. I could picture her sitting with the phone receiver in her hand at the bottom of the stairs in that dark hall with its dark green stair-carpet and cream woodchip wallpaper.

"I'm sorry, Jenny, I really want to, you know that, but my father won't let me," Sometimes it's good to have a powerful father.

"Can't we just run away to Gretna Green?"

In those days, if you were under twenty-one, Scotland was the only place you could get married without your parents' approval.

"Meet me for lunch tomorrow at the Wimpy Bar in the High Street. Bring your cousin if you like…" I held my breath.

"We can't, it's Marian's school fair tomorrow."

So her name was Marian, I played with it in my head for a few seconds, then;

"What school? I'll meet you there."

"It's Our Lady's but you can't, our mums will be there."

I tried to sound disappointed but I was already making plans.
"That's a shame, Jenny. I will try to see you some other time then, goodbye."

"See you soon, very soon, I hope..."

I ended the call. I was totally elated. I was going to see that feisty little Marian, soon, very soon I hoped.

Suddenly the phone on my desk brought me back to the present.

*

"There's a Dr Campbell for you, sir," my PA announced, "She says it's urgent."

Damn that woman, I'd told her never to ring me here. I felt my anger rising so I took a few breaths before I answered, "Put her through, Miranda."

"Sir Charles, I just can't understand how it happened, I really can't – we watched her like hawks, just as you asked, but she's gone…"
"What do you mean gone? I thought you had her heavily sedated and wasn't she using a

wheelchair? What about the alarm system on the gates and doors?"

"I'm so sorry"
"Sorry doesn't help at all." My anger was getting the better of me so I took some more deep breaths. Shouting at her would achieve nothing and I might need her on-side in the future. "What does that nurse say, the one you had allocated to her?"
"Sonya says that Marian must have wheeled herself into the garden when there was a fight between some of the other patients. All the staff were busy trying to separate them – it was getting quite vicious and it upset the other patients who started screaming and crying. Nobody noticed her slipping out. As soon as she realised, Sonya went out to get her but she refused to come back in."

"Surely, all she had to do was to grab the damned wheelchair and get her back inside. That's ridiculous!" Why is it that no one can do a simple task nowadays?

"Sonya said she was frightened…"
"Of a loopy old woman?" What little patience or control I'd had was disappearing and with good reason. I'd paid a considerable amount of money to get Marian looked after and kept out of the public eye and now they say they've lost her?

"She couldn't have got far – unless, maybe, her son Darren came for her? He was always complaining about.., well, about everything." Campbell was clutching at straws.

I slammed down the phone and made a note to stop any further payments to Dr Campbell and to set things in motion for an enquiry into the running of the Home. I do not like being taken for a fool. Dr Campbell will soon find that out.

Felicity: Chapter 15

A Woman's Work is Never Done

Felicity sat in her mini, parked by Brighton's promenade and watched the rain drizzling down on the dark pebbly beach. The bright sky with its wind-blown clouds and sunshine had disappeared and the sea and sky merged into one grey miserable mess. Now there were very few visitors enjoying the prom, the ice creams and all the fun of the fair. Yesterday's gaiety dragged itself down into the gutters, mingling with the rain, empty chip wrappers and lager cans. She was beginning to regret booking into a cheap hotel in Hove; she should just have hurried back to her safe little flat in Putney and let the world – and Marian- take care of itself. This was not the happy place of her childhood. Someone had told her that you should never go back. They were right. How our memories deceive us...

*

This is nothing like all those childhood trips I had with Mum and Ed and Uncle Charles. Dad was always too busy. That pier, with its happy noises, candy-floss smells and colourful helter-skelter used to make me giddy with excitement and, if I shut my eyes, I can almost smell the chips that we used to throw to the seagulls at the end of the pier. I quite fancy some now.

As I step out of the car, the rain spitefully pierces my face so I quickly drop back inside to safety. What a coward! Always one for the easy life. Never one for a confrontation. Then and now. I sit for a while thinking of Marian again. I can't just leave it there. There's clearly something wrong and now I'm complicit in hiding it away, just like I always do when things get too awkward or embarrassing. If nobody talks about it, it fades away until it seems it never existed.

Isn't that why Uncle Charles wanted me all the way up in Edinburgh? To stop me thinking about the situation with Marian, to take me away from it, or just to get me away, full stop? Well, fuck him. I'm going to do something I've never done before; confide in my big brother, Ed, and get him to help. I phone him from my car before I lose my nerve.

"Hi, little sis, what's up?" His voice bathes over me with a warmth that almost brings me to tears. Once again, my emotions, held down for most of my adult life, surface with such a force that it all comes out much more dramatically than I mean: the alleged mistreatment of Marian in the home, the photo of Tracey and Uncle Charles, his insistence that I only report to him, the fake medical report and on and on.

"So, you're coming to Edinburgh?"

"That is so not the point!" I get agitated and snap at him, "Yes, that's what he's offering me; a hotel, then accommodation once I'm settled, expenses and a salary a damned sight fatter than I'm used to. But, don't you see? He's paying me off. I'm not actually coming up there – at least, not yet. Will you cover for me; say I am actually there with you if he calls?"
"Ok, if that's what you want. Tell me more about this Marian. You say she thinks she had this baby in the sixties?"

"That's what Tom says. She married his grandfather when she was seventeen and it must have been some time before then…"
Then Ed articulates the realisation that hits me, strangely rather late in the day.

"So she must have been under sixteen when she got pregnant, if there is any truth in this baby obsession…"

How could I not have realised that?

"Then again, you say there's no medical evidence to show she ever was pregnant, let alone that he was the father..?" Ed sounds like he doesn't believe me, that I'm being the melodramatic little sister as usual.

"Why else would he have her locked away and get me to spy on the family?" I'm getting annoyed now; why does he always think I'm exaggerating things? "Not to mention having her drugged and constantly being told that her memories are false."

"Maybe it is all innocent, Fliss. He knew the family, feels obliged. Maybe she *is* suffering from dementia or grief… But come to think of it, I've never trusted that man. The way he used to watch both you and Mum; I used to think it was because I felt left out, jealous, but there was always something slightly sleazy about it."

I feel a shudder of reluctant recognition. I don't want to go there. Another, even worse, thought sneaks its way into my head, "What if she's not the only girl he took advantage of? What if there are other women?"

"I wouldn't be at all surprised."

I have a brilliant idea, "Could you find out the names of any women who knew him back in the day?"

He is supposed to be an investigative journalist, after all. I'm not sure where I'm going with this or how it would help Marian but it suddenly seems the only thing to do.

"Well, I suppose I could research party documents, especially the youth registers... I don't have much work on at the moment..." I can almost hear the synapses snapping into place.

"Yes, and you could send me details of likely prospects; girls who would have come into fairly regular contact with him. Maybe ones who suddenly stopped being active in the Party after meeting him..?"

I'm getting excited at the thought of mounting a campaign against him. I don't know why. It could go so wrong. Could totally ruin my career but I'm on a roll now and I feel the urge to do this so strongly, I can't stop talking, "I can talk to them, woman to woman, to see if they can shed any light on his past. Marian could just be the tip of the proverbial iceberg."

"Well," Ed is not quite so sure and he thinks it over for a while. "You say he paid for this woman to stay at the home..?"

"Apparently and it doesn't look like a place that would come cheap."

"Well, it's not like him to do anything unless it serves his interest, I guess. He wouldn't have helped out the family unless there was something in it for him."
"Or he had to. So there *must* be more to it, don't you see?" How could Ed not see?

"Or maybe it was all an excuse to get you back into his evil clutches," Ed let out a fake demonic laugh. I didn't find it funny.

"That's not funny, Ed." I tried to swallow down the thoughts gathering like the saliva in my mouth. I felt sick. I feel the tears prickling my eyes.

"Hey, I was only joking. What's wrong? You used to idolise the man, follow him around like a little puppy and he never hid the fact that he loved your company. I just told you, I used to get so jealous." His voice was almost tender, "Come on, it'll be fine. Let's check him out. We'll get to the bottom of it all."

But as soon as he agreed, I wanted to step back. What if I have gotten it all out of proportion? The old lady was quite clearly on the verge of dementia. Look how she nearly crashed the car on our way down. In the last few weeks I've so not been myself. I've been a mess of emotions, making me doubt my own judgement, even the memory of my own childhood. I'd always thought it was a happy one until the other week when Ma was recounting our golden past. I couldn't help feeling there was something not quite right. She wanted it to be oh-so-lovely and I couldn't see it. It just felt wrong. Oh, that's such crap. For some reason I need to punish Charles. I'm letting Marian mess with my head or is it because she's Tom's grandma and I miss him? Me, pining for some man? I really am so not myself right now.

"What's wrong, Fliss? This is not like you. I always thought you were the original ice-maiden."

The tears come before I can stop them.

"I don't know who I am anymore. I used to be, like you say, so cool, calm and collected. But now look at me. I've started crying over stupid tunes and even TV programmes lately. I'm completely unable to stop thinking about Uncle Charles and this bloody woman's family. You've got to help me Ed. Please say you will look into his early life. You're an investigative journalist, you'll know what to do."

I feel I'm clutching at straws but what else can I do? I take a deep breath. The next request's even more difficult to ask, "And can you find out where they sent Tom?"

*

Two days later, Ed's back on the phone. I'd just got back from watching some women swimming in the sea. It was a freezing cold, grey morning. I've read it's supposed to be good for your immune system or something. I thought they were mad. They did look like they were enjoying it; both the swimming and each other's' company. I feel a bit jealous about that.

"Are you sitting down, Fliss?" my knees make it impossible to do anything else. It's clearly bad news. Has he found something or nothing? Which is worse?

"Finding Tom was quite easy. He'd managed to smuggle in a mobile and had contacted some of his friends on Facebook. A bit silly, the centre he's at will soon find out and confiscate it but at least we know where he is. It's a small rehab clinic just outside Cape Town."

My head lurches to the left. Why hadn't he contacted me?

"The other thing I've found out is that there have been quite a few allegations made against our dear old Uncle Charles by young female members of the party over the years. Nothing serious and nothing was ever done about it but it might be worth following up. Are you still up to talking to any of these women? Of course it may be difficult to track them down as women change their surnames when they marry."

"What sort of allegations?" I'm making myself a tea, only half listening.

"They were usually filed under "unprofessional conduct" but as they only involve young women, I think it's pretty obvious what that really means." He was clearly excited and pleased with himself but I hardly gave it a thought, my mind was elsewhere, "Is Tom's Facebook page still online?

*

217

Within a few days, Ed forwarded me a long list of possible names of interest with their contact details. It wasn't as easy as I'd thought, meeting these women. Many of them refused to speak to me but those that did could not stop once they realised that someone would listen to them without judgement. After years of denial and suppression, what was done to them years ago seemed even more outrageous now and these women were finally feeling their rage. Against the man himself and at the way they had been silenced. Silenced by the way society was back then and by their own internalised acceptance. They all started by blaming themselves,

"I knew I should have stopped him…"

"I shouldn't have allowed him into my room..."

"I was a bit star-struck, he was so important and handsome, and he wanted me…"

Every time, the women felt responsible; they thought it was their job to say no and to police men's sexual advances. One after another, the women started out our conversations, berating their complicity in their seduction. But the fear, shame and embarrassment was nothing compared to their confusion when, after hearing their stories, I told them that they were not the only one abused by Charles Davidson. First came the shock that they had never been special, then came the rage.

I found it more and more difficult listening to these stories. As each woman confided their stories, peppered with emotional outbursts of shame, confusion and rage on behalf of their younger selves, I lived it all along with them. The circumstances may be slightly different each time but the feelings were not and they seemed to lodge themselves in my head and grow there. They inhabited my dreams and then my thoughts as I tried to get through each day. Soon, I couldn't tell their feelings from mine. I found myself shouting at the little TV in my tiny hotel room every time there was a mention of a man assaulting, abusing or murdering a woman, either in a drama or on the News. Until then I hadn't realised how often it happened. Their pain was my pain and I was angry. Angry at the perpetrators but also angry at the many programmes that showed women being abused or murdered and called it 'entertainment'.

I had to talk to someone, get it all out of my head so I rang my brother again after I'd emailed him a written copy of each of the conversations I'd had that first week.

"I'm not sure I can keep doing this, Ed. It's doing my head in. I actually feel every single one of their emotions, I go through all their ordeals. I'm losing sight of the fact that it happened to them; it's as if it happened to me too."

"I'm not surprised, sis. You've been tearing away at it like a madwoman. How many interviews have you got now?"

"About 15 or so, I'm not counting. You talk as if they're just data to be processed, but they're not you know, they're real people." I couldn't stop the edge to my voice.

"I know that, I'm sorry. I just meant that you've totally immersed yourself in so many of their stories so it's not surprising that you feel this way."

"No, I'm sorry. I was being over-defensive. These women have been used before, I don't want us to use them all over again, just to bring Charles down."

"Come on now, I'm not the enemy here or are you tarring all of us men with the same brush?" He tried to keep it light but to me he was just digging himself in deeper. Maybe all men *were* the same, made that way by the society we live in. Just look at the tabloids, just look at the way boys are brought up; the toys they are given, even the clothes they wear. I've just walked through the baby department of a big store and all the slogans on the girls' T-shirts were sweet and full of unicorns and rainbows but all the baby boys' tops were of aggressive looking dinosaurs and one even said "I'm going to be a heart-breaker". On a baby! How had I never noticed before? Maybe I am getting it all out of proportion. I need a really good night's sleep.

"You know what Ed? I'm going to bed now. It's probably me, and you're probably right, but I can't do this right now. Just tell me before I go, how far have you got with Marian's baby – or have you forgotten about that in all the excitement of a great scoop?"

 "Now that's not fair. You came to me, remember?" I grunted what could have implied a grudging consent. "Ok, sis. I'm trawling the local newspapers around Brighton and her home town of Welwyn Garden City for stories of babies being abandoned or women being arrested for back street abortions. I've also got a list of

institutions for unmarried mothers which
I'm going through. Ok?"

"Yes, thanks. I'm sorry Ed. I shouldn't let it
get to me like this. See you soon," and I
hung up.

*

I threw myself onto the hotel bed. Why had I
been so mean to my brother? It was me who
had asked for his help. Oh for fuck's sake,
there I am, taking the blame again. Typical
woman. And suddenly I'm laughing at
myself, despite everything. Am I finally
becoming a feminist? I'd always ridiculed
them at Uni. Maybe I'm finally growing up
and not seeing everything in clichés. Look at
these women I've just met – their
doggedness and bravery. Little old ladies –
some almost as old as Marian – still furious
and prepared to go to court after all these
years. Prepared to reveal intimate details of
their lives to some fusty old judge or
whatever. Quite humbling. No, maybe not
that. I refuse to do humble. But I am
impressed.

I went back to the minibar. It was well
stocked; chocolate bars, mini bottles of
spirits and a half bottle each of red and
white wine. A red Cabernet and a Sauvignon

Blanc. Both South African. I chose the red, of course, picked up the phone and idly scrolled through the photos of me and Tom.

Why hadn't he contacted me? Did he even think of me now that there was all that distance between them? Had he already forgotten me? Just saw it as an interesting experience with an older woman? I sipped slowly, deliberately. Maybe he thinks I groomed him..?

I had to place the glass on the side table before I spilt any. Where did that thought come from? I slumped into the small armchair by the window. Tom was a grown man! Well almost. A couple of years beyond the age of consent. It was men that groomed young girls, how could I even think like that?

A few more sips of wine calmed me down. There were similarities, though. I'd definitely used him. He was a fair bit younger, and I had all the power in the relationship... But he had stayed willingly, clearly enjoyed being with her, hadn't he? But then there were those American actresses who had to explain why they had stayed with the powerful man who had raped them. The court still agreed that they had been abused. Oh shit. I finished off the rest of the wine in one go and went straight over and took out the bottle of white. I finished it almost before I knew what I was doing. I chucked the bloody bottles in the bin. I'd like to be throwing them at bloody Charles. Every time he comes into my life he messes with my head and makes me think and do things I don't want to do. Why did Mummy and Daddy allow it? Were they afraid of him; owed him something? Looking back now I see that Mummy had probably been in love with him. Maybe even Daddy too. No, this was getting silly. Too much wine, too quickly – and on an empty stomach too. I looked at myself in the long, ornate mirror that took up most of the wall on the other side of the bed. I stood a little taller. It was time. I can't keep blaming others for my shortcomings. I'm a strong independent woman. If those little old ladies could stand up and fight for their younger selves, then shouldn't I be able to? But I can't help laughing, knowing that by the morning, once the wine's influence had been flushed through my system and down the toilet, I'd be little Fliss again, buffeted by my family, by Charles and by that bloody need to be liked.

No, I have to make sure something good comes out of all this.

I can't let that man do any more damage. So, with my hands shaking – that's interesting, is it the alcohol or nerves? - I texted the phone I'd given Marian. I said I needed to see her again urgently as I had some information for her. Even as I press send, I'm not sure it's a good idea. But it was done now and I'll have to follow it through.

Chapter 16: Marian

Don't Trust What You See, Even Salt Can Look Like Sugar

"You know Kevin and I are trying to adopt a child, Mum?" Darren hands me a cup of coffee and sits down next to me on the bright red sofa, "We met this really helpful social worker."

I open my mouth to speak but he cuts me off.

"Yes, I know you don't trust them, Mum. After what you've been through this past year, why should you? In fact, by the time we met her, having jumped through so many hoops and been let down so many times, we weren't so keen either." He holds up his hand again to stop me butting in. "She was really helpful and she knew her stuff. The point is, I spoke to her and she knows all the ins and outs of reuniting adopted children with their birth mothers and she has said she will help you."

"I don't trust them – any of them! They helped you all to put me in that awful home..."

"I know mum, but she is willing to give up her spare time to help us. I wouldn't know how to go about it, so play nice when she comes."

"Is she coming here? Today? I have to go to the Town Hall to look up records. It said so on your internet."

I haven't got time for visitors. I need to get on. The sooner I find my baby, the sooner I can get on with my life. I get up from the table and take my coffee to the kitchen area. I don't like coffee. I need a cup of tea. Why can't Darren see that I need to do this by myself? I don't want some social worker taking over. That's how I ended up in that home and, besides, it's my life, my mission. No one else's.

"She is going to take you to the records office and anywhere else that can help. She'll be here soon. Maybe that's her now..." and Darren gets up to answer the door.

I look round for a way to escape but there isn't one. If only I felt agile enough to climb down from the roof terrace. No definitely not, so I lock myself in the bathroom instead.

"Come in Carol. Mum, this is...where's she gone? Mum! Oh come on, you haven't locked yourself in the bathroom again...We've talked about this..." Darren bangs his frustration through the bathroom door.

"It's ok, Darren, let me have a try," I hear that Carol woman walking to the door and she knocks gently.

"Mrs. Norman, or may I call you Marian? It's Carol here. I haven't come to hurt you or upset you. It's just that I have some information for you about babies born in Brighton in the 1950s and 60s..." The idea permeates through both the door and my fear of social workers. After a few minutes, I open it a little and look out at her. She's holding some bulky files.

"Here are copies of all the births registered in Brighton from 1959 to 1961. I didn't look later than that because Darren told me that you met your husband Bob in 1961."

Despite myself I am so curious that I leave the bathroom.

"I've only taken copies of the male births because Darren said you think you had a little boy..?"

I sit down next to this Carol, my eyes drawn to the papers spread out on the coffee table. Could my little boy be here? I realise that I've stopped breathing and out comes a long sigh. The breath of years, no decades, of waiting is unleashed into the room.

"I have to go to meet Kevin now, will you two be ok?" Darren slips on his leather jacket and makes for the door. I'm already so engrossed that I hardly register his leaving.

*

But it's not to be. No matter how many times we each go through the lists, there's no record of a boy's birth that could have fitted the circumstances of one born to me; a young Marian Alsop. "Maybe we have the dates wrong, Marian. I know you said you couldn't be sure of the date but is there anything you can remember from about that time that would help us pin-point it more accurately?" I feel her eyes pitying me.

"I...I was very young. Yes. I can remember something he said now. He said we couldn't get married for another three years because I was too young."

"But that would mean you were only..."
Why does Carol look so shocked?

"What date were you born, Marian?"

My mind goes a total blank. It always does when I'm asked a direct question like that.

"I don't know. I've got it written down somewhere. But they took everything away when they put me in that home." The home has taken away my legal identity along with everything else. They have made me into a non-person. I can't stop the tears that embarrass me in front of this kind stranger.

"Not to worry," Carol reaches out and holds my hand. It's the first time anyone apart from Darren has touched me since the rough handling of the carers at the home. The tears flow freely now. For myself and for the baby; neither of us seem to exist anymore, at least not on paper.

"We can ask Darren when he gets back. He'll probably know or can find out when your date of birth is."

The phrase "date of birth" triggers something in my brain; the part where I store all those catch-phrases, snatches of song and things I'd had to learn by rote, like

the Co-op dividend number or the poem
Daffodils at primary school. "It's the
thirtieth of December 1944!" I splutter.

"Well then, we've been looking at the wrong
dates. We need to look at births for around
1957 and 1958. We'll have to go back to the
Records Office. Come on, my car's outside.
Dry your tears, give your face a wash and
let's go and find those records."

Mum always said I mustn't get into a
stranger's car. But I do. It seems to be a
habit of mine. Sitting in this stranger's car
today sparks off a memory of another car,
another stranger.

*

It was one day after school; he was waiting
down the road. It was during one of those
really fast April showers that only last a few
minutes but soak you through and through if
you get caught in them.

"Hello Marian, I was just passing when it
started to rain so I thought I'd give you a
lift. Hop in the car, I'll take you home," and
he smiles the nicest smile. I'm still not sure.
But he's Jenny's boyfriend, not really a

stranger. I saw him the night they had their terrible argument.

"Jenny's not speaking to you anymore," and I begin to skip off into the rain.

"Wait. I need your help. You're a kind little girl aren't you? You want to make me and Jenny friends again don't you? After all, it's your fault that we had that row."

That stops me. I look back.

"Come on, you're getting soaked. I'll take you home," so I take that first step into his car. I wish we had a car. Mum says we can't afford it. I feel so grand, sitting next to him in the front seat. He asks me questions about school and teases me about not having a boyfriend yet. Silly man, he knows I'm not old enough. Then he started on about the time I'd ruined their evening by coming downstairs when they were baby-sitting me. They had a horrible, scary row. I feel really bad but I don't know what to say.

"I haven't been able to see her since then, you know?" His face sort of crumples and I think he's going to cry. Men don't cry. I have to do something. I don't know what.

"I'm sorry," I feel the tears prickling my eyes so I look out of the window, "Jenny's really sad now." It was true, everyone at her house seemed sad and a bit angry. I don't know why.

"Is she now? Well then, I have a plan; a secret plan. You like secrets?" He looks at me with such a friendly smile.

Secrets? I love secrets. Suddenly it all seems better. I nod.

"I need you to help me to make Jenny jealous. Then she'll remember how much she loves me. Then we'll get back together and we'll all be happy."

The thought of everyone being happy again is so good that I nod at him again.

"Then the three of us could go out for rides in my car if you like. You never know, you might get to be our bridesmaid when we get married. If you help me get her back, that is."

 A bridesmaid. I've always wanted to be a bridesmaid, wearing a pretty pastel-coloured dress with a big brightly-coloured sash and several stiff, sticking-out petticoats with a garland of fake flowers in my hair. I can almost feel the starchy petticoats scratching my legs. I grin happily at him. I'm still not quite sure what he wants but I'd do anything to be a bridesmaid.

"What shall we do?"

I want to help because Jenny really has been very unhappy since her fight with this man. She'd made me cross my heart and swear on my mother's life never to tell anyone about him so no one else in our family knew about it. It's my fault that they were cross with each other. I shouldn't have come downstairs. Jenny said that I was never, ever, ever, to come downstairs when she was looking after me. After the shouting man had gone, she grabbed me and just screamed. I couldn't breathe, Jenny was squeezing me so tightly. I'd do anything to make Jenny happy again, so that she never screamed like that again. Anything.

"What shall we do?" I have to ask twice because Jenny's boyfriend is thinking so hard that he didn't hear me the first time. The silly man has gone the wrong way home. This is the way to the fields near the old abandoned farmhouse. I used to play there with my friends. That was before Mummy found out and said it was too dangerous. She made me promise not to go there again. Jenny's boyfriend stops the car in a lane by the fields, gets out and opens my door. But I won't get out.

"I'm not allowed here, Mummy says the building's going to fall down on someone one day. She says the council ought to do something about it..." I know I'll get in trouble if anyone sees me here.

"It's ok. We won't go into the farmhouse if you're not allowed. I just want to show you something and then I'll take you straight home. No one will ever know. It will be our secret,"

*

The news on Carol's car radio breaks the memory. They were on about "historical abuse" again and some rumours about an un-named politician that were going viral, whatever that meant.

Carol coughs and turns to look at me. I smile back. The silence suddenly feels strange.

"It must be hard for women who are abused so young," she says, "I'm sure they never really get over it, do they?" There's more to what she's saying but I don't know what so I just keep quiet.

"Do you mind if I ask you about your child's father..?" The question's left hanging. I feel uncomfortable and begin to worry that maybe I shouldn't have got into her car.

"Are we nearly there yet?" I ask.

Chapter 17: Tracey

Truth will Out

Tracey remembered little of the flight back from Cape Town. She had a vague memory of the kerfuffle at Johannesburg when a swarm of shabbily dressed men – all black, of course, but that didn't worry her, honestly it didn't,- grabbed hold of their cases to "help" them to get to the other part of the airport for their connecting flight to Heathrow. For some reason it involved going round lots of deserted corridors, up and down ramps, back through more corridors, to find themselves less than a pebble's throw from where they had started. A South African pebble; beautiful but very hard and no longer just for the taking as it had been under white rule.

Each man held out his hand politely, belying the menace Tracey felt was behind their broad smiles. Or was it that she was projecting her guilty feelings on to them? Nigel harrumphed and grumbled like a true Englishman but, like a true Englishman, he didn't like to make a fuss and so paid up, still grumbling.

"I can't believe you let him do that, mum," Emily hissed, "you usually spot a scam by a mile."

It's always my fault, my responsibility, thought Tracey, and she snapped at Emily,

"Your dad is big enough and ugly enough to look after himself. I should have thought it was HIS job to look after me for a change."

Emily and Nigel stared at each other, then at Tracey, totally baffled by this stranger in their midst. She had not been right for a day or so now and hearing that her mother had disappeared had clearly pushed her right over the edge.

The rest of the trip to Heathrow was conducted in total silence, Nigel retreating once more into his newspaper; the Daily Mail, helpfully placed in the pocket in front of him. He'd completely devoured the Telegraph while waiting in the airport. Emily watched back-to-back films on her I-Pad and Tracey shut her eyes to her family and the rest of the world, only opening them to request a gin and tonic from the ever-smiling stewardess every now and again.

By the time they landed she was suitably numb but, unlike most other travellers, did not feel the need to switch on her phone the moment her feet hit English soil, despite the fact that she knew she needed to sort out the mess that the stupid care home had created. She told herself that she wasn't really worried. Her mother couldn't have just disappeared; she must be somewhere in the home. They had fantastic security; Dr Campbell had taken great delight in showing her when she had first visited. It must be a mistake and the gin reassured her that all would be well in the morning.

"Mum! Mum!" Emily's voice broke through and suddenly she was once again aware of the noise, the crowds, the harsh lighting and the awful reality of where and who she was, and of what she had heard a few days before.

"Uncle Darren's on the phone. He says he's been trying to get through to you for hours and he sounds really, really angry!" Tracey gingerly took Emily's proffered IPhone.

"What's all this about you working with some guy and that evil woman at the clinic to keep mum locked up..?" Darren's voice screamed over the noise of the airport.

She didn't hear any more, she didn't need to. It was all hitting the fan at once. The top of her head spun round. It was like being on the Waltzer back in the days when the Bank Holiday Fair came to town. She'd never really liked it, disliked the dizzy feeling of being completely out of control, but always went on with Darren because he was too little to go on his own.

"I'm coming down, as soon as I can," she said as calmly as she could to Darren, "don't let Mum out of your sight. She has schizoaffective disorder and could be a danger to herself and maybe to others. You don't know what she's capable of, Darren. Even I took some convincing but she isn't the shrinking little violet we all thought she was."

Tracey pulled the phone away from her ear, "Stop shouting at me, Darren and listen. I had a long talk with Aunt Jenny while we were in Cape Town and she told me stuff about her and mum's childhood. I think it has had a serious effect on her mental health, supressed when she was with dad, but now there really is no telling what she might do next..." and she ended the phone call, throwing the phone back to Emily.

Nigel and Emily watched open-mouthed as she rushed from the baggage reclaim, through the customs exit and out into the harsh sunlit concourse without a word of explanation. She hailed a taxi and jumped in and told the driver to go, without a thought for her husband or daughter

The dark silence of the taxi contrasted with the bright noisy airport and Tracey allowed herself to calm down. She did her breathing exercises that she'd learnt at yoga and felt her heartbeat, no longer hammering in her ears, going back to normal. She thought back to the first time she'd met Charles Davison; to the time before she allowed everything to go wrong.

*

"Tracey, you have to accompany me, it's not open to question. If I'm to be the next Parliamentary candidate my wife has to be by my side at all times." Nigel's pomposity irritated me; was I just his appendage? A useful accessory? No it wasn't just that; I never felt I belonged at these sort of events. They were full of people more articulate, smarter and well, more well-bred than me. I didn't have the knack of small talk and, no matter how expensive my outfit was, it always looked cheap in comparison to those of the other women there who carried themselves confidently and always knew exactly what to say.

I've tried many a time to explain it to Nigel, but he just shrugs it off, saying it was a kind of inverted snobbery. He'll never understand. He came from a good middle-class home, cultured and socially competent. His father wasn't a wife-beating drunk and you can be sure Nigel never wanted for anything. We had no books in the house, often wore shoes stuffed at the toes with paper until we actually grew into them and rarely ate anything healthier than the pickle and scrap of lettuce you got in a burger. He gets cross when I go on about my childhood and I know I'm still resentful about it. Mum eventually dragged herself out of her depressions and made something of her life but those early years have a strong effect on how you view the world. I just didn't belong in the rarefied social events that Nigel insisted I attend.

When he first told me he had been picked as the Party's candidate, I thought he meant as a local councillor. That's how much attention I'd been paying. Whenever politics were discussed at home, Nigel and the two children instantly took up opposing positions, whatever the topic might be and it got quite hostile. I kept well out of it. I'd learnt a long time ago how to make myself invisible in aggressive situations.

"I tell you what," Nigel said in an effort to placate me, "why don't you buy a new frock or something, to give you confidence? I'll pay, and I promise I'll be by your side as much as possible during the evening. How's that?" What else could I do? It was my duty to be by his side; Lord knows, he's stood up for me every time my mother's antics caused a fuss.

It was as bad as I thought. The 'soiree' was held in the London house of one of the Party's ministers; very grand, stylish and reeking of good taste and a hell of a lot of money. There was no way I belonged here and Nigel was soon whisked away to meet various important people. Mum had taught me that, if you found yourself alone in a party, you should pick up a plate of party food and offer it round, introducing yourself. But here, there were maids in little black and white uniforms serving people, so I just stood there, feeling more and more embarrassed as the minutes went by. Eventually a tall, well-dressed man, quite old but still handsome, took pity on me,

"You must be Mrs. Dawson, Nigel's lovely wife." He shook my hand, lingering a little longer over the handshake. I couldn't stop a little shiver of excitement. It's been a long time since anyone gave me such intimate attention.

"Don't you just hate these events? I do, all that small talk with people you don't know, have nothing in common with and will probably never see again," and we chuckled together in mutual recognition. He handed me a glass of wine from a passing waitress's tray and we chatted for some time. He really put me at ease, I was so grateful. I even told him about Mum, I don't know why but he was just so easy to talk to. He was very sympathetic and even when I told him about the swimming pool incident, he didn't laugh or step back in horror - the way most people react,

"That must have been so difficult for you," he said. No one else had talked about *my* feelings. I felt my eyes prickle and my throat contract.

"Here, come into my study and let's see if we can sort something out for you." Only then did I realise that he owned the house we were in and so he must be the celebrated Charles Davison. Even I had heard of him and not just because Nigel idolised him. He was so jealous afterwards when I told him I'd spent almost the whole evening with Charles.

"Charles?" He'd spluttered, as if I'd uttered an expletive.

"Yes, he told me to call him by his first name. He was so lovely, Nigel, not at all pompous, just very friendly and down to earth. He was very sympathetic about Mum; says he wants to help find a suitable home for her. He's given me the name of a psychiatrist who will assess her needs too." I showed him the card.

"We can't afford Harley Street! Probably won't be able to pay for the home either. What's wrong with the council one that Darren found her?" He almost threw the card back at me. I couldn't help feeling more than a little pleased with myself as I played my winning card,
"He said she needed special treatment. He wants to discuss it with you, man to man. I got the impression he might even help financially."

Torn between his pride and lack of funds, Nigel soothed himself, as I knew he would, with the idea that the great Charles Davison wanted to talk to him. I never found out exactly what happened between them but from then on, Nigel's campaign for selection went from strength to strength and he suddenly became very interested in Mum's welfare. We had her assessed and committed to Golden Meadows within the month. We even held a dinner party in Charles' honour at our house. It normally would have terrified me but I knew that, by his very presence, Charles would make it a success. Emily took a photo of the three of us and we put it in pride of place on the dining room wall.

But that was then.

I know different now. Aunt Jenny had told me on the phone that when she was a teenager she'd got pregnant and was made to have an abortion and that was why the family had immigrated to South Africa.

"That's very sad, Jenny, but why are you dragging all that up now? It must be so painful for you." I'd said.

"I think you should sit down for a minute, Tracey." Puzzled, I did as I was told.

"The father of my child was Charles Davison." I couldn't control myself; I yelped a little. "And that's not all. I think he may have started on your mum after me. First she ran away from home, then she was sent away for months. She was never the same when she came back. We were always

so close before, but she refused to talk to me
- just when I could have done with her
support after my… you know, my situation.
My family were barely talking to me and I
wasn't allowed to go anywhere unless Mum
came too. They were so ashamed – and so
was I. It hurt, losing her, and I'm afraid I
didn't take it well and didn't try hard enough
to find out what was happening with her. I
decided to ignore her like she ignored me
and my pain. Silly, childish behaviour but
then we were still children really. Once we
left for South Africa we completely lost
touch. I can't say for sure, but looking back
now, I think he may have got her pregnant
too, when she was still only thirteen."

How I didn't drop the phone I don't know. I
wanted to throw it as far as possible away
from me and to shout to Jenny that it
couldn't be true. But I couldn't do anything.
I just sat there, stunned, until Jenny asked if
I were all right. I mumbled my thanks and
said I'd be back in touch once I'd processed
what she had said.

And now Mum has mysteriously
disappeared from that high security home.
What has he done with her? What have I
done?

Marian: Chapter 18

Every Cloud has a Silver Lining?

The woman at the records office is friendly but, in the end, unhelpful. After about fifteen minutes she comes back to the reception desk, "Hi, I'm really sorry but I can't find any records that fit the details you've given me." I look at Carol. That's interesting, she doesn't look surprised. The woman gives us an official smile. "I suggest you check the newspaper archives downstairs."

Is this woman just trying to get rid of us? What does she think we could find there? Still, it might give me a chance to get away from this Carol woman. Something she said in the car, I can't remember what it was now, but I don't think I can trust her. Also she seems determined not to let me out of her sight. She reminds me of Sonya. Sometimes these people treat me like a child; always *looking after* me, never letting me have any control. I know I had control once, then it was taken from me, just like my baby.

"I need the toilet," I say as I walk away. She begins to follow me and takes out her phone.

Who is she going to talk to? What's that saying? *Just because you're paranoid doesn't mean they're not out to get you.* I do not trust this woman, I don't care what Darren says; he's another one who tries to belittle me. I don't want that any more.

"I'll come with you." She says while raising her phone to her ear.

"No, I'm quite capable of going by myself, thank you." I stretch up to my fullest height, only five foot one but head held high.

"But I need…" She puts the phone back in her bag and looks really worried.

"*I* don't need minding. I've had enough of that lately. I'll meet you in the archive section!" I can still use my teacher voice, even now. How good is that? I thought I'd lost it at the home.

As soon as she's out of sight I go back to the records woman to check once more without Carol looking over the poor woman's shoulder. My baby must be there somewhere. But still, no. The loss hits me again and again. How many times can you lose the same baby? I have to get away, to get some air into my body before I suffocate from this latest disappointment. I try to catch my breath as I head for the sign that says "stairs". I decide not to use the lift because, when Carol starts to look for me, as I'm sure she's been told to do, she won't think I'd use the stairs. It was such a long way down. As I start my descent my chest tightens with the effort. My knees begin to crackle and ache and it's as if I'm descending into Hell. And my only thought is, where could my baby be? What have they done with him? Why is there no sign of him?

The relief at landing on solid ground brings back some of my breath but I need a cup of tea and maybe just one of my little pills to calm my nerves. My trusty brown handbag used to be full with all the stuff that good mothers keep, like wet flannels in a plastic bag, hankies and emergency sweets but now all I have is my purse, my make-up, that phone and the pills I've hidden in the lining.

As I leave the council building, I turn towards where I remember the Lanes used to be. Somehow my mind remembers the way and, after I stop thinking and just trust myself, I find them. So I haven't forgotten everything. The crowds are busy here, no one caring when they nearly knock me flying, or they stop so suddenly in front of some jeweller's shop that I bump into them.

"Careful, love. Where are you off to in such a flaming hurry?" The burly man with the bald head and tattoos all over his arms seems to think it's my fault. I step back but then his huge face breaks into a massive grin as he makes a dramatic bow and waves me past, "After you my dear. Mind how you go." I'm so embarrassed that I dive into the first café I come across.

It's the strangest café, or I should say tearoom, I've ever seen. There are teapots everywhere, of every size and style, although most of them are floral-patterned china. Vintage, I think they call it. The walls are covered with pictures of the Queen. Not just the usual ones you see; some of them are in bright fluorescent colours, some have her doing things that I'm sure she would never dream of doing. So many people squashed into the higgledy-piggledy mixture of tables and chairs. Nothing in this place matches. But somehow it works; somehow the atmosphere seems safe. The young people there, for all their weird clothes, are chatty and smiling and no one looks at me – an old lady, clearly flustered, - as if I shouldn't be here. Even the young girl who serves me speaks so gently that I can forgive her for spoiling her looks with all those piercings and tattoos. I make my tea last for ages. Once again, I feel as if I cannot move. Even in my deepest depressions when the kids were young I had never felt quite as stuck as I do now. I go back over the day; there was something that Carol said that was important. What was it? My date of birth. That was it. But then we were looking for my baby's date of birth and it was only a few years later. That can't be right. There was something she said in the car too...

I think back to when I first got into his car and he took me to the fields. How old must I have been then? I can't work it out. I was definitely still in Miss May's class because I remember trying to pluck up the courage to ask her about what had happened and if I should tell my Mum. I never did find the courage. Mum would have been so cross if she'd found out that I'd got into a stranger's car. I never did tell her either.

Sometimes, when I try too hard to remember, my mind refuses and goes unassailably blank so I concentrate on the tea-pot covered in its knitted Union Jack tea-cosy, the garishly camp waiter chatting loudly anyone who will listen and the pictures of the Queen adorning the tiny café's walls. But it's no use, my mind keeps taking me back to my childhood. The

childhood taken and lost so long ago. I must have been eleven, no probably twelve, when it started. First year of grammar school.
Yes. I truly loved him. He noticed me. Little old me that no one else took seriously. He made me feel good, made me feel like a woman. I was so sure we would be together for ever. That he loved me too. Was it all a lie? He left me. Left me to face all the shame and the guilt on my own. That means well over 60 years of lying to myself: 60 years and more of living that dirty lie.

"All right my love?" I feel a hand on my shoulder and look up. The young man with the cropped, very blond hair is by my side, kneeling down so that his blue eye-shadowed eyes, brimming with concern, are on a level with my own life-weary and teary ones.

"I…I just realised something bad," as I say the words I know they don't make sense. Nor do they explain my shameful epiphany. I struggle to connect my thoughts and speech but the memories are drowning out everything with their noise. I have to get away.
"I think I need to be alone for a while. Thank you for the tea and… and

everything," and my fingers fumble around in my bag for my purse.

"It's all right lovely, have this one on us. Are you sure you don't want me to call someone?"

Who could he call for me, after all this time?

"No, but that's very kind of you. Thank you," and I wander out of the café towards the pier.

This time it really is the sea calling me. Here I am stood on that same old promenade, almost before I've left the sanctuary of the quirky cafe. The world has moved on without me. I don't belong in this new, brash Brighton with people everywhere. People push past me. As if they can't see me. Maybe I only belong in the time when Brighton was greyer, colder and quieter. I try to ignore this frantic rushing, the smell of the constant traffic and the tall, young people who make me feel so small.

I step onto the beach, away from the crowds. The sea remains the same, I can take comfort in that. Still cold and grey, sweeping over the cold, hard pebbles. Back and forth, going nowhere. Like my memories. I pick my way carefully over the treacherous stones. It would be easy to fall and, as usual, I've no one to catch me or pick me up after. Why do I bother? Nobody cares now. The mother that Tracey and Darren loved no longer exists. It was all based on a lie. I can't be that person any more. I was never any good at it any way. The sea calls. It would be so easy.

I take off my shoes, put my handbag under my coat and hobble on the sharp stones towards the unwelcoming sea. Closer and closer. But, oh my goodness that water's cold. It hurts. Even more than the stones. My feet go numb, then as I creep back away from such a silly, selfish idea, they tingle as the blood flows back into them. Painfully at first but it's a reminder that I am here. That life does renew itself if you let it. It flows, back and forth like the sea, except, unlike the sea, there are things I can now control. And there still is one more thing I must do, whatever anyone else says.

I put on my shoes and coat and go back to join the noise and bustle. Walking along the front, I look at the big houses with their *No Vacancies* signs and try to remember the room at Mrs. Blakely's boarding house. He must have brought me here. If I'd come with Mum, we would have gone to Aunty

Olive's. If I shut my eyes now, I would see it all – did I want to? No, but if it helps me piece together those days then it might help me to find my baby. I sit on a bench and shut my eyes.

*

The room was on the first floor and smelt of damp carpet and old fish. There was a small window but the yellowing net curtains and the black metal fire-escape blocked out most of the light. The walls had originally been covered with cheery floral wallpaper. You could just about see the pattern through the brown sheen of years of cigarette smoke. Shiny emerald green eiderdowns topped the brown blankets on each bed and there were extra blankets in the big walnut wardrobe that took up most of the room. At the time I thought it was lovely and said so which, for some reason, had made Charles laugh.

 That laugh. I can hear it. I open my eyes. Is he here?

No, it's just my memories, so strong that they invade the present, flashing into my life, unbidden. The flashbacks now are worse than my dreams. More vivid. And the worst of it is - I know they're real. This all really happened to me. I check for my purse again. My useless fingers shake with shock, the arthritis doesn't help, but I manage to undo the clasp. Let's see, I still have my credit card. Luckily, I'd had the sense to hide it inside the lining of my bag when they took me into that awful home. I'm sure they'd have taken it otherwise. I need a brandy. It's good for cold. And shock.

I walk along the prom, past the pier and on towards Kemp Town, enjoying the way the sea air fills my lungs so completely, so full of life-giving energy, but it's getting late so when I come across a hotel on the corner with a bar over-looking my beautiful sea, I pluck up my courage and walk in. I don't think I've ever been in a bar by myself before but lately I seem to be doing lots of things I'd never done before. If Bob could see me now! He wouldn't approve and that eggs me on. Before my courage fails me I walk up to the bar and order a brandy. The young barman is very friendly and doesn't seem to find it strange that a little old lady was ordering brandy in a bar in the middle of the day.

The bar's empty apart from a middle-aged couple so it felt safe, not like a pub; I could never walk into a pub alone. I choose a lovely spot, by the window overlooking the sea, a little distance away from the couple who now don't seem so happy. They argue in whispers. I can't hear what they're saying but I can tell it's not anything pleasant. I block them out and look at the sea. I have my own unpleasantries to sort out. I try to control my trembling thoughts but the flashing memories keep knocking them sideways. My shaking hands spill some of the brandy on my coat but it's ok because I have some tissues to clear it up. I drink what's left too quickly as I try to remember what happened all those years ago.

*

That terrible day in the fields, how could I have forgotten? As we get out of the car, he holds my hand a bit too tightly and points to the asphalt track leading from one of the other council estates into the old town, "I've got a really good plan to get Jenny to want to be my girlfriend again." I look at him, he's so clever. He has such a lovely smile. Everything's going to be all right.

"Jenny's friend, Sally, will be coming along here soon. If she sees me kissing a new girl-friend she'll tell Jenny. Then Jenny will get jealous and ask me to go me back with her. I can pretend to give up the girl for her sake, she'll like that, and then everything will be back to normal. What do you think?" He looks so excited but I'm not so sure now.

"Yes, I think, I suppose so - but where is your new girl-friend. Is she coming soon?"

"Hmm. That's the problem. I love Jenny so much that I couldn't kiss another girl." He looks puzzled. Suddenly he clicks his fingers.

"I know! *You* can pretend to be a girl-friend; I'll show you what to do. It'll be ok because you're her cousin so it won't matter if I kiss you. We're almost family. We would be doing it for Jenny."

He knows I'm too young to be a girlfriend. What is he thinking? I shouldn't be here. We're right by the fields where the old farmhouse is that I'm not allowed to play in anymore. I'm going to get into trouble.

"I…I'm not sure…" My knees aren't working, nor is my mouth. It's so dry that each word feels like it's full of the communion wafers the priest gives us on Sundays that stick to the roof of my mouth.

"Come on, you love your cousin don't you? I promise I won't hurt you. We'll just lie here and pretend. Nothing else." Why is he holding my hand so tightly? It's beginning to hurt as we cut through the hawthorn hedge, into the field. He smiles encouragingly as he pulls me down onto the tall, slightly damp grass. Mum will be cross if I get my school clothes dirty but he is a grown-up, and they don't like it if you answer back.

"Why are you looking so serious? It's a happy thing we are doing," and he begins to tickle me gently round my waist, then my legs, then under my arms, accidently touching my chest. I like it, I can't stop giggling. He's laughing too but then his hands move up under my skirt. That's not right, is it? I squirm away but then his hand goes through the leg of my knickers,

"Hey, that's rude. You mustn't touch me there!" and I pull away completely.

"Sorry, my hand slipped. I didn't mean to do that."

I think he's really sorry and I do like him.

"But you're a little girl and little girls like to be tickled. There's nothing wrong in that, is there? I bet your friends tickle you sometimes, don't they? We're just friends. You are my friend, aren't you, Marian?"

Am I his friend? I know I'm too young to be anyone's girlfriend but I like the idea of being friends with a grown-up. It makes me feel important. Then he looks at me so sadly that I feel bad for shouting at him; Jenny's really missing him and he only wants to get her back.

"Yes, of course I'm your friend. Shall we go home now? "My voice is a bit shaky.

"Soon, but we haven't finished our plan. Sally hasn't come yet..." he looks up "Oh, wait a minute, I think I can see her coming. Quick - let me get on top of you and pretend to be kissing you," He sounds so panicky and he moves so fast that, before I know what's happening, he's on top of me in the long grass. His heaviness crushes my ribs. Stealing my breath. Yuk! His fat tongue fills up my mouth; his spit along with it. Why's he doing that? It's disgusting. I can't breathe. I pull my face away, take a deep breath and wipe his spit onto his clean blue shirt. Oops. It's left a dirty mark. I hope he doesn't notice. His hands pull on my knickers again and this time I can't move...

"Thank you, you're wonderful," he whispers as he brushes across my ear with his sloppy, noisy mouth. What's he saying that for? Then he just lies there, puffing and panting on his back. And, as if some magic occurred, he's stopped being so scary and he's my cousin's boyfriend again. It's like Beauty and the Beast, only he's both. Then he holds me gently and it's lovely, nothing like the nasty grabbing that had gone before.

"Did you see Sally go by? I did." He looks so happy. "She saw us and I know she'll tell Jenny and now we'll get back together and all because of you. Jenny would be so pleased with you but you must never tell her. Can I trust you not to do that?"

I can only just about whisper, "Yes."

"And you do trust me don't you? You know you're special to Jenny and because of that you're special to me too, don't you?"

"Yes."

I don't remember walking back into the car but I must have done because, within what seemed to be a few seconds, I'm sitting uncomfortably in the car at the end of our street. I'm scared but I don't know why. My big, grey school knickers feel strangely wet. Neither of us has said a word since the fields.

"Listen Marian,", and again he smiles at me, "Don't tell Jenny you've seen me and we'll get together again soon to plan another way to help Jenny and me get back together. You *do* want that don't you?" He looks so intensely into my eyes and I can't, or don't want to, look away.

"Yes," Why can't I say anything else?

And what just happened out there in the cold, wet fields? Jenny's boyfriend is acting as if nothing at all has happened, so why do I feel so ashamed and embarrassed? All I remember is his face and body over mine and the weight of him making it hard to breathe. Then the strange noises he made and the grabbing which turned to pain. Pain down there. Most of all I remember the sky. Not the blue sky like in drawings but a nasty sky, almost black with its rainclouds. I'd concentrated very hard on them, willing myself to disappear into them, away from these strange feelings. I just wanted to float up into those storm clouds and drift away.

"Are you still my best friend after Jenny?" It's like he's begging me, like a new girl who comes to school and doesn't know anyone.

"Yes,"

"So please don't spoil our special secret by telling anyone. Ok? Next time we meet I'll bring some Tizer and sweets to share. Would you like that?"

"Yes."

"Ok. Now you run along home and remember, not a word to anyone. Especially not Jenny, but no one else either. It's our special little secret. No one else would understand. You do trust me don't you, Marian?"

"Yes."

I stumble out of the car and run home as fast as I can, up the stairs and into the privacy of my bedroom. Oh no, my knickers have got blood on them, Mum will be so cross. I stuff them into the corner of the big dark wardrobe that Dad got off a demolition job in the old town. Will anyone notice if I have a bath, even if it's only the middle of the week? Luckily, Mum and Dad are still at work and my brother David never notices me, whatever I do. Afterwards I change into my pink winceyette nightie and slide into my bed, trying not to ruffle the covers too much so that everything is still neat and tidy. I snuggle up to my beautiful Princess Ann doll with her blonde ringlets and trusting blue eyes and fall into a deep sleep, happy and grateful that I've helped Jenny get back with her boyfriend.

*

I wrap my coat tightly around me; the memory's gone wrong. I seem so young. I tell myself it's probably a false memory but whatever it is, it'll have to wait. It's getting quite late in the afternoon now and I'm still sitting in the bar, two more brandies helping me to steady my nerves. I try to marshal the stories and pictures that flash in and out of my brain, but they're never there long enough to catch; to see what they mean. I know they're important; they could help me find my baby. Baby? The child would be a grown man by now.

I won't find out anything by sitting here and drinking like my Bob did. I'm sorry, Bob, that I couldn't be a proper wife to you. No wonder you were always so angry. I got what I deserved. But the kids didn't; "Suffer the little children…" Did my baby suffer? The brandy shivers in the glass as I raise it to my lips.

I need to find somewhere to stay for the night. Why don't I want to go back to Darren's? Have we had a row? I can't remember. Or is it because I'm worried he'd send me back to Golden Meadows? Maybe. No, I won't go back. Not to Darren's, or Golden Meadows or anywhere else. I won't have anyone tell me what to do any more. I'm not a child. Do you know what? I've always wanted to be the kind of person who lives in Kemp Town. Why shouldn't I do it now? I shall find myself a B&B there until I know what to do next. I could do with a little lie-down...

*

Where am I? This is not my bed. Why aren't I in my little house in Finchley? So many changes lately. I look around the strange room. Of course, I'm in that sweet little B&B I found yesterday in Kemp Town. It's quite an eccentric kind of place with each bedroom in a different style. Mine is very kitsch, with a big high bed covered in a dark pink satin duvet and so many cushions, each patterned with different flowers, that it took me ages to remove them and get into bed. I put them on the Victorian chaise-longue so they didn't get dirty on the pale pink painted floorboards. Look at these chintz curtains with their cheerful yellow flowers, so cheerful, that I feel jealous. I look at my watch. It's nine in the morning. I should get up and dressed, I have things to do but I love this strange little room so much that I don't want to leave. I've never been anywhere quite like it. There's a tap on the door,

"Mrs. Norman, did you want some breakfast, love, only we are closing the kitchen in a few minutes. Wouldn't want you to miss out now, would we?"

"I'm coming, won't be a minute. Thank you." It never hurts to be polite.

I make my way down to the little basement dining room; tables and chairs fighting each other for space. A man in a shirt that could only have come from somewhere tropical stops chatting to the young couple by the window and gives me a huge smile as he goes behind the most gorgeous woven curtain into the kitchen at the back. Almost immediately he brings me tea and toast and offers me a choice of breakfasts.

I love a full English breakfast, I've not had one since before going into Golden Meadows. Darren seems to thrive on oats; either muesli or porridge. Tasty and nutritious enough, I suppose. But a full English! It reminds me of Sunday mornings with Bob and the children. Mind you, we never had quite this much. Thank goodness I have their little dog Daisy under the table. Bob always insisted that none of us ever left food on the plate.

"Oh naughty Daisy! Is she bothering you? I'm so sorry. She's a greedy one, that one." And he scoops up the little chocolate-coloured cockapoo and pretends to scold her.

"No, she's fine. I love dogs. I've always wanted one but…"

"Oh you can have this one, she's a complete diva and a pest," the dog licks his face, "but no, I'm only joking. Stuart and I would be utterly bereft if we lost her.

I laugh. It's been a long time since I heard myself do that. Not since Gwen.

"She is lovely. My name is Marian," and I hold out my hand but instead of shaking it, the man bends down and gently kisses it.

"It's a pleasure to meet you and have you stay in our little hotel, Marian. My name is John, but most people call me JJ." He holds my hand just a little longer and it feels rather nice. I'd almost forgotten how it felt to be touched in a way that was not medical.

JJ looks out the window and sighs, "What a dreadful day, my love. Such a shame for you on your mini holiday. What are you going to do in all this rain?"

I withdraw my hand as subtly as I can without upsetting this nosy man. What business is it of his? Does he know Darren? Is he in cahoots with him? Going to report back? No, of course not, I'm just being silly. And then I before I can stop myself it comes out;

"Do you know my son Darren? Some of his friends call him Dazzer, although I don't really like that. He's gay like you." As the words leave my mouth I can feel the awfulness of what I've said hit the atmosphere in the room. Luckily JJ isn't offended and within seconds he gives a snort of friendly laughter,

"No sorry, being gay doesn't give me special powers to find out the whereabouts of every other gay man in the world. Wish that it did…" and he bends down and whispers close to my ear, "only don't tell Stuart I said that."

I'm about to tell him that Darren lives in Brighton so it isn't quite so ridiculous, but then I would have to explain why I'm not staying at his place. Even I don't know the answer to that one.

"I tell you what, if you're on your own and fancy it, Stuart and I are going to watch a DVD this afternoon. You're welcome to join us. There's not much else you can do. This rain is set in for the day. It's got Judi Dench in it and she's trying to find out what happened to her little boy. She was sent to one of those awful places run by nuns in Ireland when she got pregnant. It's had great reviews. Just pop up to the TV room on the next floor if you fancy it. No pressure." He smiles at me as he clears the plates. I'm no longer able to smile back.

"I think I'll go to my room for a while." I remember the nuns.

"That's fine. We'll be showing it at 2pm. The couple from room three are coming too, so if you do fancy it…"

I can't even stop to be polite, I have to get away. Somehow I make it to my room and onto my bed, my mind lurching around inside my brain. The nuns. Of course. And Father Michael. I'd almost remembered it once, back at Golden Meadows. Now I realise. I must have been taken there because

I was pregnant. They must have taken my baby. Tiredness overwhelms me. I give in.

The dreams this time give me no clues; no nuns, just screaming sea-gulls and chocolate-coloured dogs scampering along endless grey corridors until the alarm set them free. I don't want to go but JJ is there at my door, reminding me about the film. Watching it, though, did make me realise that I, like Philomena, needed someone to help and the only one I could think of was Felicity. She's a bit giddy and unreliable but she did get me out of the care home and Tom seemed to trust her, although maybe his head's been over-ruled by his loins. She owes me an explanation of why she lied to Darren at the very least.

I trawl through my handbag. There's the phone. Caught inside the lining of the bag next to my pills. No wonder Darren couldn't find it. Men are hopeless at finding things if they're not right there in front of them.

"JJ, can you make this work for me please?" Daisy jumps up to be fussed as I knock on the door of the kitchen where JJ was preparing dinner.

"Of course, my love. I think I've got a charger upstairs that will fit it. Won't be a jiffy."

He comes back with a plug and lead and shows me what to do. It's not difficult. Later, once it was fully "charged" as they say, he showed me how it all worked.

There's a 'missed call' again. It has to be that girl's.

"Here, take the charger. I don't need it. It's from an old phone."

"Thanks JJ, I think I know what to do now." Such a nice man. I retreat to my room. I try to ignore the twisting pain inside my stomach and with shaking hands I ring the girl's number.

Felicity + Marian: Chapter 19

Ignorance is Bliss?

I still can't stop my hands shaking as I pour my tea. I love this little tea-room with its fancy mismatched china, beautiful tea cosies and lists of rules on laminated brightly coloured cards to show you how to behave in a "decorous" manner.

They've made me so welcome since that first time and I'm fascinated by the people with their bright make up and garish clothes. I can't tell if they're boys or girls but nobody seems to care and neither do I. It feels so safe here. This is why I've chosen to meet her here. I was surprised when she said she wanted to apologise for abandoning me before and really wanted to put things right. I trust her even less than I did before but I know Tom adored her and he's a better judge of character than his mum. She married Nigel, for heaven's sake. I remind myself that the girl's called Felicity, I'm getting better at remembering names since I escaped from that home. Felicity; a happy name, but she seems unhappy to me.

Here she comes. I straighten myself up.
She's far too old for my little Tom. Why
didn't I notice that before? Very attractive;
long legs, long blonde hair, she could almost
be a Barbie doll but she has an intelligent
look in her eye and she's dressed in jeans
and a jumper, nothing flashy or overtly sexy.
Maybe she chose the outfit especially to
meet me,

"I'm so pleased you agreed to meet me," she
gushes. A posh voice. No, Tom wouldn't fit
with her at all. What is going on?

"Sit yourself down, do you want tea? And
they have the most delicious cakes here,"

"I'd rather have a flat white please." Then
she takes in her surroundings. To her credit
she seems not to mind the bearded man in
his bright turquoise1950s style dress who
serves us but it seems that's the way of
young people today. So much better than in
my day.

"Only tea, my love. We have a selection
written on the board up there." He turns to
me, "How about some cake, Marian?"

"Yes please, I'd like the lemon drizzle
please."

We sit in awkward silence while waiting to be served; she focusses on the pictures of the Queen, the knitted tea-cosies and the decorated tea-pots. I focus on her.

As soon as we have been served, I launch straight in. No point in delaying. I need answers before I decide whether or not to trust her. "Why did you leave me at Darren's, pretending you didn't know me at all? That was very unkind. He still thinks I made you up."

"I'm so sorry, Marian. I panicked, I…"

But I talk over her, "You encourage me to leave the home, then abandon me. Just what are you up to? And what are you really doing with my grandson? You're not right for him."

Maybe I'm being a bit rude, aggressive even. But I'm not sure, at my age, how much time I have left to sort everything out. And, I am still annoyed at her. I can see I've shocked her. I'm glad. I might get some more truthful answers.

"I…um, Tom and I, uh. Oh lord, it's all such an awful mess. Typical of me. But I'm trying to fix it, I'm trying to help, honest."

She looks so wretched and so young. I actually take pity on her. And I do need her help.

"All right. Calm down, just tell me two things: why did you get me out of the home and what is your relationship with Tom really about?"

"Ok," and she looks around to see if anyone could overhear, "do you know a Charles Davidson?"

Oh my goodness, I was not expecting that.

"I knew a Charles a long time ago and I've heard of Charles Davidson. He's a politician, isn't he?" I'm not going to show her all my cards.

"He is; a very prominent and powerful one." Her voice becomes a whisper. "It was him who paid for you to go to Golden Meadows."

The inside of my head does what my body can't - a series of brilliant back-flips. I hold on to the table for support.

"He employed me to get to know Tom and to keep an eye on you."

I want to get up and leave, but I'm far too dizzy. I sit there. My legs itch and my stomach threatens to jump out of my throat. I have no words that I can say out loud so I just look at her. She has no idea how much her words have shocked me, I can tell, as she goes on,

"You probably hate me now and I don't blame you, but I truly do want to put things right. That's why I got you out of that home. I was beginning to worry about you and I wasn't really sure of anything anymore. I didn't know why Uncle Charles had sent you there and why he wanted me to keep an eye on you. And I really am fond of Tom…"

What? Did she really say that?
"*Uncle* Charles?"

I do something I would never have done before; I shout at someone in a public place.

"I think you should leave… Now!"

I expect her to flounce out but she sits there. Silent. I want to throw my tea in her face but I just can't do it. So our teas grow cold, the cake is left untouched. At least things are now becoming clearer. It wasn't just the drugs making me paranoid. Somebody *was* out to get me, as they say. But Charles? My Charles? Why – after all this time?

"Everything all right, ladies?" The waiter wants to clear up. I look around and see that we are the only ones left in the tea-room.

"Yes, sorry. We'll let you get on. She'll pay," and I get up to go, knowing that she'll not be able to leave it at that. She's a pleaser, vulnerable; like Gwen said. I walked out and across the road to look at the sea. Sure enough, once she had paid our bill, she followed like a troubled puppy.

"I'm really, really sorry, Marian… Mrs Norman. Please let me explain."

"Does he know where my baby is?" I round on her. Why did I think I could trust her?

"What?"

"Has he and that Jemima adopted him, or maybe one of his friends did?"

"I…I…I don't think so." She's near to tears but I feel no pity.

"You would say that, wouldn't you? How do I know you're not lying?"

Passers-by turned to stare and before today I would have been embarrassed enough to moderate my voice or even just give up the questioning. The past few weeks have taught me that there's no point trying to be what other people expect. Mostly they don't even see you, let alone care who you really are; they already have their preconceived idea of you.

*

Felicity didn't answer any of my questions. I gave up asking. She was far too distressed and ashamed to say anything helpful. Instead we stand on the edge of the beach and watch the sun begin its descent into the sea. I always thought the sunset skies looked as if Heaven was trying to break through into our boring little world. To bring it colour and light. Now, glorious pinks melt into baby blue and, falling into the sea, there was a golden halo – like those on medieval pictures of Christ. When was it that my faith failed me? Tonight's sky is still beautiful and it calms me as it always has but I no longer believe in Heaven or a just and bountiful God. Lost, along with my baby and my childhood. After standing together for a while, Felicity turns to me,

"Please believe me, I didn't know what was going on." She touches my arm. I shake her off. I move away to sit on a bench. The waves pound at the silence between us. The possibility of another reason for this girl's involvement strikes me.

"You don't happen to have an older brother?"

"Yes, Ed. He's been trying to…."

"Charles is an old family friend, yes?"

"Yes but I don't see…"

Then her face gives her away. She knows what I'm getting at.

"No, Ed couldn't be your son."

"Maybe your brother Ed found out he was adopted and started asking awkward questions. That's why Charles tried to silence me by putting me in that home."

"No, you've got it all wrong. He can't be your son. He's only 30. Younger than your Tracey."

"Then why has Charles, after all these years, started to worry about me?"

"He saw the video of you in the Lido. That's when he got me involved."

"That? So much fuss over a silly mistake. But why should he worry about me after all this time? Or does he want to find our baby too?"

"I don't think so, Marian." Her voice has an edge that worries me.

I look towards the sea. Not so welcoming now. The sun has gone, the skies are turning grey. The tide's rising and I can't help feeling that the incoming waves are warnings of more revelations to come, one after another. Perhaps I just don't want to know any more.

"Can I ask how old you were when you had your child?" For such an impertinent and personal question her voice was incredibly gentle.

"No, you *may* not." Don't they teach children the correct usage of words, like *can* and *may* in school anymore? She really is infuriating.

"I'm concerned that you might have been a victim of child abuse."

The waves crash louder and all I want to do is to get away from this silly girl with her preposterous accusations. I block it all out, covering my ears but she stays next to me. Why won't she go and leave me alone? I just need to find my beautiful baby.

"I wasn't a child. I was thirteen," As the words come out I am forced to finally accept how young I had been. At the time I had felt grown-up and that feeling, fixed in time and in my memory, had never left me. Until today, looking back as an adult and also remembering Tracey as a thirteen-year-old. Still a child. But, no, I can't let go of my memories so easily. I have to fight for them so that they are still true, even to my adult self.

"And besides, it wasn't abuse. I loved him. We loved each other. The world was different then. We grew up quicker. Your generation's been molly-coddled into being children so much longer, in fact some of you are still children well into your twenties. We went out to work at fourteen. We were adults and took responsibility for our own lives."

"But the age of consent was still sixteen, even back then."

"Well, I was happy to consent. Just because something is the law doesn't mean you have to agree." My daughter would definitely have taken me up on that but she isn't here, is she? I can say what I like. "There were lots of girls who followed the big name groups, did very well out of it. They weren't sixteen. You didn't hear then complaining."

"But they do now. Have you not heard about the "#MeToo" movement?"

"Load of nonsense. They just want to make money out of the poor men who they willingly went with years ago. They made their choices back then. They can't complain all these years later."

Felicity looks at me as if I've let out a stream of swear words. They don't like being contradicted, these youngsters. She lets out the biggest sigh, no a complete rush of air. Quite aggressive, I think.

"How can you still believe that, Marian? How would you have felt if it had been Tracey or your granddaughter being made pregnant by an older man who then abandons her?"

"No, Charles didn't abandon me, he said he would marry me. He called me his special girl." That day on the pier. I was so happy. I only had to wait three more years. What happened? Why did I lose him?

"Exactly, just like he said to all the others." She caught her breath as if the words had come out by mistake.

"What do you mean? What others?" I ask but, silly me, she must mean other men, with their broken promises of course, but Charles wasn't like that. He really wasn't.

Felicity steps back from me, as if she wants to run away. We both stare towards the horizon but now you couldn't see where the sea ended and the sky begins. Everything seems menacingly grey. Neither of us wanted to make the first move. To take that step away from when everything was fine and rose-coloured. Felicity battles against the cold wind that is blowing her hair into her eyes, sighs, moves back closer to me and sits on the bench. Then she takes hold of both my hands and looks me straight in the eye.

"I didn't mean it to come out like this but you'll have to find out eventually, I guess. Charles has a history of abusing – or seducing if you prefer – young women." I try to pull away. I don't need to hear this but she has me in a firm hold.

"I've already spoken to twenty of them now. Each of them thought they were special. Many of them were afraid to speak out because he could wreck their chances within the Party. Some were even forced to have abortions." I really don't want to hear any more but she is relentless and, like so many times in my life, I find I can't move, can't speak, can't say no.

"Almost all of them were made to sign non-disclosure documents so they could never tell anyone what he did - not then nor at a future date. Ed and I have been working with your Tom. We're trying to expose Charles' past, to bring some justice to you and all the other women he abused."

My head reels. My ears begin to ring. I pull my hands away with all the strength I have left and I bend over as far as I can to bring back some sense into my head.

It can't be true. He loved me. We had a baby together. I need to find my baby. Other women? Abused? I just won't accept her lies. And Tom? He knows?

They all knew. They knew about the things I did with Charles back then. They knew how I'd kept our dirty secret. They knew things about Charles that I didn't. Things I won't believe.

"I need to go back to my lodgings. I can't take this all in." I tell her, but without conviction because I still can't move. I need to go to the toilet. I sit there, immobile. I just can't move. I don't even care if I mess myself. Nothing matters now. The mess I'd kept inside, my shame, those sinful secrets – for what? A man who had never loved me. Really? Lots of other women? I'd always thought I was special. That was the biggest shock. Everything I'd gone through and I was never special to him. I just sit there, unable to speak, move or even think.

"You've got a lot to process, I'm sorry, Mrs Norman."
"I need to go."
"No we must talk all this through. It's been a shock, of course, but we can help you get through it."

I can't trust her. I can't trust anyone.

"No! Leave me alone. You've done quite enough, thank you. Just let me go so I can think about all this. I'll phone you later, once I've had a chance to think." She helps me up off the bench. Once again I shake off a hand that was gripping me too tightly. I feel sick, my legs don't want to support me and I just want to lie down. Here, or anywhere. I literally can't stand this.

Somehow, I don't notice how, Felicity gets us a taxi. Maybe she used her phone or maybe one was just passing. It doesn't matter. Nothing matters now. She helps me into it. I always seem to be getting into cars without thinking, despite my mother's warnings. This time, though, it feels safer than listening to what this girl wants to tell me.

"You've had a shock, Marian. Let me come with you. See you home."

I tell the driver where to go and shut the door firmly against Felicity and her lies.

"You ok, love?" He looks into the mirror at me, "Hey now, cheer up, it may never happen."

I realise as I look into his mirror why he'd been so concerned. My mascara has run; in fact it's still running with the tears that won't stop, in the pallid wasteland of my face.

Cheer up? Yes, put on a happy face, other people don't want to see your misery. Cheer up! But it had already happened.

Chapter 20: Felicity

Sufficient Unto the Day Is The Evil Thereof

Did she believe me? I don't know. Should I have told her? I don't know that either. She looked dreadful as she drove off in the taxi. I thought back to that weird medical report with its random mentions of personality disorder and something like schizophrenia. Maybe I've done more harm than good.

She was so desperate to get away from me. Shit! Have I caused her some dreadful psychological damage? Stupid. That's a no brainer. I've just demolished the past she thought she'd lived, her childhood and the one true love she had treasured, despite the pain and the trauma.

I do what I seem always to be doing lately; I phone my big brother, but before I could speak he almost jumped down the phone to me,

"Fliss, a bit weird, but I had a phone call from Uncle Charles. He said he needed to see you urgently." Ed sounded worried.

I held the phone tighter and found myself pacing around in a circle on the prom, trying to walk off the nervous itching in my legs. The reason I'd phoned Ed was lost in my panic at the thought of seeing Charles again, knowing what I know now and because of what I'd done. Did *he* know? He always had eyes everywhere. People said that's why he'd been such a successful Home Secretary.

"He must know. Oh Ed, I'm scared. Should we just drop it? It's not too late, is it? We haven't told anyone official yet."

"Calm down, it may be nothing. He just wants to see you. He's always had a soft spot for you," and Ed laughed, "maybe he'll proposition you as well and then we can really go to town on him."

I couldn't believe he'd make a joke like that at a time like this. Or any other time, come to think of it.

"Don't keep saying things like that, it's not funny," and I felt that old saliva rising in my throat again. The thought of that old man – silver fox or not – pawing me, triggered a myriad of feelings. Feelings of guilt and shame, disgust and fear. What? Supressed memories or just distortions from all I've heard from Marian and all the women I'd interviewed? I don't know any more.

"You ok?" Ed asked, "I'm sorry, that was in very poor taste, especially after all the work you've done with the women."
"Don't worry about it. I'm fine." I watched the seagulls wheeling about in the sky, free and unafraid, "So, does he want me to ring him?"

"No. Apparently he needs you to go down to a meeting with him again next week. He has some new information he wants you to see. He still thinks you're here in Edinburgh"

"What? Where?"

"He's at the Royal Albion in Brighton." Brighton? Shit!

"No, he can't be. How did he know? You don't think..? Did he have me followed? Does he know she's here?"

"Is Marian in Brighton, then?"

I grunted, it was all I could manage.

"Oh shit. I don't like it, Fliss. I think you should step away from it all." His voice had an urgency that frightened me but after what had just happened between us on the beach there was no way I could leave her to it now.

"At least I need to warn her. I've messed everything up as usual. She kept saying at the care home that she thought her life was in danger. What if it's true? What if it he really thinks he needs to silence her completely?" She lowered her voice as two little girls on scooters sped by her.

"Surely not. None of the other women you've interviewed have felt threatened like that."

I knew that was true. But then again, he didn't know that they were now prepared to name and shame him in court.

"He doesn't know about our investigations, does he? Or that there are other women now prepared to talk about him. He'll think that Marian is his only danger. The one he never silenced at the time." I was gabbling now, clutching at stupid straws. Marian could well be in danger.

 I've just forced her into seeing that her whole adult life had been based on the lie that she had once had a child with her one true love and all she needed to do was to find that child and make her peace with the past. She'd be easy pickings for Charles, the state she was in. I'd destroyed her in a single afternoon. Now the man she thought had loved her was right here in Brighton, ready to finish what he had started when he had her confined to that home. Shit, shit, shit!

"Yes, but he wouldn't harm her. Far too extreme. He probably just wants to pay her off." Ed was trying to downplay the issue and get me out of here. He'd already told me he was beginning to worry about my mental health and that I was becoming overly close to Marian.

"No, I need to warn her." I tried to sound as if I were in control.

"Ok, but get Darren on side first, she'll probably listen to him and besides, he's family and you're not. You have to step back, Fliss. Promise me?" He knew I wasn't able to; in fact I was totally out of my depth.

"Ok," I lied.

First I had to settle things with Uncle Charles. Even after everything, I still wanted a career in politics and, until the investigation into the claims against him proceeded, he was still my boss and capable of making sure I never worked again, except maybe as a cleaner or bar assistant. Until it was all over, I had to make him believe that I was still on his side.

I did not sleep well. That dream again. The door opening, my teddy tossed aside. Waking up in terror, not clear why but too scared to go back to sleep.

By the time I arrived at Charles' hotel I thought I was as low as I could get. But no, I'd underestimated his ability to mess with my head.

*

"No way. She couldn't have done it. She's not that good an actress." I can't stop the paper fluttering in my hand. I'm in his suite overlooking the Pier.

Charles takes it gently from me. The smile he gives me makes me feel sick. He's won some sort of game. He's the only one who knows the rules. I wish I hadn't come. I barely make it to the plush armchair by the window. I sink into it. I'm drowning. No, it can't be true. I don't want it to be true, it's just too awful. She couldn't…

Do I actually know her? Am I confused because of my feelings for Tom? Or the accusations of the other women? Has that clouded my judgement of him – of her? That encounter in the toilets at Golden Meadows comes back to me. The rapid changes in mood, her harshness underneath that vulnerability. Pretending she couldn't walk on her own. Had she been playing me? But she was broken when I told her about him yesterday. Maybe she *is* a good actress. She and Uncle Charles might have been made for each other with their game-playing and lies.

"Here, you need a drink." Charles hands me a large brandy; not really a favourite but I down it in one. It's supposed to be good for shock.

"It may not be true, I agree, but it's the correct year, according to the age Tracey says she was at the time." He refills my glass without asking.
"Tracey? You've been in touch with her? Recently?" The brandy burns my throat, why did I drink it?

"I'm going to tell you something now in confidence - and don't forget about the non-disclosure papers that you signed when you came to work for me - that I have never told anyone. I had an affair with Marian's older cousin, Jenny. Marian found out and became totally obsessed with me. Her cousin found her diary one day and she told me about all the fantasies Marian had constructed around the idea that the affair I had with Jenny was actually with her. She'd even fantasised about having my child. I had to end it then with Jenny," and his voice crackles with sadness, "and move away."

He could make any lie seem totally believable.

"I lost contact with the family until several months later when Marian's mother pleaded with me to help her. Marian had gone completely off the rails and had run away to live in a squat in Brighton. I had her traced to a hospital in Lewes but then lost her again. Her mother thought she had been pregnant but lost the baby. I was able, through Social Services to return her to her family eventually but her mind was severely damaged by all the drugs and alcohol she had taken but most of all by the experience of apparently losing her baby."

Could this be true? Had it all been a fantasy? He was very convincing and the newspaper report does suggest that she was not of sound mind at the time.

"All my life I have felt vaguely responsible for her. She is very good at making people feel a responsibility towards her."

That was true; I had spent the last few weeks feeling that way.

"But now, reading this information, I feel my action in getting her into a secure and caring environment is all the more essential for her well-being."

He waves the newspaper in front of my face then turns to look out of the window.

"I trusted you, which is why I needed you to read this for yourself. Now can you see how far your recent actions are completely out of line?"

He walks back towards me. The wistfulness has gone, replaced by the smile of someone ready to smash my world.

"Naturally, you'll remember her brother Darren? He remembers you: his description of you was accurate, if somewhat unflattering. He was not at all impressed by your little charade when you dropped her off."

Oh I hate that smile, so dazzling that you almost miss the threat behind his words. But here I am, wrong-footed again by his ability to know everyone and everything. I just can't guess where he's going with this. I need some air. It's not just the brandy that's making my mouth dry and my stomach queasy. I look down out of the window at the cheerful holidaymakers and day-trippers, so carefree, so far away. Why can't I just walk away and join them?

"Darren said his mother thought she had a phone. You wouldn't know anything about that would you? Or perhaps you'd say it was just another example of her, shall we say, loose grip on reality?" Charles laughs the mirthless laugh. The one that means that he's going in for the final blow. He fixes me with his eyes. I can't look away.

"Or maybe that's how you arranged her sudden exit from Golden Meadows?"

Oh shit! I sit upright. I need to think quickly. It has to be convincing. Until the case being set up by Ed and Tom against him has been securely proven, Charles holds my career in his hands. No, it's more than that. I realise now that, although I used to love the treats he gave me and the outings we had, I've always been scared of him. I'm scared of him now but, for once, I'm even more scared of what he might do to Marian if he found her. I don't think I believe his latest set of lies.

"I'm very concerned that she is now unsupervised. She could be a danger to herself or the general public. As I'm sure you read in the confidential medical report before you gave it to me." He shushes my pathetic attempt at denial with another smile and a wave of his hand, "I'd be disappointed in you if you hadn't, my dear." He pours himself a small brandy.

"That report. Extraordinary. I knew she had problems even before I read it. Her parents or rather her mother - the father always remained uninvolved - contacted my surgery when her daughter was a young teenager. I was their MP. The truth of the matter was that while the girl was living in the squat she was consorting with much older men and quite possibly having sex with many of them for money or cheap alcohol. As I said, the mother begged me to help find her."

Even if some of what he says is true or more likely just lies, I can't let that ride. It all sounds too familiar,

"Why do people always blame the girls..?"

Charles, however is in full flow and totally ignores me.

"I later heard that the mother had contacted her priest and he had arranged for her to be sent to a Catholic institution for 'troubled' girls. In other words, a mental asylum."

I try to process this new information. He holds up a hand again as I try to speak then walks over to the mini-bar and pours out two more brandies.

"I was then offered a safe seat in London and forgot all about her until her daughter, Tracey, recently asked my advice about finding her a secure placement for her after that ludicrous incident in the swimming pool. I'd met her husband through the Party; quite a promising chap, I thought. At least you were useful in finding that link with the family."

I hear every word but can't really make sense of it. How much of it is true? I think again about the newspaper report he's just shown me. Was it possible?

"If it all happened like you say, why does she keep going on about finding her baby? That's no act. She really means it."

"She has suppressed the memory, Felicity. I imagine *you* would understand that."
My stupid legs itch to run away again. My heartbeat clamours in my ears. I don't want to remember anything. I need to focus on Marian.

"Can I have another look at that article? Why are you so sure it's *her* baby?" I stand up and walk around a little, try to make my brain combat his dreadful accusation.

"I have absolutely no doubt that it's hers. Lord knows, I wouldn't wish this on anyone, but work out the timing. Also, she had an aunt who lived here then. Which church do you think she attended?"

"Not St Mary's?" My hearts sinks as I begin to accept that it could be true.

"Precisely! Here, take it. Read it again, if you will. Then perhaps you could explain to me your reasons for taking Marian out of Dr Campbell's care at Golden Meadows."

 I read it a second time. I have to sit down. The heating in his flashy hotel suite must be full on. The colours of the carpet swirl round; orange, brown and black.

"A time will come when she remembers what she did back then. At that point she could become a danger to herself and possibly to other people."

More like a danger to his reputation, I think, but, look at this article. What if there is some truth in what he's saying about her past? What if our talk yesterday shocked her into remembering more of what happened? There's no knowing what she'll do to herself. I must get her mobile number to Darren as quickly as I can. He'll have to look after her. I'm totally confused now.

"But how can you be so sure she will ever remember if it's been buried all these years?"

"Think, girl. Where did she want to come to when she got out of the home? Directly to the place where it all happened and, I can assure you, it wasn't because Darren lives here. You have to trust me on this, all I want is to keep my promise to the family to look after her."

I need time to think so while he starts pouring yet more brandy I excuse myself and then and lock myself in his en-suite.

Maybe she does need more help than I'd realised. But, Charles –really - the best person to help her? With his record of seducing young girls. Their stories have been harrowing to hear. Marian is convinced that he is the father of her child, despite what he's just told me. If it's true does that make him such a bad person? From what I've seen in the media lately and what Marian said, almost all men of that generation were pretty predatory.

Of course, he doesn't know about the work Ed, Tom and I are doing behind the scenes; still thinks his reputation and career are safe. He thinks it's only Marian that might pose a threat to his reputation. God, I haven't felt this confused since I was a child. What is it about this man that still makes me doubt my own judgement? I walk back into the room having made up my mind to ask him what he was going to do next.

"A penny for your thoughts, little Flissy,"

Charles' voice crashes into my head. He's the only one who's ever called me that. Memories that should never have come back flood my brain and before I know it, I'm shaking and backing away from him, all doubts killed stone dead.

"I... I've just remembered something. I have to go. Right now." All pretence gone.

"Don't be a silly goose, we're only just beginning to get to know each other again," and he sashays across the room, convinced that he's still a player; a charming, powerful man. I look towards the door, wondering if I could make it should he try to stop me. I wouldn't make it in time; it's too far. He sees me looking.

"Good grief, I was simply teasing you," and without a flicker, he completely changes his mood and laughs at me. "Sit yourself down, relax, just one more drink with your poor old uncle. I think you ought to tell me what you think we should do about Marian, considering I've told you all I know about her. Lord knows, it would only be fair."

"No it's fine, *Uncle* Charles," trying to put the distance between us, "I do have a mobile number for her, just as you said, but it's in the sim-only phone and I've left it behind…" Quick thinking, hoping he didn't check my bag while I was in the bathroom.

"Excellent; you're finally seeing sense. We can drive back to your hotel in my car and get it. Where are you staying?" He's walking towards me, keeping himself between me and the door.

"No. I mean; no, I haven't got it here in Brighton. I left it in Edinburgh. I'll have to go back up there to get it." My voice betrays my fear; I sound like a child again.
"Even better. Surely you could phone your brother right now. He could tell us the number." Damn! He's always outwitted me, brushed aside my excuses. He'll find out for sure that I haven't been to Edinburgh. I want to cry but I'm not a child, not any more. Think, girl, think.

"No, I mean, it's not at his place and … and any way the battery's probably dead now." Do I sound convincing?

"I'll text Ed, see?" I'm gabbling.

He just smiles as he walks towards me. I get out my phone,

"Ok, I'll phone him right now, get him to go over, charge it up and then I can text you the number tomorrow."

He actually laughs at me but it is not a genuine laugh. It is the laugh of someone who has caught me out in a lie. The sim-only phone was there in my bag when I went off to the bathroom. He could easily have seen it. It is the laugh of a man who has just realised he has won. I can see he's no longer fooled, no longer interested in what Ed might do.

He stands so close I hold my breath, dreading what will come next. Could I handle it now? For what seems like forever we stare each other out. It's too intense for me and I drop my gaze. He really has won. I give in. He rests his hands on my shoulders.

Just at that moment room service arrives with a three course meal for two and an ice-bucket of champagne that Charles failed to tell me he'd ordered for us. I have never been so pleased to see a waiter before. It snaps me out of the hypnotic hold I was in.

"I have to go. So sorry, Uncle Charles I can't stay for dinner after all."

I rush past the confused waiter before Charles can say anything and stop me. Relieved to escape, I'm still totally confused about how I feel about Marian now. She could have severe mental issues – just look at that news report – horrific. All I know for sure is that I have to get out of this nightmare for the sake of *my* mental health.

Chapter 21: Marian

If You Play With Fire, You Will Get Burnt.

Thank goodness JJ isn't around when I get back from meeting Felicity and I'm able to reach my room unnoticed. I can't speak to anyone. I can't do anything. I just want it all to go away. Sleep. That's what I need. I'm aching to the very core of my body. I'll just stretch out on the bed for a little while. But my mind won't let me be. I try concentrating on my breathing to block out the thoughts. Charles Davidson *was* my Charles from back then. I've always known. I just couldn't believe it. It doesn't fit with my life. I was ordinary. He was somebody. Somebody special... He'd told me *I* was special and I always thought I was, when I was with him... All those afternoons when he took me to our secret room. He used to buy me my favourite penny sweets: Flying saucers, Black Jacks and the pink bubble gum that Mummy never let me have. I loved being with him, enjoying the attention. It was only after, back home with Mum and Dad, I felt the shame. And all those nights when I couldn't sleep...

Back at Golden Meadows I'd had fantasies about him when he came on my TV. I told myself that was that all they were…
Apparently not, according to Felicity…
Good God, my head hurts, all these stupid thoughts… But what about all those other women? She'd said there were others. Was I really not his special girl? What had she said? Oh I don't know, can I trust her? She lied to Darren about not knowing me… Something else… She said that it was my Charles who paid for me to go to Golden Meadows. How? Why? Tracey organised it. I had to sell my house to pay for it… What happened to all that money? And Tom…. How can he be working with this Felicity and her brother? He's miles away in a foreign country… This girl is manipulating me and all my family. Why? She's either on my side and lying for some purpose I don't know about, or she's involved in some scheme – again I don't know what - with Charles… Yes, come to think of it, she'd actually called him *Uncle* Charles. I remember *my* Charles telling me so often, "Say nothing. Trust no one."

I sit up. It's useless chasing sleep like this. My head throbs with the worry of it all. Maybe I'll take just one little pill… JJ will wake me when it's time for dinner. I sink into my soft pillow. I pull the satin duvet tight around me like a cocoon. That feels safer. I can't tell if I'm awake or dreaming. I'm a little girl again, in a hospital this time. I know it's a bad time.

*

I'm not asleep. I'm not even pretending to be asleep. I just can't open my eyes and face the world. How is it that everything is carrying on as normal? People come and go; nurses, probably. They talk in whispers around me. Why aren't they shouting at me, forcing me to get up out of bed and face up to what I have done? Maybe, like in the stories I write in school, I'll wake up and find that it's all a dream. The pain tells me otherwise. So do the voices chattering inside my head. Round and round they go, telling me how sinful and disgusting I am. A voice I recognise silences them. The one I want to hear most of all. The one I dread too.

"What have you done to yourself, my poor baby? Why didn't you tell me, you silly girl. Oh my baby!"

Is that my mum? How did she get here? The shock that Mummy must know everything forces my eyes to open and the tears to fall. Still I have no words. No words to explain the awful thing I've done; the shame, the guilt. The blackness of my mind gives me sanctuary.

"Nurse, nurse! She woke up and looked at me! She recognised me! I'm sure she did."

Mum's dishwater-rough hands crush my fingers. But the pain of it is a relief; like the smack that you know you deserve finally hitting your legs, reassuring you that, even when you're bad, you are still Mummy's little girl and that Mummy is still in control.

*

 JJ knocks on the door. I wake up fully and think about all the things I can now remember from that time. Even the antiseptic smell of the hospital comes back as the memories clarify in my mind. I remember that Mum sat by me for hours, then days and finally a week, before she was able to take me from the hospital and back to Aunty Olive's house. One night, when they thought I was asleep, I overheard them talking. Talking about a baby, my baby. I heard them say that he'd "gone to a better place". So there definitely *was* a baby. I remember lying back, grateful tears seeping through tightly shut eyes. My little baby, looked after by people who could give him everything that I couldn't. He was in a better place.

For a long time when I got back home, I couldn't speak. The longer I kept my silence, the harder it was to begin to even think about opening my mouth and forcing any sounds out of it. Nothing was going to come out of my body ever again. I would keep it all inside, safe. Everyone pretended that things were back to normal and if the teachers at the school complained that I wouldn't speak up in class, Mum would argue that they should be grateful.

"It's not like she's causing trouble or disrupting their precious lessons, is it?" Mum would demand of her friends on the few occasions that the change in my behaviour since my 'holiday' with Aunty Olive was ever mentioned. After a while everyone stopped asking questions, reassuring each other and any health worker, nosy neighbour or concerned member of the family that I "would come round in time", that I was "best left alone" and that "time is a great healer – she's young, she'll soon forget". Dad was not consulted. He was never told what had happened and he knew better than to ask. This was women's business.

"Teenagers are often moody and secretive. She just likes to keep her thoughts to herself. She'll come out of it and start talking again when she is good and ready." He and everyone else was told. But I never was good nor ready. So, with building pressure from the school, I was assessed by a child psychologist and admitted to Sacred Heart Sanctuary, a nearby psychiatric hospital. The Loony-Bin, we kids called it.

*

"The nuns will look after her," Father Michael reassured my Mum in the dingy entrance hall of the grim building, "they will care for her soul as well as her mind and body and you know full well that her soul is sorely troubled, Marian."

"Yes, Father," and she watched me being led away along the echoing grey corridor that stretched into the darkest place on Earth.

*

"It's time for your treatment, no need to get dressed, you can come in your nightie." Sister Dominique appears in the dormitory, silently as always. I've been here a week and no one has said anything about treatment but the ashen looks from the other girls urge me to run.

The nuns hold me tightly, one on each arm. No need. I was never going to struggle. I know I deserve to be punished.

I'm not sure I can stand up. The panic has turned my legs to water. The nuns grip my arms, almost carrying me along. Along those long dark corridors again. A door opens and as I'm dragged in, I see the bed. No pillows, just brown paper sheets. And thick leather straps with vicious metal buckles. At the head of the bed the machine waits menacingly. Still I allow them to strap me down. Maybe this will take away my sinfulness; make me normal.

The leather strap in my mouth hurts the most. I can't stop myself from gagging. They tighten more straps to my arms, legs and around my body. I'm so scared but I refuse to even whimper. I deserve this. I need this. The coldness of the metal cap freezes my shaved head. I concentrate on a crack in the ceiling. I try to float up and disappear into that crack. What are they going to do to me? No one speaks. No one explains.

The silence in the room as they unstrap me afterwards is fractured by a very quiet sobbing. Is it me or the youngest of the nuns – the only one who ever showed us girls any kindness?

I don't remember much about the place after that day but I do remember Mum coming to collect me. She dressed me gently in my old clothes and cried when she saw how small they were on me. That was all so long ago that it seems like it happened to someone else; a different me. I feel so angry for that little girl. No wonder I was such a bad mother to Darren and Tracey – and such a useless wife to Bob. I'd always thought it was because I was weak. Now I know I'm not. I survived all that. Somehow. At least I can remember some things about that time now. My boy was taken to a better place. Mum said so. I know he's alive. I didn't lose him in Father Michael's institution. The nuns took my mind, not my baby.

*

"Marian? Are you ok?" JJ sounded worried. Had I been crying out in my sleep?

"I'm fine thanks JJ. I just had a bad dream but honestly. I'm fine now."

"If you're sure, my pet. I'm here if you want to talk. It's lovely out there now, if you fancy a little walk," and I heard his footsteps fade away.

I was fine, honestly. It had been a bad dream but at least I felt reassured that the nuns, who had haunted my dreams on and off for years, had not taken my baby. All I have to do now is find details of adoption agencies and see if they can help. My face hurts from smiling. Everything was going to be all right.

Outside on the street, I blink into the bright sunlight. It was as if I had a magic compass or maybe the sea just called me, I don't know, but somehow I found myself at the promenade almost before I realised I'd left the B&B. My mind refuses to accept this noisy, brash Brighton with loud people everywhere. The screeching seagulls seem angry and their calls bring back a memory of another day; a beautiful sunny day when the seagulls made me laugh. I find myself an empty deck chair on the pier to enjoy the day and my memory.

*

The seagulls wheeled and screeched above me as I threw chips for them to catch off the end of Brighton pier. Charles laughed at me when I was too scared to walk along the boards of the pier but I could see the waves breaking under me through the cracks. They seemed threatening. Even with Charles standing next to me, I still didn't feel safe. Then he made me run, grabbing my wrist, until my terrified screams turned to shouts of laughter as we reached the safety of the fish and chip shop in the middle. I knew he would never let anything bad happen to me. After I threw the last of my now cold chips to the greedy gulls, I hugged him tightly,

"This will always be our special secret place, eh? No matter what happens?"

He smiled a beautiful smile down on me,

"Yes, my love, whenever you need me, I'll be there. But we must go now. This nice lady I told you about will just check that everything is all right down there; that everything is working properly. It might hurt a little bit but she'll give you a drink to ease the pain. You'll be fine, I promise." We started to walk on, away from the bright joyfulness of the pier. I tugged at his jacket.

"But you'll be there too, won't you?" I pleaded even though I had somehow guessed the answer.

"No, my love, I'd love to but this is women's work and they don't let men stay. I'll have a taxi waiting for you to take you to our room at Mrs. Blakeley's B&B. You can go straight to bed when you get there. We won't tell anyone, especially that nosy landlady. There may be a little blood but that will start your periods off and then you'll be a real woman."
"And then we can get married?"

"Not yet, you're still only thirteen, remember? We have to wait another three years and who knows, you might have met a young man more your age by then."

"Never! You will always be the only one I'll ever love, I promise."

"I know, but look, we're here now," and he takes my hand and smiles as if he was taking me to the fair or a sweetshop, or somewhere nice. But no. He leads me down crumbling steps to a basement in a terrace of three huge old houses. The smell of cats-wee stings my nostrils and makes my eyes weep. My legs sag beneath me so I stumble and cling to him for support. I really want to run away, to tell him I've changed my mind but I daren't. I feel him put his arm round around me but instead of a hug, all I feel is a push towards the underground doorway. Without speaking, he rings the doorbell and leaves me standing on the doorstep, terrified and alone.

"Come in quickly. You can't hang around on the doorstep. Someone might see you. Shut the door behind you," and the woman yanks me in by the elbow.

The room smells bad; the fetid smell of dried blood and bleach mingles with the old woman's body odour. The darkness of the hallway can't veil the griminess of the walls, the cracked lino or the threadbare blanket hanging over the middle of the room. My hand recoils from the greasy door-handle but I do as I'm told and shut it firmly behind us.

"Drink this, all in one go, take off your knickers and hop on to this table" the scary woman says and goes to boil a kettle behind the curtained-off bit of the room. Even the curtain hangs in a musty torpor of sadness, blocking me off from the window and its murky light.

I do as I'm told and pour the drink down my throat as quickly as possible. It really burns and I can't stop retching. Now I feel even more queasy than before. Please don't let me throw up in front of this woman. She is so scary; she has my life and my body in the very bowels of human existence. I think of the fearful pictures of Hell on the walls at my school. The room turns, my ears fill with noise and everything disappears.

*

"No!" The word is out of my mouth before I have time to stop it. The flashbacks are worse than my dreams. They are more vivid. Some passers-by sharing a bag of doughnuts turn to look then turn back to each other and laugh when they realise it's just some mad old lady shouting out. The smell of the doughnuts mixes with the fear of the flashback and I desperately want to be sick but I can't move. So I sit in the brightly coloured deckchair, surrounded by happy children racing along the pier with the cheerful songs of the funfair mocking me.

To think, less than an hour ago, I'd been so sure I would be able to find my baby or at least find out what had happened to him and then I could put the past behind me and get on with what was left of my life without the shame and guilt that I've been carrying in secret for decades.

Chapter 22: Felicity

Forgive and Forget?

I hope I can find Darren's flat. My hands shake on the steering wheel and my legs are still prickling from my encounter with Charles. I refuse to think of him as an "uncle" any more. It makes me feel like he can define me. His face as he approached me in the hotel room! So like the feelings in the dreams.

I'm still not a hundred percent sure if the dreams come from my memories or from the stories of the women I've spoken to. To be honest, I don't even care anymore. If he did do stuff to me when I was younger, I just want to forget about it. We'll soon get him for all these other women, thank goodness. Then I remember Marian. Although, seriously, my feelings for her aren't quite as sympathetic now I know what she must have done. Memories are very strange.

I need to find Darren and warn him that Charles is here in Brighton, looking for her. What did she say about where he lives? She thought was such a good joke. Oh yes, near Queens Park. Now all I've got to do is find

that ridiculous rainbow flag. I drive slowly
round and around the streets near Queen's
Park. Then remember, a bit late, that we'd
used the sat-nav. God! Why can't I think
straight? I turned on the sat-nav and I was
soon - too soon - outside number twenty-
three with its grubby rainbow flag.

I can't stop shaking. I'm not sure I can do
this now. He's going to kill me. I don't do
confrontations. Oh, stop being such a wuss,
girl. What's the worst that can happen? I get
out of the car, narrowly missing the huge
dog turd that's still there, slowly
decomposing. I superstitiously count each
crumbling step and reluctantly press the bell
by the big old door.

The voice on the intercom asks what I want.
Good question. I could still run away. Have
nothing to do with it all. That's what I really
want but I'm in too far now. As soon as I
give him my name, the intercom clicks dead
and I wait for the inevitable onslaught. My
heart beats stupidly fast and my mouth is so
dry that I won't be able to speak by the time
he gets down here. He wrenches the door
open,

"You? You've got some front, coming
here." I step back from his anger.

"No… wait. Have you seen her? Do you know where she is?" he shouts.

I want to run away. He looks furious. I can't help taking more two steps down before trying to answer. I don't blame Darren for being shocked and angry at seeing me on his doorstep. I just can't speak. I'm so frightened and it's all I could do to not just run back down the rest of the steps.

Before I finish that thought, he grabs me and hauls me inside,

"Well? Do you..? Do you know where she is? Is she all right? Come in, come in." He almost drags me up a very steep, darkened staircase to his flat. The door to the flat is open. There are oversized paintings of men in a variety of positions looking down at me as I step into the room. I'm not really intimidated by them, but they are unsettling.

Once he's shut the door to the flat he lets go of my wrist. I rub the soreness away and walk quickly away from him towards the large open window. I look out to give me time to gather myself. It's an amazing view. Beautiful, yes but it's very high. He follows me and stands way too close behind me. My legs do their usual itchy tricks. I'm about to step to one side when I see a guy who, I suppose, must be Kevin. He's sitting on the roof below which they've turned into a make-shift terrace. He smiles at me, which is a surprise, but thank God for that. Then he stands up, puts down his glass of prosecco and climbs back into the room. He walks past me without a word and puts his arm around Darren.

"What's wrong, love, you look like you've seen a very unpleasant ghost?"

"I have. This is the woman I told you about. The one who's been messing around in our family for the past couple of months. Oh, why didn't I believe Mum? She told me this… this woman was involved…"

Darren shrugs off Kevin's arm and comes straight for me. I'm still stupidly stood by the open window. Oh shit. This is so much worse than I expected. I glance behind to the streets far below. The siren from an ambulance wails its warning down in the street. Once again I thank God Kevin's here.

He puts his arm back around Darren and leads him gently away to one of the two white sofas on the other side of the room. "Don't blame yourself, your Mum didn't always tell the complete truth, now, did she?"

Then he sits Darren down, pats him reassuringly on the shoulder and turns to me. He smiles again, and I feel a little better. I sit down opposite him on the other sofa. Away from the window, the itching in my legs is not so bad but I still can't bring myself to face Darren's anger full-on. So I concentrate on Kevin sitting next to Darren, both of them opposite me. Like an interview. Or police interrogation. Will he help me explain? Can anyone?

"We need, Felicity, to know exactly what you were doing with Marian, how you got to know Tom and most of all why you're involved with this Charles Davidson. But first, I think we all need to calm down a little so I propose a lovely calming-down glass of prosecco. It's nice and cold." He goes and pours out three fresh glasses. Thank god he didn't leave me alone with Darren to get his glass from outside.

The drink *was* nice and cool. I took a gulp and that, along with Kevin's kindness, made it easier to get my voice working again.

"I am so sorry for the upset I've helped to bring into your family"

"Really? Sorry? Is that the best you can do? That man is manipulating my whole family with your help. God knows why. We're just an ordinary family. And you're sorry?"

Kevin gently places a hand on Darren's arm. Not a restraint. Just a gentle reminder. Darren slumps back into the sofa. I try again, "Charles Davidson has been a close friend of my father's since they were at Eton together. So when he asked me to look at the video of your mother at the swimming pool, Darren, and find out where she was, I didn't think much of it. Uncle Charles said he wanted to help her. My family worships him and I couldn't - or didn't want - to believe he could actually hurt anyone."

"Oh no, not good old *Uncle Charles.* Wouldn't harm a fly, I'm sure. Other than abusing my mother and countless other young girls. God. How these men get away with it! Oh no, they're so well respected, they couldn't possibly do anything like that; despite the evidence."

What? How did he know about the other women? We've been so careful not to reveal Charles' identity until we have all the evidence. It could only have been through Tom.

"You've heard from Tom then?"

"Of course! We're in the middle of a family crisis. My mother's gone missing and that man's involved, as are you. You even used the poor boy to get to her."

"We need to stay calm." Kevin's voice of reason.

"Calm? I think she should explain herself to the police as an accessory. We should be getting this man charged… Stay calm?"

I haven't had much experience of anger in such close quarters; no one in my family or friendship groups ever expressed such a basic emotion. It was always a stiff upper lip or, among my friends, staying cool and aloof.

"I'm sorry." I put my glass on the coffee table that thankfully separated us. Preferably before I spilt any more, my hand was shaking that much.

Stay in control, girl. You've got to make them understand.

"After I met Marian, we thought that we would look into Charles's history. To see if he had mistreated anyone else. I just couldn't believe it at first. I'm working with Tom and my brother, Ed. It was my job to talk directly with the women that Ed and Tom suspected of having been used by Charles. At first, even talking to those women, I still couldn't believe what I heard. Some of them were very young when they encountered him. I told myself there must have been misunderstandings, that the women had given out mixed messages, or that the time back then was so different from now. My excuses for him came thick and fast. He was my Uncle Charles, Daddy's best friend. How could the man I'd been hearing about be the same man? But gradually, the feelings, the excuses, and the shame these women described..." My throat closes up on me. I can't go on. I'm crying again. It seems to happening a lot lately.

Darren gives me a vicious look, sighs angrily and gets up to stare out of the window, fists clenched. Kevin pours us all another drink.

"And what Felicity? You've come this far. Come on, tell us." The prosecco, the soft tissue Kevin passes me and his gentle probing finally does it for me. For the first time I feel, not just permission, but also acceptance and support. I take a large swig of Prosecco, almost choking myself.

"I recognised their feelings, despite not wanting to admit to it. It made me reassess my past. When I was a little girl, Uncle Charles always came up to tuck us in and kiss us goodnight when Ed and I were at home in the holidays. He never seemed to stay very long in Ed's room but longer and longer in mine. Ed used to get jealous." I take another sip. Darren comes back to the sofa and stares at me.

"Then the kisses on the lips started. I didn't like it but he was a grown-up. I couldn't say anything. When he started stroking me, he told me it was a way of helping me get to sleep and I believed him. He was Mummy and Daddy's best friend. They would be cross if I made a fuss. So really what happened next was my fault. I shouldn't have let things get that far. I should have told somebody."

"But you were a child!" Darren's anger at me was now redirected, even though I had lied to him and, worse still, possibly put his mother in danger.

"Mum had always warned me that men have strong urges and that I had to be careful not to give out mixed messages. All the women I interviewed said they felt the same responsibility."

"But nobody thinks that now; attitudes of both men and women are changing," Kevin said, handing me the whole box of tissues.

"But it's too late for some of us. It's obviously too ingrained. I still feel the need to be careful, to feel ashamed and responsible when a man goes too far. It must be way too late for Marian, at her age, given what she's been through and what she did."

"Whatever Marian may or may not have done is not for us to judge, just remember she was very young when this man entered her life." Kevin reaches across and touches my arm.

Should I tell them about the newspaper clipping Charles had shown me? I don't want to believe it. Why should I let it muddy the waters?

"Hang on, what about my Mum? Aren't you two forgetting that she might be in danger, either from herself or this... this toe-rag of a politician? He seems hell-bent on finding her." Darren's voice once more shatters the fragile peace.

"Of course, Darren. Felicity, you *have* to give us her number now, don't you see? You're far too deeply implicated in all this…" and Kevin comes and sits next to me, his arm around me is so comforting that I start crying again. "… I think you could do more good by following up the other women and getting them to agree to testify. Maybe even testify yourself, it would help you face up to your past, so you can let it go and start to live more authentically in your present. I could introduce you to one of my fellow counsellors, if you like. She's done a lot of work with women survivors of child abuse and runs a self-help group at our clinic."

Not so long ago I would have pooh-poohed all this as just a load of mindful, hippy nonsense, but today it all seemed to make sense. I take Kevin's card with the address of his clinic. It's here in Brighton, so maybe I should stay around a bit longer, not for Marian, but for me. I pass him my burner phone and I feel a great relief; I no longer have to carry this burden alone. I'm suddenly bone-tired, all adrenaline seeping away.

"It's the only number on that phone," I tell him.

"Thank you," said Kevin, copying the number into his and Darren's phones, "Are you ok to get yourself home? Do you want me to take you?" He passes the Nokia back.

"Yes, I mean no, I have my car outside. Thank you."

 And I leave them and my responsibility for Marian's safety behind. Surely they will be able to find Marian. Brighton's not that big and they can get their friends to help.

I shall concentrate on building the case against Charles; for the abused women I have met and for myself. It's going to cause a huge rift in my family, they'll probably never forgive me and Ed, but I can't live my life, always looking for their approval. I'm an adult now and whether they accept it or not, that is not my problem.

Chapter 23: Marian

The Wages of Sin is Death

All morning I lie in my room at the B&B, trying to remember more of what happened, but memories flash in and out so quickly, a smell, a thought, a feeling. Nothing tangible. I fall asleep listening to the radio and soon I'm thirteen again…

It hurts. I feel sick, I think I've wet myself. Good. I want it all out - to be empty. I curl in on myself. Hide under the smelly blankets. Away from the world, away from the pain, away from everything. Even Charles and my mum. The shame crawls over me. Oh God. What is this? I lift the blankets. It's disgusting. Blood oozing from between my legs, messing up the sheets. I put my hand down. I can feel a sticky softness. I breathe hard and look. A lump of blood-marbled jelly. I shake it off. So much blood! Please just make it go away. My feet and fingers are numb with cold. I'm shivering, my teeth chatter. I can't stop sweating. I can't stop crying. Snot joins the tears that cover my face. I hide under the covers again but come up gasping for air. The smell of blood! I throw off the covers and slither on to the

*cool of the lino floor. Still the pains come,
tearing me apart. Why isn't anyone helping
me? What have I done to deserve this?*

*Deep down I know. What I did with Charles
was dirty and sinful. This is my punishment.
"God pays debts without money." You were
right Mum. I'm in Hell. Something inside me
is ripping me apart. I can't look, I can't. But
it insists; pushing out from inside me. A ball
stuck between my legs. With hair. No it can't
be. Please not that. The nuns at school were
right. It's one of the satanic helpers. Inside
me. It made me do bad things with Charles.
Just like Eve. If I get it out, I can be saved.*

*"Hail Mary, Mother of God, pray for us
sinners…" I crawl to my suitcase. It hurts
every time I move. I use the pain to push
open the case. My manicure set. I take out
the shiny nail scissors. The creature pushes
my insides out. I pull on its head. If I don't
get it out I'm going to die. Die in sin and
eternal torment. I gasp as the ball shifts. I
look down and it turns inside me. A
shoulder, then another slides out. It looks
like a tiny baby, not a devil. I pull at it and it
slithers out onto the lino. Oh God. It's
joined on to something else inside me! Eve's
serpent. I grab the nail scissors and hack at
the disgusting snake attacking the baby. If it*

is it a baby. I manage to tear it away. So
much blood. I pick it up. It stops crying.
Even I stop screaming. The pains go and I'm
no longer scared. The last thing I see is that,
whatever it is, it's male and it's mine.

*

My pillow is soaking wet when the banging
wakes me up.

"Marian, you ok? You asked me to call you
for dinner. It'll be ready in ten minutes. Do
you need some help?"

I struggle up out of the dream and force
myself to answer confidently,

"Just coming, thanks JJ." I've never asked
anyone for help, maybe I should have. Pride
is one of the seven deadly sins.

I sit for a while to gather my thoughts. So
there really was a baby. Despite the horror, I
feel lifted. I *did* give birth to him. Not a
good birth. But he *was* born. He'd be about
the same age as JJ. Wouldn't it be nice if I
found out JJ was my son?

When I reach my table I see he's set it with
a small bunch of flowers and a candle in a
decorated jam-jar. So sweet. He pulls the

chair out for me and serves me with mock formality, tea-towel over his arm,

"It's pommes de terres frites et poisson today, madam," he says, placing a huge piece of battered cod, mushy peas and fat golden chips in front of me.

"I don't know the French for mushy peas," he whispers in my ear, "but I do have a very nice glass of Chablis, should madam desire?"

"That would be perfect, thank you my man," I quietly imagine he's my son and I can't help feeling how lucky I am to be here, joking with him instead of sitting at one of the care home's Formica tables.

My handbag suddenly starts playing a tune. A tune I'd heard before,

"Your phone's ringing" JJ says. So that's where I've heard it.

"Shall I answer it for you?"

I pass it to him. "Can you see who it is please JJ? It's probably that girl again."

But it isn't and I shake my head when he mouths "It's Darren."

"I don't want to speak to him today," I tell JJ and he shows me how to "decline" a call just by pressing a little red button. How easy it is to be rude nowadays.

Then the phone makes a small tinkling sound and JJ tells me I've been sent a message.

"How biblical that sounds. What does the "message" say and who is it from?"

And he shows me:

Mum, I'm so sorry about everything. Please talk to me.

Love Darren. xxx

I feel a little triumphant. Now he wants me to talk to him! But I'm not ready yet. My whole family let me down badly. I shall sort things out for myself.

"I'm just going for a little walk, JJ. An evening stroll to walk off that delicious dinner. I need to do some serious thinking."

*

As it's a bit chilly at night by the sea-front, I put on my camel coat and brown scarf. I'll take the phone, keep it in my pocket. It's

336

such a good idea; a phone you can carry around.

Ah, there's my favourite sight – the pier all lit up with the helter-skelter near the end. So many happy holidays with the kids here. And of course when I was younger although, now I realise, they weren't quite so happy. The sickly smell of the candy floss mingles with greasy chips and car exhausts; on top of a stomach full of fish and chips it makes me feel a little sick. I need the fresh sea air. I try to cross the road. But the cars hurtle along, music blaring, young people hanging out of the windows. I step back. I'll go to the crossing. Safer. What's that sound? My phone. How come everyone seems to know I'm here? Oh no, it's Darren again. Another message:

I'm sorry. Meet me at the pier. Our special place. I'll be there at 7.30. I miss you Mum. Please forgive me. Love Darren xxx

Stop hooting at me. Can't you see I'm going as fast as I can? They never give you enough time at these crossings. I deliberately slow down until I reach the safety of the kerb, then wave sweetly at the angry driver. People are so impatient.

I can stop now and look at my watch. A quarter past seven. I suppose I should meet him. I'd like to see him. Maybe he can help me after all. I swallow down my pride along with the nausea. I'll have to walk a bit faster to get to the pier in time. All these people! Brighton has really changed, but I'm revelling in the liveliness of it all. Look at that girl with the green hair; you wouldn't think it would suit her, but it does. I wish I could have done that; maybe I can now. Who would care, if I lived here? A couple of girls walk by, hand in hand, and then – oh my goodness – they're kissing each other. Right there in the street. How embarrassing. I don't care that they're both girls but… in public?

Suddenly I am grabbed from behind and two strong arms wrap me in a beautifully warm embrace. I turn to my Darren. No! I try to step back. I don't like it. I feel sick again. It's not him. Who is it? This is like the towel man at the lido all over again. I struggle to rid myself of this human straitjacket and call for help but my voice cracks into tiny gasps. A deep laugh from many years ago turns my legs to jelly.

"It's you! Charles. Is it really you? What are you doing?" It's him. For a split second I'm happy to see him. Then it all comes flooding back.

"Hello Marian. It has been a long time since we last met. Too long. It's extraordinary good luck that you're here too. Here in our special place. You look just the same, my dear. What are you doing here? I'm in Brighton for a conference. I couldn't believe my eyes when I saw you standing there. I thought; no, it can't be her, she looks too young. How are you? I'm sorry if I startled you."
He doesn't quite let me go; keeping one arm tight around my shoulder the whole time.

"I'm meeting Darren…" I manage to splutter.

"Darren? Your husband?"

"No, no, my son."

"Your son? How splendid. I shall wait with you. I would love to meet him," He steers me over to a bench, "we can talk over old times."

Old times? He is so genuinely pleased to see me. I feel myself blushing. I push away my bad memories for a while. Even the possibility of those other women. I need to keep him sweet, no, maybe I *want* to keep him sweet, despite everything. The time passes quickly; he is a charming raconteur and I find I'm enjoying his view of our past. I'd like it to be mine too but then I remember why I'm here in Brighton. To find my true past, not this sugar-coated one.

"Charles, that's all very lovely but I remember a baby. Was it your baby?"

I am chilled by his silence. I've got it wrong. He doesn't like me talking this way. I need to go to the toilet again.

Apart from his silence, he gives no sign that he's registered what I said or even that I've spoken at all. I flail around for suitable words. There are too many and saying any of them scares me so I, too, just sit as the last of the noisy Sunday trippers in their happy-bright clothes mill around us. I can't bear it. My heart is thumping so hard in my chest. My mouth is dry. Then Charles breaks his silence; his voice has that dark quietness that always used to scare me.

"You shouldn't be here alone, Marian. In fact you should not, all thing considered, be here at all. Darren told me that you have not been well. I was deeply distressed to hear the news that you'd been sectioned and placed in a home. Perhaps I should take you back there." He stretches a hand towards me. I really need the toilet now.

"My Darren? You've been in touch? He told you that?" I'm looking around for somewhere to hide. I was right. They all knew. Why had I doubted myself? Why did I let them persuade me I was wrong? They *were* all in it together. What did they do with my little boy?

"Is that Carol in on this too? Is that why Darren made me go with her, to make me believe there was no baby?" I get up, I need to keep moving. "I was there; I know he came out of me. I can remember the very feel of him." It's true; buried for more than half a century, fractured memories of that night burst back into my consciousness once again with a force that makes me dizzy. I'm forced to grab Charles' outstretched had to prevent myself from falling over. Suddenly, he grabs my waist and tries to lead me away from the crowded pier. I pull back.

"I'm sorry," I force myself to look up and smile, "would you excuse me a moment, I need to find the Ladies."

That laugh again. Where is Darren?

"Come," and he pulls me along beside him.

"Where are we going?" I try to pull back.

"You say you're in need of the toilet. I couldn't expect you to use the facilities here on the pier. My hotel is across the road – just there, see?" Slowly we walk towards the roaring cars, the dirty lorries and a huge double-decker bus. Right to the very edge of the kerb. He reaches around my back and has hold of both my arms. We stand on the edge as the traffic roars by. So fast, so noisy. I'm really scared now, thinking about my conversation with Felicity, my incarceration in the home and Sonya's pillow. Is this it? The bus approaches. I close my eyes and wait for the push. Now a bright yellow car with its hood down, music so loud it almost drowns my fears. Then another car; a blue one. As each vehicle goes by I wonder if he'll do it now...now...or now? The waiting is agony, I'm tempted to step out myself just to get it over with but I seem to be made of lead; immoveable.

Suddenly the lights change and it's as if he's Moses at the Red Sea making the traffic part. He strides out. I can't keep up. My legs aren't as long as his. I do my best, he's holding me so tightly. Out of love? Affection? No. It's definitely something else now. Why had I come? Why did I top to talk with him? I've only myself to blame – again. I struggle to shout out but I can't even whisper *no*.

"Wait." Safely across the road my voice comes back. I pull one arm free and look at him again. "I'm waiting for Darren."

"Oh I can't imagine he will be coming now, can you?" His smile unnerves me.

Was he ever coming?

I stumble as he "escorts" me up the steps at the entrance to his hotel. He squeezes in beside me as the doors revolve. I'm completely helpless again. How did he know I'd be here? Had Darren told him? Had he seen me when I was walking along the prom all those times? How did he even know I was in Brighton? Darren, Tracey, Carol or Felicity; it could have been any - or all - of them. I don't know any more.

We pass the reception at the hotel. Why can't I find the words to tell the receptionist that I don't want to be here? I beg her with my eyes. *Please understand.* She just gives me her corporate smile. She's more interested in Charles as he charms her and gets his key. There's the Ladies. "I need the toilet." I pull away but he's too quick;

"Behave yourself."

Then out loud, "Come my dear," he shares a smile with the people waiting for the lift, "We'll soon be in our room."
"No, I need to go now…" but the lift pings and he gently pushes me in. "Too much brandy," he mutters to the other couple. They smile at me. I can't find the words I need to explain. I only need one word. But my fear is so deep it's drowned my voice. Soon it will drown any chance I have to resist. What is he going to do? We leave the lift and there's no one else around.

"My darling, you look terrified. Why?" He's smiling again now. I let him guide me to his door. "You have nothing to be afraid of. It's me, remember?"

He locks the door behind us and pockets the key. "We have such history together." He sits me on the bed. "A man never forgets his first love."

He picks up a single glass and pours a large drink. "Here, have a brandy; that will calm your nerves." And to my shame, I do exactly as he asks.

The brandy works and I begin to feel I could talk again, but I have no words.

"You asked me on the pier if we had a child together. Extraordinary." He draws up a chair to sit opposite me, our knees almost touching. "My dear girl, that's the question I have been asking myself for decades. I long for a child; a son and heir. Jemima and I never quite managed it."

What? He's talking about my baby. The baby he tried to have murdered in that basement. Even before he was born. A mortal sin. Anger replaces fear. My voice returns. "You took me to that place. To that horrible woman. You left me there. You knew I was pregnant. You wanted it taken away. I didn't know what was going on." His scornful laugh stops my voice again. "Come now, dear girl. You knew exactly what was happening. You enjoyed every minute we had together. Then you had to get yourself pregnant and spoil it all. I just helped you out. Your life would have been ruined if people found out." He gets up and pours more brandy. "Drink up, my dear. You're looking quite peaky."

It may be true but it isn't my truth. I struggle to remember; to counter this version of my life. He sits down too close to me. His voice is gentle. Like it used to be when he told me stories of how our life together would be. How special I was to him. How our secret was the most treasured secret in the world.

"In fact I had to pay a substantial sum of money just to try to protect your reputation. You obviously realised back then that you could never have kept that baby."

I take a deep gulp of brandy to give me courage, I need to hold on to my story, not his.

"Why did you leave us there? Why didn't you come back? How, if you loved me like you said you did, could you do that?"

"You tried to catch me with the oldest trick a woman can play on a man, getting pregnant."

"But I wasn't a woman, I was thirteen years old. I didn't know I was pregnant. I didn't know what was happening. You seduced me when I was just a child. They call it "grooming" now."

"Oh, for goodness sake. Not you too. I thought better of you. You always came back for more. You never once tried to stop me. You never said *no*. We had such fun together. You loved it."

"No, Charles, I loved *you*."

And as I say the words out loud, I realise that what I had loved was a fantasy, fed by my mum's romantic paperbacks and the overwhelming premise of those days; that young girls were quite rightly attracted to older, powerful men. That they should trade their bodies for love, attention, even the enjoyment of being used, if it meant keeping their man. I had traded mine for a few penny sweets and the promise of a love that was never there.

I suddenly see him for what he is. I feel, for the first time since I was a child, in control. I now see a weak man who was given, as a birthright, the feeling that he could do exactly as he wished. No one had ever challenged that assumption. I feel angry for all the girls like me and Jenny that he, and men like him, have damaged with their feelings of entitlement and power.

I surprise myself by bursting, not into tears, but derisive laughter. He's neither the longed-for lover of my fantasies, nor the powerful man who had overwhelmed me with his sophistication and physical strength.

"How could I have ever loved you?" I spit, "you're pathetic, a laughing stock. Did you need to seduce young girls like me and Jenny because the posh women you should have been with despised you? The newspapers will love my story."

That cynical laugh again.

"I don't think you'll want to tell your story to the world. Yes we had a son," his smile does not prepare me. Nothing could prepare me for what came next.

"You killed him." His words hit me like a physical blow. Another gulp of brandy. I can't let him do this to me again. Distort my sense of truth.

"No! Our baby *was* born alive, despite your efforts, and he was adopted. I'm going to trace him. If you really mean what you say about longing for a son, you'll help me find him. It's not too late." Not that I'd really let this man share my baby, he doesn't deserve that.

"Adopted? What makes you think that?" That insidious, self-assured smile.

"My mother said so. When I was in hospital, after…after that woman did what she did to me. She told my aunty that he'd gone to a better place," and as I speak her words out loud, the first shudders of doubt begin to creep in; after all these years.

His laugh this time is real.

"You sweet, innocent little girl. That's what Christians always say when someone dies," and his laughter goes on and on and on. I can't stand it anymore.

"Stop it. He can't be dead. They'd have told me. I'd have known." I hurl myself at him, just as I had the first time we met, when he was hurting Jenny.

I hit him time and again, trying to stop the lies coming out of his mouth but he's far too strong for me. He pushes me roughly away and I fall, crumpled like a rag doll to the floor. I have nothing left. I just want to curl into myself and disappear. Why can't I?

He's gone when I look up. I might be able to get to the door, away from this story. This is all wrong. I want *my* memories back, not his. As I start to get up, he returns, smirking, with a piece of paper. He lifts me, oh so gently, and sits me back down on the bed. His kindness confuses me once more.

"Before you go to the newspapers, or whatever, you might like to read this," he says, handing me the sheet of paper. "But first, remind me where your Aunty Olive used to worship?"

Aunty Olive? How can know about her? I don't understand his games. Yet, once again, I obey. I try hard to remember, like a good little girl.

"St Michael's, I think" I watch his face to see if I'm right. Apparently not. I try harder. "No, I'm sorry, it was St Mary's" His look tells me I'm right.

"Read this. You'll find it interesting." He hands me what looks like a copy of an old newspaper report.

Abandoned Baby Shock

A newly-born baby was discovered outside St Mary's Catholic Church, Kemp Town, last night. The Gazette was informed that the infant was wrapped in a small, heavily blood-stained and grubby towel but was otherwise naked, despite the recent drop in temperature. Father David, vicar of St. Marian's parish, told our reporter;

"I have never seen such a disturbing sight in all my 30 years of ministry here. The poor child was stone cold but the most horrifying thing was that someone, the wretched mother who abandoned her child, I suppose, had shredded the umbilical cord to pieces. There were also multiple bruises on its little chest. The baby bled to death. It had no chance of life."

A police spokesman said that initial studies indicated that the baby was extremely premature and would probably not have survived long after the birth but that this did not detract from the heinous nature of the vicious assault and callous abandonment of this child.

A door-to-door search of the local area has been mounted, along with a check of local hospitals in a bid to find the child's mother. The mother will be in need of medical attention and health officials have made a plea for her to come forward for her own safety.

*A full post mortem report on the
infant is expected next week.*

The paper trembles in my hands. The words
jump around the page, trying to escape. "No.
My baby? Attacked? Who could have done
that..? He's dead? No. It can't be true..!" But
doubt is already whispering in my ear. Then
shouting, filling my head. The room spins
and I fall again, this time into the deepest of
hells. I can't come back from this. I don't
want to.

I'm glad our baby is dead.

No, that's not true, I would have loved that
baby had he lived. I was just too young. I
have to hurt this man who blighted my life,
made it impossible for me to have decent
relationships, even with my own children. It
was him who made me constantly doubt my
own sanity and took away my voice. And
yet, now, I need him again. I need him to
hurt me one last time; I need to be punished
for killing our son. How could I have done
it? I must be mad, or evil or both. This has
to end here. Sins must be paid for.

Chapter 24: Charles

Desperate Times Call for Desperate Measures.

Why did I allow myself embroiled in this? I don't know what to do. Stop panicking – think! There she is just lying on my hotel floor. Such an insignificant little life and yet she could destroy me. Me..! I've done so much for my country and my party. Not that the media will care about the good I've done. Oh my God, I can see it all now; "Senior politician involved in historic sex scandal" or "Woman found injured in Brighton hotel room accuses senior politician of historic sex abuse."

I don't know what to do. I usually have other people to clear up my messes. Who can I trust with this? I could call the home, get Dr. Campbell to take her back. We could always tell the family she was found wandering Brighton's streets. She should never have been allowed to leave the home. It's not my fault. Campbell assured me she had her under her control, sedating her and arranging several attempts at an accident to send her into her 'better place'. It's her fault really, she can explain it to the family, but how much has Marian told Darren?

 Damn! She's beginning to come round. I should have hidden her somewhere in the hotel. Or never have brought her back here. My father was right; I never think things through. Once again I hear her derisive laughter rattling around my head. The newspaper article soon put paid to that. I just don't see what to do next. That's not like me. She's really messed me up. And she could do worse if I don't deal with her once and for all. No, I can't wait for Campbell; she'd only get it all wrong again. You just can't trust women.

"Up you get, Marian," She stinks of brandy and just lies there, snivelling about the son she killed. My son. My only son. I can't help it, her weakness goads me and before I know it I've kicked her. Still she lies there irritatingly small and snivelly, just like the younger boys at school, just asking to be kicked. So I do it again. Why won't she get up? Fight back? I can't take any more; I need a reaction so I tell her about my going back to the B&B and seeing them both lying there, blood everywhere. I'll never forget it; it haunts me still. I'll never forgive her for that.

At last! Now she's awake, ranting at me like some brandy-sodden streetwalker. It's quite funny really but I'll have to shut her up before someone comes to see what all the shouting's about. Come here, woman; as I grab her she falls back, hitting her head on the table. Once again blood everywhere but I can't run away this time. She's in *my* hotel room; booked in *my* name. That was stupid but who knew this would happen?

How can I get her out of here looking like that? Maybe the smell of brandy can help? She's coming round again; here my sweet little drunken wifey, take some more. It's going everywhere. Still that will only make her a more convincing drunk, the stench of alcohol will convince everyone within a mile radius and give a reason for her unsteady gait. Brilliant. I pull her hat over the wound on her head and tuck away the blood-stained hair.

"We're going to our special place my love, to get you some air," and to find somewhere to dump you. With her track record, no-one will believe a word she says about how she got there or what happened here. In fact, I doubt even she will remember what's happened, given the amount of alcohol she's ingested. I'd better clean up a bit, all this blood. I can do a better job once I've dumped her and come back here. I can sort my alibi out later, just in case anyone finds her before she freezes to death and believes the wretched woman. I drag her up, drape her arm around my shoulder and arrange my smile,

"Come on my love, I think you've had a bit too much to drink. Let's get you some fresh air," I say it loud enough for any casual listeners to hear as we stagger to the lift.

With any luck, the head wound, loss of blood and the cold night air will send her off to that "better place" before she's found in the morning. That's quite funny, I think, or would be if she hadn't forced me into all this. Time to get rid of her once and for all.

Chapter 25: Marian

Needs Must When the Devil Drives.

It feels like I'm swimming up from deep blackness. Charles is standing over me. His face terrifies me. But what that paper says I've done, if it's true, is worse. It must have been me. I was on my own, I'm almost sure of that. Why can't I remember? I was so frightened. There was a lot of blood, I think, and a...snake? No that's ridiculous. I'm remembering a nightmare, not the truth. Do I want to remember? I don't think so. Not now. I look at the man who says I killed my baby.

He looks like he wants to kill me. Actually, I want him to kill me. His kicks, when they come, feel like a blessing, or at least a penance. I curl into a ball cradling the pain.

"Get up," he growls and drags me to my feet.

"You killed my son." Spittle from his angry mouth hits my face. "I saw you at the Blakely woman's house. Blood everywhere. I thought you were both dead. For years I believed you were dead. But then there you were, flaunting yourself again. All over the media, with nothing but a towel to cover you." He thrusts the newspaper once again at my face. "Now I find out you murdered our son!" The words take a while to make sense in my head. Too much going round and round inside. Then I realise.

"You saw us and you left us there to die?"

I'm so angry that I have the strength to crawl away from him and haul myself up, clutching the back of the chair. I begin to shout. No stopping the words now. My voice is the loudest thing I've ever heard. All the stored-up anger and pain I've endured over the years scream out. And with my screams, I cry. I cry for the son who was never able to cry for himself. I pour shame on this man who abused me as a child then left me and my son to die. He tries to stop me and I fall back and crack my head on the corner of the table. I fall into darkness once more.

I can't breathe. My nose and mouth fill up with water. No, not water: thicker, sweeter. Something else. I swallow. It's brandy. In my hair, on my clothes and covering my face so I push it away, struggle to sit up. Still the brandy comes, floods my eyes, my nose and my mouth. One more effort. I bide my time. I lie still, willing my body not to cough, not to react. I feel his hold relax a little. I shake my head violently and push him away. I can't stop coughing. I feel sick. My head is spinning. From the violence or the alcohol? Who cares? At least now I'm sitting up. He steps back and laughs at me.

"You're stronger than I thought. And more calculating. I can't help but be impressed."

I am covered in brandy and, it seems, a fair amount of my own blood. I touch my head. My fingers come back bloodied. Once again my head spins.

"Look at what you've made me do now. People have seen us together. What shall I do with you? Here, put on your hat before we go out. You won't look quite so unpleasant."

He pushes my hat painfully down over my ears. He hauls me up and I vomit at the sudden movement.

I grab the chance to catch my breath when he drops me back down. He returns from the bathroom with a wet towel. I shut my eyes as he dabs at the blood and vomit. Like a child, being made smart by her mum. No of course it's not the same.

"Come, that will have to do," he laughs again. "You'll make a very convincing drunk. I think we both need some air and time to think."

My arm is wrenched over his shoulders and we stagger along the corridor together, like a macabre version of the "Gay Gordons" that I loved dancing with my dad every New Year. My mind drifts back, away from this mess back to my happy childhood, before Charles. Stop. Don't think about the past, stay here, and stay awake. It's hard. My head throbs. My eyes keep closing.

The lift comes. No one in there to help me. He's pushing me in, then up against the side to steady me and he presses the button. The doors close in on us. The lift drops slowly down, each swaying movement bringing up the bile to my throat. I can't be sick again. I clench my teeth together and take some deep breaths.

It's stopping at the third floor down. I've got to pull myself together. Thank goodness; there's a lovely young couple waiting. I stand up straighter, ready to ask for help. But their horrified stares stop me. I, too, catch sight of the dishevelled drunk reflected in the polished sheen of the metal lift wall.

It's hopeless. I close myself down once again.

"Sorry about this. It's my wife's birthday." He tells the couple. "She's overdone it a bit," and he smiles indulgently at me while hoisting my slack body a bit higher. "Taking her out for some fresh air." They share his smile. Why can't I form the words to deny his lies? My mouth is too dry. I have no words left anyway. I silently plead to them, "Help me," but they don't understand. All sympathy is with my doting "husband".

The bell rings. The lift jolts to a halt and the doors shudder noisily on the ground floor. The noise and the movement make me want to vomit again. I can't. They'll only think it's because I'm drunk. I give up. My baby is dead. There's nothing I can do. Just let me go.   The cold air on my face wakes me. He's dragging me along the promenade. Towards the pier. Our pier. No. Not any longer. He lied. He left us to die.

No, I won't let him get away with it unpunished. I no longer care for myself: I deserve whatever is coming but he has to be made to feel at least some pain, if not remorse. My mouth fills with saliva and my stomach heaves again with the smell of the doughnuts and the clamour of the crowded pavements. What can I do? He's holding me so tightly. I'd fall down if he didn't. It's hopeless. I am hopeless. One arm in a grotesque embrace around his shoulders, the other uselessly stuffed in my coat pocket.

Just a minute, what's this? The phone. It has that girl's number in it. Hers is the only one on it. If I press the bottom button it will come on. But he won't stand by while you call her, silly girl. Still, I switch it on. Now what? I glance up at him. He drags me along, eyes on the pier, uncaring whether or not I am even conscious. Slowly, slowly I pull out the phone, glance down. It's on. I see the green phone symbol.
"You've come round have you?" That laugh again. "Not long now."

He hasn't seen the phone. I hide it back in my pocket and, I pray to all the saints I can remember. *Let me press the right button.* I take it out for a quick look. Yes. We are on the bit where it tells you about recent calls. Felicity. Yes. That's her name. I put it back in my pocket and press again. I can hear its ringing, muffled in my pocket. I look up at him once more.

"I have such a treat for you. Remember how much you loved running to the end of the pier?" His face is a picture of self-assured

362

power. He doesn't hear the ringing above the noise of the crowd. He can't imagine that I might still fight back.

"Why are we going to the pier, Charles?" I shout. I need to drown the noise of the ringing. And I'll need Felicity to hear me. "I don't want to go to the pier."

"You used to love it." He quickens our pace.

"But I like it here on the promenade." The phone isn't ringing any more. Please let her be listening. "Let's not go to the pier, Charles. I'm frightened." I shout.

We pass through the gates, past the doughnut stand. This time I can't stop myself; I vomit into a nearby bin. A group of teenagers laugh at me but are silenced with a look from Charles.

"Let's not go any further Charles," I shout again. "The fish and chip café will only make me do it again and people are staring." This time he stops. He looks directly at me. My head and hands prickle.

"You're up to something. What have you got in that pocket?" He lets go of me. I try to run but my legs won't cooperate and I drop to the floor. I crawl into a ball. He's grabbing at me, pulling at my coat. I cradle my body around the precious phone; my lifeline and, with God's will, his downfall.

"Steady on, mate," a man calls from a safe distance. One look from Charles and he moves on, muttering to his wife. Everyone gives us a wide berth. As always, Charles is in control.

He pulls me back up and drags me to the railings. Pushed up against them, my breath is crushed out of me one more time. My hand is wrenched from inside my pocket. The phone's still working. I shout into it once again that Charles has dragged me to the pier. He throws it far out into the sea. His face is ugly with rage, his once beautiful blue eyes bulge with fury. I'm not sure he can even see straight any more.

He yanks me off the railings. I try to resist, to hold on, but he is far too strong for me. I see the people stare as I am pulled along, stumbling and crying towards the end of the pier.

"She's drunk," he shouts at them, "She needs fresh air, that's all." His anger has taken him beyond the pretence. Still no one intervenes.

It's like that first time, in the fields. Back then it was lust that turned him into a monster. This time it's a mixture of fear and anger. I realise that he can't let me go. My story would ruin him. He's so strong. I am the biddable, weak one once more.

No, I refuse to be weak. What's that saying about what doesn't kill you makes you stronger? Not sure it's true. I killed my baby when I should have had the strength to give him a life. I should have remembered what I did but my mind couldn't accept it. I should have paid a penance but I couldn't confess it. I should have died with him but my body couldn't let go of life. I grew stronger, true - but badly damaged - and that damage has followed me all my life. It's time to end it.

"Come on, you stupid woman," he hisses at me, as he drags us through the screams coming from the funfair at the end of the pier. Once again he's dragging me into darkness; the grey clouded night meeting the blackness of the waves as they hit the end of the pier. No hungry seagulls now, no chips to throw, no joyful laughter like the last time he dragged me along here. That was the last time I was truly happy.

A group of teenagers are playing around a little to the right of us. I know how to make amends. Redemption, not rebirth, in a watery baptism.

"No Charles!" I scream. Why didn't I scream back then, when it all started? "No, you can't do it, please don't Charles. Let go of me."

He looks confused. I struggle like a woman fighting for her life, screaming his name over and over. I manoeuvre us closer and closer to the protective railings. I don't want protecting. It's all so very late for that.

"Help me, he's going to kill me!" I scream towards the shocked teenagers. They look as stunned and as helpless as I had been, all those years ago, unable to move.

In the darkness they won't see the detail. They'll believe he pushed me in. I lean backwards over the railings, pulling him halfway over with me. I shall never be used by him again. I can't help laughing at the irony as I use his body. I use it by pulling my knees up onto his chest to lever myself over the railings and into the blackness.

The water is cold, grasping the breath out from deep within my lungs, freezing my skin so it crackles over my old broken body like cling-film that has suddenly lost its tender softness, its shrunken brittleness digging into the flesh. I don't mind. It's quite comforting; the pain is almost soothing. No more bad dreams. No more loss. No one can hurt me now. No one can be hurt by me. I can give up. It is over at last.

*

They say your life floats by you as you drown. I see only darkness, hear only the blood rushing in my ears. My lungs bursting to find some air. Am I sinking down or floating up? I think of my baby. I think of the girl I used to be before. I think of my other children. No! Stop. I don't want to drown. I want to live – if only to see that man get what he deserves. I kick out again and I find the surface. I swim. I hear my son. The living son. My Darren. I should have taken better care of him. I wish he really *was* here.

"Over here! She's over here" It is his voice. It *is* him. He *is* here. I splutter my way towards him. Hands; warm, gentle hands hold me and haul me out of the water and on to the pebble beach. A coat is wrapped around me, a welcome enfolding this time, and Darren hugs his warmth into me. I cry and hug him back.

Sirens sound and blue lights hurt my eyes.
What's this? I'm being wrapped up yet
again, this time in tin-foil. Like a chicken.
So odd. Am I dreaming again? I fly through
the air and land on a sort of bed in a strange
van. No! They're trying to stop me breathing
again. Covering my face. No, take it away. I
try to push it away. They're stronger than
me and soon there's a mask over my mouth
and nose. I gasp, about to hold my breath.
But this is not Sonya's pillow nor Charles'
brandy; this one helps me breathe.

Chapter 26: Marian

Tomorrow is Another Day.

Once again in a hospital, no Mum there this time. I'm the mum and my family is sitting around me. "We got him, Gran." Is that my Tom?

"What? Who have you got?" I struggle to speak. There's something over my face, smothering my voice again, suppressing my words, my truth. I struggle to sit up. Someone helps me, taking away the oxygen mask at the same time. It's my Tracey. Why is she crying? What have I done wrong? I try to remember. Jumbled images come and go n terrifying succession; the sea, Charles, brandy, a dead baby. No, *my* dead baby. I shut down, sliding back into the safety of the bed. I turn my face into the pillow and feel its softness envelope me. I can't see, I can't speak. It's safer that way. It's always been safer that way. Until the need to speak out led me to this pain.

"Mum, it's ok. You're safe now," Tracey's hand on my shoulder tries to bring me back but I can never come back from this. All those years; waiting until I could look for him, but he'd already gone. I feel numb; I have no right to grieve, certainly no right to feel safe. I push my face further into the pillow, trying to escape this awful reality. Why hadn't Sonya finished me off back in the home? It would have saved my family from finding out the dreadful truth about me. I could have gone quietly, just a mother and grandmother who they could simply mourn, thinking I'd gone in a state of grace.

"Mum, honestly. Everything is fine. Charles can't hurt you any more…"

It was no longer Charles that hurt me. It was my own sinfulness. I would soon have to atone for my actions. Atone before God and before my family. As I realised that I dreaded the latter most, I sank deeper into sin and depression. I can't face them. Why won't they go away and leave me alone?

"I think Marian needs to rest. Perhaps you should come back tomorrow?" Someone, maybe a nurse comes to my rescue.

*

I sleep, how long I don't know. It's the same drug-induced sleep of the past but without the dreams. It was a sleep so deep that I am disoriented when I wake to find my family smiling down at me.

This bed reminds me of the care home and yet all my family is here, smiling at me. For a moment my heart sinks. Have they taken me back there? A nurse, in a proper uniform actually smiles at me as she passes by and I know I'm not in that awful place.

"I told you, we got him Gran, all because of you," and my lovely Tom is there, his sweet face full of smiles.

"Who dear?" I take his hand. He really is a good boy.

"Charles Davidson of course. We…" and he points to Felicity,

"…we built up a case and took it to the police. He's been charged with more than twenty counts of sexual abuse." He looks so proud. I love that boy - but what on earth is he talking about?

"Not to mention attempted murder, Mum," There's my Darren - he looks just as proud.

"Murder? Who's been murdered?" I still can't understand what they are talking about or why I'm here. The last thing I remember was looking for Darren by the pier.

"No, you daft old thing. You. Or rather he tried to. He must have knocked you semi-conscious, then dragged you to the pier. He told the receptionist you were very drunk and that he was taking you into the fresh air to clear your head. No one else confronted him."

"You obviously made a convincing drunk, Mum." Tracey's here too. How lovely. I haven't seen her for ages. I've no idea what they're talking about.

"Why am I here? Is this another home?" I try to get away but I don't seem able to move much. Darren lays a gentle hand on mine.

"No Mum, you're in hospital. Don't you remember? He tried to kill you."

My head hurts. I try to rub it better but I'm covered in bandages and drips. It's all too much. They keep talking at me. What are they saying? I don't care. I'm just happy to hear their voices.

"Felicity heard your call, Mum. On the mobile. That was amazing. So clever." That's my Tracey's voice again, I turn and see that she's smiling at Felicity. The girl's eyes are shiny with excitement as she takes her turn next to me.

"I couldn't work it out at first. Thought you'd rung me by mistake. Then I listened and realised you were in trouble and sending me a message. I contacted the police straight away and then Darren." I'm beginning to remember now. Oh, that phone in my pocket. It's coming back. So all that really did happen?

"But guess what Mum? Darren and I were already out looking for you." That's my Tracey again – never lets others take the limelight for long. "It was me who remembered how much you loved taking us to the pier at night when we were kids. Our special place, you called it."

"Don't ever call it that again!" My voice comes out loud and shrill. Thankfully no one cares or even notices. So pleased with themselves.

"We saw him dragging you along and we ran to stop him but he pushed you over the pier railings and into the sea. Darren dived in after you. Charles just stood there screaming obscenities. Then some teenagers grabbed him and held him until the police came."

"I don't understand. You say were out looking for me." I looked at Darren. "But didn't you send me a message to meet you at the pier? I waited but you never came..?"

"That was my fault, I'm afraid," that Felicity girl. There you are; maybe I shouldn't have trusted her after all. What did she do this time?

"It was Charles who sent you those messages. I'm so, so sorry. I'd had a meeting with him at his hotel." Why was she meeting him? Why aren't the others asking her? They seem to think she's on my side, just letting her go on with her excuses.

"When I went to the bathroom, he must have checked both my phones and got your number off the Nokia; that's the one I've been using to contact you, Mrs Norman." Interesting, her being so formal. "I realised as soon as I'd got into the bathroom that I'd left my bag out there with him. I was so worried that he'd take the Nokia. But when I got back and they were both still in my bag I thought I was just being paranoid."

"Paranoid is what you need around that old skunk," says Tom, putting his arm around her. So they are still together. I wonder how Tracey copes with that.

"But what were you doing in his hotel room anyway?" At last. Tracey is on it like the Rottweiler we all know and love.

Suddenly the atmosphere changes. The girl's hiding something.

"Um, he wanted to show me something," her face - and then everyone else's - tell me exactly what the something was. The shame when it hits me, is as strong and as complete as the light that blinded Paul on the road to Damascus. Unlike Paul, though, I am not blinded. No, completely the opposite. For the first time in ages I can see. For years, I was unable to see what happened on that wretched night. Then Charles put an end to my foolishness and my sense of innocence. It was there in black and white. I have to confront my guilt.

"The newspaper article?" I suggest and relief floods the room.

"It wasn't your fault…"

"You were just a child…"
"You didn't know what to do…"

I turn my head away from all their talking. So they all know. I killed my own baby.

Tracey stops them and tries to explain it away.

"When you cut the cord, you cut it far too close to the baby, the scissors were obviously not sharp ones and it was all a bit of a mess and you didn't know that you had to clamp or tie it to keep the blood in.."
"So I let him bleed to death?" I can't bear it.

They try to reassure me but I can't talk to them and eventually they all leave, all pride and happiness at my rescue turned to a limp sadness.

Chapter 27: Marian

A Friend in Need is a Friend Indeed

I'm crying as I wake from the fitful sleep. Fitful but no longer haunted by dreams of the past. That's something at least. Now I know what happened, I can make sense of the flashbacks and bad dreams and come to terms with them. The guilt and shame are my penance, I suppose, although Felicity refuses to listen when I try to explain.

She has been by my side at all the police interviews I've had to suffer. I didn't want Tracey to be involved. She would have to listen to all the sordid details of my past. What daughter needs to know about her mother's sexual experiences? Her pride was hurt when I told her I didn't want her there but I think she was also secretly relieved.

"But Mum, you need someone to support you. I've always been there for you. Why do you want Felicity to be with you? She's not even family."

"That's exactly why, my love. Please don't think I've not appreciated your support. I did and still do. I'm just not always good at

expressing my feelings but I do love you."
As I said it and saw Tracey's reaction, I
realised I'd never said so before. I'd been
too afraid to love anyone after Charles.

Two female police officers came this time.
The young girl visiting her grandmother in
the bed opposite was intrigued by the fact
that I was being visited by police officers in
uniform and kept trying to listen in but they
were very discreet. As they left, they said
my statement was the most important
because I was so much younger than most of
the other women. That shocked me. I didn't
know there were others.

"He told me I was special." I whispered to
Felicity as she handed me yet another tissue,
once the officers left. I didn't want the girl
to overhear our conversation either.

"Me too," She said and for the first time, I
realised just what it was that we'd somehow
recognised in each other that first time we
met.

"With him..?"

"Yes. It took me a long time to remember
and then to process and accept those
memories. In fact, if I'd never met you and
then all the other women, I doubt if I would

ever have remembered. I'd have just carried on thinking I didn't need a loving relationship and choosing all the men that would confirm my warped view."

"And Tom?"

"He's different. Maybe because he's younger - and don't think that I can't see the irony there, Marian. It does worry me sometimes. But there's no power gap between us. In fact he often seems more mature than I am. We both know what we're getting into."

" That's exactly how I felt about Charles and what those girls who claim they've been abused say. They – we – went into it willingly. Charles didn't force me and I kept going back for more. Surely I'm to blame too?"

"See the little girl over there?" I nodded.

"Guess how old she is?"

"I can't tell ages any more. She's not very old, I shouldn't think. Why?"

"She's here so that her grandma can wish her a happy birthday and give her a present. Obviously the mother bought and wrapped the present but the girl doesn't know that.

Anyway, I overheard the mother reminding the gran that she's thirteen today."

"So?"

"How old were you when you met Charles?"

No, I can't have been the same age as that little girl. Surely I was older than her... I'd felt so grown up. He told me I was his girlfriend. Looking at this girl, I see how inappropriate that was. It's true that in the hotel room I'd screamed at Charles and accused him of grooming me and stealing my childhood for some penny sweets. But they had been words. I'd meant them but now, looking at this young girl on the edge of puberty, it all became so much more real.

I was not to blame. I was a child.

I felt hot, sick and elated all at once. My Damascus moment. Absolution.

But no, not quite.

"I still killed my baby. A mortal sin and something I can never forgive myself for, no matter how young and scared I was. Why haven't the police charged me? They haven't even questioned me about it."

"You're talking about that newspaper report..?" I nod, unable to speak.

"You shouldn't believe everything you read in the papers, especially when Charles is using them to his advantage. That was only one report out of many about the same incident and the editor had to retract it once the post-mortem report came out."

What? Maybe he wasn't dead after all. No, she said "post mortem".

"It said that the baby was way too premature and probably died during the birth or even in the womb. The bruises on the body showed that someone – that must have been you – had tried to give him CPR but there was nothing anyone could have done to save him. Not even a trained midwife and you, at thirteen was certainly no trained midwife."

"You're right. I had no idea what to do, what was happening. I had no idea where babies came from. Mum never spoke about any of that."

Felicity squeezed my hand. "You were just a frightened child, caught up with stories of guilt, shame and sin. With no one there to comfort or help you."

"But surely there must be an investigation?"
"No, the worst you could be charged with is unlawful disposal of a body with a view to conceal the birth of a child. My brother Ed looked it up. But you didn't do that. According to your cousin Jenny in South Africa, you were far too ill – in hospital, in fact. She thinks it may have been your Aunty Olive or that landlady - Mrs Blakely, wasn't it? Anyway they're both dead now and the CPS are not pursuing it."

My poor little boy. No one to fight his corner.

"Does he at least have a grave?"

"Yes. The congregation of St Mary's Church back then raised enough money to have him buried in the churchyard there. You could perhaps have a headstone erected there and visit him when you're well enough."

So that's what we did.

I said goodbye to the little boy who had been with me almost all my life, sadly hidden in a shroud of guilt and shame. Confronting Charles I saw that I had nothing to be ashamed of or to feel guilty for. One day I shall believe it too.

The nightmares have now faded, as has my anger over what Charles did to me all those years ago. I may never fully forgive him as I know I should.

He will probably die in prison, disgraced in full view of his family, friends and the media. Surely that's enough? It's enough for me.

I've confronted the suffocating shadows of my past. I want to concentrate, in the years that I have left, on loving my family and friends.

I've carried the sadness of my lost baby boy for so many years that it is now a part of me, just as he was, for too brief a time. The sadness will fade but the love never will.

Printed in Great Britain
by Amazon